THE DEAD OF SLED RUN

THE DEAD OF SLED RUN

A PIPER BLACKWELL MYSTERY

JEAN RABE

Boone Street Press

Boone Street Press

Cover design by Juan Villar Padron
Interior design by John G. Hartness
Editing by Janet Deaver-Pack

Published by Boone Street Press Tolono, IL.

First Boone Street Press Edition:

Name: Rabe, Jean, author

Title: The Dead of Sled Run, a Piper Blackwell Mystery / Jean Rabe

Description: First Edition. Boone Street Press

Identifiers: ISBN 13: 978-1-7325267-5-4

Printed in the United States of America

This one's for Jenny
Who showed exceptional taste in naming her cat Basil Meredith

1

---

11 p.m. Friday, December 11th

The keening wail of a smoke detector shredded his dreams. Oren Rosenberg jumped out of bed and slammed into his slippers. Acrid burning scents attacked his nose and throat, making him cough. Faint light showing through the window hit the rolling haze hugging the ceiling.

The wail continued, joined by another, and another, until all the detectors in the house screamed a cacophonous chorus that terrified him.

Shaking, he scooped up Cipin, the bonus gray tabby who always slept with him. Next came Razzleberry, another bonus cat, a tuxedo who had been curled on the bedside rug. Cursing for leaving his cell phone on the charger in the kitchen, he looked for the other two cats along the way.

"Freya! Buttons!"

A section of the house had been rewired a handful of days ago after a few shorts and an electrician's warning that things needed updating. Had shoddy work caused this?

"Freya!" he shouted, voice competing with the alarms' dissonance. "Buttons! Freya!"

The smoke was thicker in the hall. He held his breath and fumbled through the space, hearing the sizzles, pops, and spitting, finding Buttons, a Hemmingway—his third bonus cat—hissing under the kitchen table. He fumbled for their carrier sitting by the wall, somehow persuading all three squirming bodies into the mesh and canvas enclosure meant for two, ignoring the claws raking his hands and arms. He closed the zipper and stood, the carrier tight in one fist.

Everything looked blindingly bright, flames reflecting in the stainless steel of the refrigerator, licking up the walls, racing across the ceiling like yellow-orange flowing water. Sweltering, Oren felt like he was roasting.

Something fiery dropped on his shoulder. He brushed it aside with his free hand, a piece of wood trim from the ceiling, burning his fingers. The fire moved fast, growing in all directions, its crackling competing with the wails. He smelled something plastic burning, melting, sickly sweet. Everything blazed.

Oren ripped the cell phone from the charger by the sink, punching in numbers, fighting down horror and struggling to find air amid all the smoke while still managing to hold the cat carrier's handle.

So damn hot. He was solid sweat.

"9-1-1. What is the nature of your emergency?" Candace, the new hire for the 11 to 7 shift, the one who dressed like she was about to have a photo shoot for some fancy woman's magazine, perfect hair, manicured nails.

Oren tried to talk.

"Say again. What is the nature of your—"

He worked up enough saliva and shouted: "This is Oren! Oren Rosenberg."

"Yes, Chief Deputy Rosen—"

"My house is on fire. Sled Run in Santa Claus." He squeezed the cat carrier tighter and started hacking so loud he couldn't hear if she said anything in return. The phone slipped from his sweaty fingers, lost in the smoke swirling on the floor.

Oren retreated by feel, shoulder pressed to a wall, keeping hold of the struggling, yowling, confined cats, coughing even harder as he went.

So damn hot and hard to breathe. So noisy: the fire roared.

He was missing a cat. "Freya! Here, kitty!"

Save these three, he thought. *Get them safe. Come back for Freya.*

Bare-chested and in his pajama bottoms, he stumbled, gasping, out of the house, losing a slipper somewhere. Scorching inside, frigid out. The below-freezing winter air warred with the smoke he'd inhaled and made his chest tight and painful. He hurt terribly everywhere. Snow mixed with ice came sideways in a strong wind that battered him and made the walk slick.

Head and heart pounding, he half-ran, half-slid to his truck. Sucking in as much fresh air as he could manage, Oren only for a heartbeat considered using the truck's radio to call the dispatcher again to make sure the fire department was on the way. The call would eat a few more minutes, so he decided against that. He shoved the soot-covered carrier full of hissing cats into the cab, slammed the door, and whirled back toward the inferno.

Oren's chest heaved. He wobbled, catching himself against the front fender and forcing down dizziness. He headed back up the side-walk, vaguely registering people coming out of front doors across the street. He owned a corner property. Across the other side stretched Lake Noel.

He heard one of the neighbors shout to call 9-1-1. Why did it have to be Candace on duty? Candace the fashionista. Why couldn't Teegan be at the desk? Teegan with all the tattoos and piercings. Purple hair. He always gave her a hard time about her strange appearance, but he wished she had been on the desk. A seasoned veteran of the depart-ment, he trusted her, didn't really know Candace, didn't know if she was competent, if she'd get the fire department out before he lost everything and himself.

Someone shouted: "I just called 9-1-1!"

"I don't hear sirens!"

"Isn't that the sheriff's house?"

"The deputy's."

"That's Rosenberg!"

"We should hear sirens!"

Oren didn't hear sirens either. But he heard his heart hammering, the wind whistling, and the whooshing, snarling conversation of the flames. The fire was so loud. He continued taking stuttering steps toward his porch, his bare foot registering the needle sensations of ice on the pavement. His arm hurt from the cat claws and something else. Burns, he was burned.

Sliding, staying upright.

"Don't go in there!"

"Rosey, stay out!" That sounded like Dave from a few doors down.

Not one part of his home wasn't burning, the house on the other side of his was on fire, too. Good thing the Laubensteins were vacationing in Florida. But what great news they'd come back to. Oren had a double lot, half of it taken up by an over-sized garage for his hobbies and boat. The wind kept that building safe, at least for the moment. But if it shifted, he'd lose that, too.

"Rosey, what the hell are you doing? Stay out!" Dave again.

There were more voices, but the flames drowned their words.

Oren kept going, sliding, feeling the heat and the snow, numb.

Move faster, you old fool. Freya's in there!

Oren's wife would have stopped him from going back inside. She would have told him to stand next to his truck; that he'd managed to save the bonus cats—the two he took in nearly a year ago when their owner had been slain in the tiny town of Fulda, and Razzleberry, the little one he'd gained shortly after that when the owner was arrested for a cold-case murder.

His wife would have held him at the truck where he could breathe.

Where it was safe.

Where the fire couldn't reach.

His wife would have stopped him.

But she lived in Alabama now and wouldn't be his wife much longer. She had filed divorce papers. There was no one to keep him from wading through the smoke and flames in search of Freya, the beautiful long-haired Norwegian forest cat he adored. Freya was not a bonus cat; he'd acquired her a dozen years ago from a breed rescue when she was six weeks old.

Freya was still in the house, somewhere, hiding, certainly petrified. He couldn't let her burn. He'd get her out or die in the attempt. Oren figured his sixty-six years on the planet had been a reasonable run, no regrets. Well, not many.

Oren slid on the icy porch, losing the other slipper, just managing to keep his balance and stepping through the front door into the raging furnace-of-a-home in search of his beloved Freya.

The intense heat walloped him like a sledgehammer and his chest burned from trying to gulp in the scalding air. He tried tiny breaths instead and concentrated to stay on his feet.

"Freya." A hoarse croak followed by a coughing fit.

The fire played along the curtains, bookcases, and a walnut curio cabinet. It danced across the throw pillows and the back of the couch.

"Please, kitty."

Nothing mattered in this moment except the missing cat. Not his collection of jigsaw puzzles; irreplaceable photographs of family and friends—some of whom were years gone under the earth; his 1968 Jonny Bench rookie card; the so-called important papers in the file cabinet, like the useless marriage certificate. He was going to lose it all.

Except the cat. He would not lose her.

"Freya! Here, kitty!" One more step and the smoke yanked him to his knees. The heat pulsed from the floor up and down his legs.

If he could just find the cat.

Oren crawled fast, his fingers fumbling across a rug that was hot to the touch, but not yet blazing. It would catch fire soon enough. Down the hall, he closed his eyes and kept going. Oren knew the house by heart; he didn't need to see.

"Freya." A whisper.

The smoke, searing and awful, burrowed to the bottom of his lungs. The detectors had stopped wailing, had probably melted. He felt like he was melting, too.

Oren still didn't hear sirens, just the angry voice of the fire. Dizzy and sweat-soaked, he kept crawling toward the study, Freya's favorite haunt. She would hide there. He risked a look. Through watery eyes all he saw were bands of swirling gray shot through here and there with tongues of fire.

"Freya! Please, kitty." Hard to talk, all the smoke, thicker and darker than moments ago. Harder to breathe. Couldn't breathe. All he smelled was ash, burning wood, and heat. He swore he could smell the heat in the hell that his house had turned into.

"Frey—"

He reached to his office chair beneath the crocheted afghan, felt her brush against his arm. He couldn't see her for the smoke, but the double-coated fur was familiar. He thought she meowed, brushed by him again, then collapsed.

No! Freya, no! He had to think the words, his throat was an oven that kept the sound inside. He couldn't tell if she breathed. *Don't be dead. Don't. Be. Dead.* Oren fell next to the chair, trying to find one more swallow of air.

Get up. Get up or she's dead for certain. Get your sorry old ass up and get out of here.

The fire screamed even louder, and the smoke wrapped around him ever tighter, trying to anchor him in place. Wobbly, he forced himself back up to his knees, gently cradled the cat and held her against his chest, then somehow managed to get to his numb feet. Oren shuffled backwards, the way he'd come, using his memory of the home he'd lived in for twenty years.

It felt like hours had passed since the smoke detector woke him. Likely just minutes, he thought, terrible minutes. The fire gobbled it all so fast. He managed to reach the front door, where the shot of cold fought with the heat, both of them winning.

So tired and so hot, fading, falling.

So cold.

Strong hands thrust under Oren's armpits and lifted, pulling him up and out onto the porch.

"I've got you," Basil Meredith said. His voice, remarkably calm, cut through the roaring fire.

Basil picked him up and carried him down the sidewalk and toward the street, laying him on the icy lawn. Oren still cradled Freya, her cream-colored fur the shade of cold ashes.

"I've got you," Basil repeated. To the gawking neighbors, he hollered: "Blankets. Get some blankets!"

Oren opened his mouth to say something, but the words stayed down. He stared at Basil, detective for the Spencer County Sheriff's Department, who lived only two blocks away.

"The fire department is coming!" someone hollered.

Faintly, Oren finally heard sirens. Finally.

His fingers tangled in Freya's fur.

He knew the trucks would get here too late.

2

Sheriff Piper Blackwell drove into the Sled Run color barrage. Red and blue strobing lights from fire trucks and police cars melded with the glow of Christmas decorations along the curvy street. The dazzling hues bounced against the icy pavement and walks, seeming to fragment and change patterns in the sleet. Adding to the dizzying display were the fires that continued to burn at Oren's house and the one next door.

She parked at the only open spot of curb. Everything so painfully glaring, she closed her eyes for just a moment, refocusing, and took a slow, deep breath of the last good air she'd smell for a while.

Out of habit she turned on her body cam, opened her door, and carefully stepped onto the icy slick street. Piper wrapped a winter scarf across her nose and mouth, yet still the strong, acrid scent of fire and char winnowed inside and settled like lead on her tongue. The noise overpowered—loud voices from firemen and police, the *whoosh* of water, crackling from the fire, and the buzzing conversations of the gawkers who had braved the nasty weather to feed their curiosity. Thirty, maybe a few more, she guessed, many in pajamas with coats over the top and knitted caps, a few carried umbrellas, all smart enough to stay on the safe side of the street.

Piper edged toward Detective Basil Meredith, posed in front of the gaggle. Six feet tall and with espresso brown skin, he stood out amid the white faces. She'd told him to get to Oren's as fast as he could and figured he must have jogged. She didn't see his department car.

"Sheriff," Basil said as she approached.

It had taken her twenty-two minutes to get here, lights, siren, and cruising way the hell too fast for the roads' wintry state. Under normal conditions and following the speed limit, the ride would have been double that. Spencer County was small in population, but spread out, and Piper lived in Hatfield, well west of Christmas Lake Village in Santa Claus. She typically wouldn't respond to a fire in a town that had its own police department. But this was different, her chief deputy's house.

"Word on Oren?" Piper asked.

Candace had dispatched fire and ambulance first, contacted Piper next, and Piper immediately called Basil because he lived two blocks from Oren.

"The ambulance took him about ten minutes ago," Basil told her.

"How is—"

"Not good, Sheriff. Serious burns, smoke inhalation, shock. They're transporting him to Memorial in Jasper. But that's just to stabilize him. Helicopter will take him from there to Ascension St. Vincent in Indy. I'm told they have a top-notch burn center."

"Bad," Piper said. Her throat tightened and her hands shook from the horrid news. She forced the tremor down and squared her shoulders, tried to keep the emotion at bay.

Piper had run for sheriff against Oren Rosenberg the previous year. Forty-two years her senior, he had a wealth of experience, but she'd won. Maybe because of her last name. Blackwell. Piper's father had been the longtime sheriff of Spencer County. Maybe people thought they were voting for her dad, who had stepped down the year before because of a cancer diagnosis. He'd encouraged her to campaign when she came home to take care of him. Paul Blackwell recovered, was the police chief of Santa Claus now, and he stood near the pumper truck talking to one of the volunteer firemen.

"Yeah. Oren's in bad shape, Sheriff," Basil continued. Softer: "I heard one of the paramedics say he was circling."

Piper shuddered and all the colors paled and blurred as she sucked in a lungful of the smoke and ash-filled air. She was tough, tours in the Middle East, downrange assignments before leaving the Army and running for sheriff. She'd dealt with a lot of death and injuries. Not inured to any of it, she nevertheless managed a stoic mien.

Behind her a loud gawker speculated that Oren had set the fire to make sure his wife couldn't get the place in the settlement. Common knowledge, Oren being depressed over the pending divorce. Piper didn't know Oren personally all that well, though she'd seen him on and off while growing up, infrequent barbecues in the backyard during her childhood, Fourth of July gatherings in the park. Oren and her father had spent decades in local law enforcement together and were close.

Piper had trained as an MP at Fort Campbell; she wouldn't hit her one-year mark with the sheriff's department for another twenty days. She'd worked with Oren for roughly a year, a wholly professional relationship, no friendship involved; he kept his distance and occasionally let her know he should have won the election. Maybe he should have, she thought, all his experience compared to her short MP stint.

And while their relationship always had been business, not personal, she knew Oren would never burn down his own house. Angry, depressed, stressed ... he could be all those things, but he just wouldn't have done this.

A terrible accident appeared to have caught Oren's house first, then the neighbors'. The dispatcher said those neighbors were fortunately snow birding in Florida.

She watched flames shoot out the windows of the house next to Oren's, and then the roof collapsed with a sound like thunder. Total losses, both places; the fire department worked to keep the blaze from spreading to other homes. Oren's boat storage building remained upwind, but they hosed it down anyway. She noticed the blackened husk of Oren's department Explorer in the charred remains of the garage attached to his house.

"Circling," Piper whispered. As in Oren was circling the drain.

"Yeah."

"He has cats," Piper said.

"Four," Basil returned. "They're okay, singed, one of them needed oxygen. They're in his pickup. I pulled it across the street to get it out of the way. Found an extra set of keys under the mat." He pointed down the block, where the truck sat under a lamppost from which dangled a blinking red and white candy cane. All the lampposts on the street had lighted decorations hanging from them. "I can take the cats home with me, get them to a vet's when one opens, have them checked out. Or I can pass them off to Millie. Does Millie know?"

"Yes." A pause. "About the fire. But not about Oren." Millie, Oren's granddaughter, and Piper's most recently hired deputy, had the eleven to seven a.m. shift this week. "She's covering an accident near the monastery. Semi- and a sedan in a ditch. A few inches of snow on the ground, tonight's ice was unexpected, most figured it would just be more flurries. People forget how to drive on ice when the weather's good."

Behind them, the nosey neighbors complained about the cold and the sleet while continuing to speculate on what caused the fire. Piper and Basil stepped away and into the street, close to the pumper truck, which had the name *Blitzen* painted on it. The Santa Claus Volunteer Fire Department vehicles were all named after the famous poem's reindeer.

"Millie'll come here when she's cleared the scene." Piper had to raise her voice to be heard over more shouting. She twisted her foot against the ice. "Then I'll send her up to Indy." Provided Oren lived to reach Ascension. "It would be great if you could watch his cats. Thank you."

Basil turned and pointed to a gangly-looking man in red sweatpants and a puffy black jacket balancing on the curb. "Neighbor from across the street and one house down, Dave ... Halm. David Halm.

Told me Oren had some rewiring done, used an electrician Mr. Halm recommended."

"So maybe faulty work," Piper said. She squinted, the sleet striking her face, tiny ice darts that faintly stung. Why didn't the lookie-loos go home, get out of this weather? Their nosiness overwhelmed their common sense.

She watched the fire a few more minutes, then returned to the gawkers and honed in on a conversation between David Halm and a thickset man in a plaid jacket, their shoulders hunched against the wind.

"Left his Christmas tree lights on, Davey. Caught the drapes on fire, I'll bet. Every year it happens in any city. Christmas trees cause fires."

"Jewish. Jewish. No Christmas tree. Jewish," Halm said.

"Does he smoke? Maybe he fell asleep with a cigarette and—"

Halm frowned. "No Christmas tree lights. No cigarettes. I never saw Oren smoke anything."

The firemen barked orders back and forth, and the east side of Oren's house fell in, smoke belching and fire shooting up with fire-work-like sparks. The red glow above the ruins painted a false dawn in the neighborhood.

"Not a smoker, then. Ah, Davey, now I remember him being Jewish. Maybe he had one of them Jewish candle thingies lit. Too close to the drapes."

"Menorahs," Halm explained. He had a wide face and a long, narrow nose, dark eyes, and gray hair that marked him late middle-age. "It's a candelabrum with seven or eight branches. Kinda pretty."

"Maybe the candles caught the drapes on fire."

Halm shook his head. "Menorahs are lit on each night of Hanukkah. And the first night of Hanukkah isn't for another week. Rosey wouldn't have lit a candle."

"You Jewish? I didn't think you were Jewish, Davey. You got a Christmas tree. Got lighted nutcrackers parading across your lawn. You decorate every year."

"I'm not Jewish. Just educated."

12

Piper couldn't help herself listening to the pair. She'd talk to David Halm later.

"Maybe faulty wiring then," the thickset man concluded. "That was probably it. Used that same cheap electrician you did. Told you that guy was a shyster."

"A shyster's a lawyer," Halm cut back. "And that electrician is my brother-in-law."

The thickset man shrugged, spun away, and walked past an inflatable snowman toward a saltbox house.

Basil joined Piper. "Fire's come down quite a bit. They're starting to get it controlled. But nothing will be salvageable."

"Faulty wiring," Piper mused. "I wonder."

"Faulty nothing." Basil lowered his voice and leaned to her ear. "No accident, Sheriff. Screams arson to me."

Piper made sure her body cam recorded all the cold, pink faces of the onlookers, and then turned to Basil, who was staring at the fire. The sleet continued to spit at her cheeks. She took shallow breaths through the weave of her scarf, finding that made it easier to manage the pungent burnt smell.

"Arson. Really? You're a superb detective. I envy your skills. But from out here on the street, not close to the house ... what makes you possibly say that—" She almost called him Sherlock, a nickname he'd acquired in the Gangs and Narcotics division of the Chicago Police Department. He'd worked years there before answering her ad for a detective in his bid to leave the gun-plagued big bad city behind. The nickname well suited him, and he'd taught her a lot. What did he see that made him think arson?

"Did you fit in some fire training? A course on arson?" Piper knew it could take hours, days, to sift through the wreckage and determine a cause. And if they deemed the fire suspicious, debris would have to be analyzed to find any accelerants. All of that was beyond the capabilities of the Santa Claus Volunteer Fire Department. The simple explanation was faulty wiring, an accident. Yet Basil apparently didn't buy simple.

"Take a look at Sled Run, Sheriff. A *good* look."

Piper glanced away from the fire, which had practically hypnotized her. What did Sherlock see that she didn't? What did his experienced eyes notice? His training? Look through his eyes, she thought. Really look.

The Sled Run houses were a mix of large ranches with vaulted ceilings and two-story saltboxes, several with fancy facades. The entire Christmas Lake Village included almost a thousand homes, with an almost equal number of vacant lots still available. Twenty-six miles of streets, the gated community featured three lakes—Christmas, Noel, and Holly, and butted up against an expansive golf course. Many of the streets carried holiday names: Mistletoe Drive, Silver Bell Court, Jingle Bell Lane, Blitzen Lane, Sleigh Bell Drive, Prancer Drive, Snow Ball Lane, and on and on. And, of course, Sled Run.

"What do you see?" Basil asked her.

Basil did not patronize her, Piper knew, he was nudging her.

Besides the homes and the noisy neighbors, voices still buzzing, cell phones out recording, she noted few cars in the driveways, modest models … Fords and Chevys with a thin coat of ice that would require scraping unless the temperature warmed in the morning. None had bumper stickers or decals, nothing to proclaim school or political affiliation. Likely any nicer vehicles were in the garages.

"I see Christmas decorations," she said. Christmas two weeks away, a lot of people in Santa Claus—in all of Spencer County—strung up lights starting well before Thanksgiving. All she'd managed this year at her own house was a large wreath on the front door. Inside she'd done a better job at decking the halls. She had a seven-foot-tall artificial tree in the living room, covered with ornaments from her childhood and others her husband Nang had added to it.

"Many Christmas decorations," she said.

A saltbox looked as if it had been dipped in glitter, icicle lights hanging everywhere, white fairy lights wrapped around trees, a lamppost, and the chimney. The ranch next to it had a Grinch theme with oversized inflatables from the cartoon spread across the front yard and green lights dripping from the eaves. Another residence displayed a life-sized manger, complete with lighted wise men, camels, and sheep.

It seemed each neighbor tried to outdo the next.

The lone Craftsman-style house on the block had every window ringed with multi-colored lights. An old-time steam engine outlined in small red bulbs chugged across the roof of the front porch. It pulled three equally-bright train cars loaded with wrapped presents, all the wheels spinning. A glowing Santa perched on the house peak, leaning on the chimney.

Next door to it a half-dozen pines wore thousands of miniature lights, and along their bases light-encrusted reindeer and elves slow-danced. Two houses down an inflatable Charlie Brown and Snoopy, easily both ten feet tall, stood outside an inflatable doghouse with a big silver bell. Across from Snoopy, life-size nutcrackers tussled with elves riding polar bears, illuminated by a spotlight that alternated white, red, and green. On the roof of that house Ho Ho Ho flashed, alternating with MERRY CHRISTMAS and HAPPY BIRTHDAY JESUS.

A snowman trio stood back from the curb of a small ranch, and grinning snowman faces peered out of each window. More white icicle lights dangled from the roof.

Every house on Sled Run had an impressive display in the front yard.

Except Oren's and his neighbor's—E & S Laubenstein, according to the mailbox.

"Arson," Piper agreed. "A hate crime."

"Looks that way to me," Basil said. "Oren told me he built this house twenty years ago because it was right across from Lake Noel, easy access for his boat. Liked the neighborhood. Hell, I like the neighborhood. Twenty years and now someone takes exception to him being here."

Piper's scarf-muffled voice became a whisper, too soft for Basil to hear. "So, who suddenly took exception to Jewish people living on this street? Who has that much hate?"

The gawkers had thinned a little, but the ones remaining continued to loudly chatter.

"He didn't have a Christmas tree," one of the lookie-loos stated. "Didn't you listen to Dave? Rosey's been here as long as me and he's never put up a Christmas tree. No damn Christmas tree caused that house to burn."

"Candles, then," a woman in a fuzzy bathrobe argued. "He lit the menorah too early."

3

Tthere was a fire on Mistletoe Drive two years back." The Santa Claus Volunteer Fire Chief removed his helmet, let out a long breath, and leaned against the fire truck named *Blitzen*. Despite the sleet, sweat beaded on his forehead. His name patch read: James "Jimmy" Wollach. He and Piper watched the other firemen roll the hoses and gather equipment, the darkness cut by truck headlights and streetlights. "That Mistletoe fire, Sheriff Blackwell, was after Thanksgiving, right at the edge of December. Nice house. Two levels, new construction. Electrical problems set it off."

Piper guessed Wollach to be mid-fifties, about the same age as her dad. She knew he owned a gas station at the northern edge of Santa Claus, had served on the county board, and been president of the school board a few years back. Apparently a civic-minded soul. His blue eyes looked kind.

"Burnt to the ground, that house. Just like these," he said, making a sweeping gesture at the charred remains of Oren's place and his neighbor's. "And two years before that, fire took a split-level on Sleigh Bell Drive. That was because of Christmas tree lights, real candles in

17

the windows. All things merry brought that one down. It was right around New Year's. They'd had a real tree, let it dry out. Total loss. And wholly preventable if they just would've kept it watered. They wrestled with the insurance company for months."

Piper felt numb ... from the cold, from worry over Oren, disgust that this was a hate crime. Basil was right, the destroyed houses had been the only two not decorated for Christmas, owned by Jewish people.

And there was the spray paint.

Anger, hate, prejudice had sent Oren Rosenberg to the specialized burn unit of a hospital in Indianapolis. What the hell was wrong with the world?

She shuddered and nearly gagged. The stench from fire, burnt wood, plastic, and all the other things that had gone up in flames remained strong in her mouth. It felt like it had taken forever to knock down every last bit of fire. All the gawkers had given up a while ago. Piper had recorded a lot of names so she or Basil could talk to some neighbors later. A few hours of sleep and she'd be back to question them when it was light.

"This wasn't an accident," she said.

"Can't say that yet," Wollach replied. "I'll be out here later today, when the sun's bright. Take a close look then."

"Not an accident," she said more firmly. She'd walked the property before settling next to Wollach. She knew it was deliberately set. She'd noticed the paint.

"I get that's what you and your detective think. I think the fire was set, too. In fact, I put a call into the State Fire Marshal before midnight. I want an arson investigator here ASAP. But you and I and your detective? We can't make the determination. We need a trained investigator to make that call."

"A hate crime," Piper said softly.

"And just because Oren Rosenberg is Jewish, you can't say that this is some sort of hate crime. Not yet." He made a huffing sound and nodded to the fireman climbing into *Vixen's* cab. "We'll have someone out of Indy take a real close look. We don't have a fire inspector in the county. And we don't have an arson investigator." He paused. "And you know that, Sheriff Blackwell. We have twenty volunteer fire-fighters in Santa Claus. They're good men and women, but none of them have that training."

Piper was well aware of what she considered her county's short-comings. Spencer County had fourteen fire departments, all of them with volunteer contracted firefighters, serving a population of roughly twenty-one thousand across four hundred square miles. It figured to about one fire department per twenty-eight square miles. The county was ranked ninth in Indiana for fire departments per capita.

Santa Claus had built a new fire station in 2014, had updated trucks, everything as red and shiny as Rudolf's nose.

Despite the number of departments in the county, all the equip-ment, and good volunteer firefighters, often houses that caught fire burned to the ground. Firefighters weren't at any station twenty-four-seven. When a call came in to the dispatcher at the Spencer County Sheriff's Department, it was routed to the applicable fire department. Men and women were summoned from their homes or businesses, and they had to travel to the station to gear up. Houses burned in the time between.

Most of the Sled Run neighbors had turned off their outdoor light displays, but an inflatable Grinch still glowed eerily green several houses down, his menacing smirk disquieting.

Her radio faintly crackled with a report of a car in a ditch. Rock-port city limits, not her concern.

Basil was probably headed back across the river from the all-night Walmart in Owensboro. He'd gone to gather cat food, litter, bedding, and another carrier so the cats could go to a veterinarian in the morning to be checked out. He would grab a few hours of sleep, and meet her in the office at nine. Then they'd come back out here.

Her father had been pacing around the remains of Oren's house, the big beam of his flashlight skittering across charred debris. The scene reminded Piper of burned stretches she'd encountered on downrange assignments in the Middle East. Paul pivoted away from the still-smoking ruin and walked to the boat garage, then paced around it before heading toward Piper. She could tell that he hadn't noticed the spray paint.

"Thanks, Chief." She stepped away from Wollach and met her father halfway across the front yard that resembled an icy-snowy marsh.

"No report on Oren yet?"

Piper shook her head. "Millie's still on her way to the hospital. She'll call as soon as she knows something."

"We'd have heard if he'd died," Paul said. "Someone would have radioed us. So no news is good news, right?"

Piper had no reply to that, recalling the comment about Oren "circling the drain."

"Basil has you convinced this was deliberate."

"Yes. The fire chief agrees." Piper futilely brushed the ice pellets out of her hair. The sleet seemed gentler now, mixing with snow. "But we need an arson investigator to make the call."

"A hate crime."

"Yes. I think so."

Paul scowled; the features of his face difficult to see. "I can't buy that antisemitism, Punkin'. Not in this neighborhood. Not as long as Oren has lived here. No doubt Basil saw a lot of hate crimes in Chicago. Black. White. Hispanic. Asian. Race so often an issue. Maybe religion, too. The disparity. The anger. He automatically looks for it, expects it. But he's looking through big-city eyes at little Spencer County. No one has it against Oren for being Jewish, or his neighbor either. Coincidence, accident." He dug the ball of his foot into the watery lawn and got a semi-frozen squish colored gray with ashes. "I was over here last night, for dinner. I brought one of those big take-and-bake pizzas, and Oren and I ate it and garlic breadsticks, and we had a couple of beers. We're being sued for an old case, claiming wrongful arrest, from thirty years back. We talked about it. It's a pain in the ass, is what it is. A time and money waster. We'll have to get an attorney. Like Oren needs that on top of his divorce and burned house." A pause. "Like I need this. Pain in the ass.

Hell, maybe Oren was so upset last night he forgot to turn off the oven."

"This wasn't an accident, Dad. Did you get a *good* look at the boat garage? There's a six-pointed star in drippy red spray paint. Hard to see, but it's there. The size of a dinner plate. That's hate. And you being sued? When did this come up?"

Paul waved his gloved hand between them. "Not the time to talk about it. Your department will probably get sucked into the suit, too. Maybe the whole county. You'll hear plenty about it soon enough. But not now. I don't want to talk about it now." He gestured to the burned houses. "Got this to deal with first. I'll poke around the wreckage when the sun's up. Get a photographer out here. I'll look into it if you're so sure it was deliberate. If you think that spray paint means something. Good eyes, you have. But I think you'll see that—"

"*I'll* investigate this, Dad," Piper said. She worried about his lawsuit, would pester him later for more information. Maybe she'd ask DA Scales about it; she had a meeting with him Monday, their regular monthly conference about county concerns. Maybe Scales would know and spill the details. "We'll handle the investigation. Basil and I."

"It's my jurisdiction. Santa Claus." Paul drew himself up and squared his shoulders. Around him firemen carried the last of the equipment to the trucks. A moment later, *Vixen* pulled away. The fire chief remained leaning against *Blitzen*, watching them. "Oren's my friend, Punkin'. We go way back. Decades. This is my jurisdiction, and I have a helluva lot more experience than you."

Though true, that last bit stung her.

"It's because of those decades knowing Oren that you *shouldn't* lead the investigation," she countered, feeling determined and remorseful at the same time. She'd never encroached on someone's territory before. "Yes, you're the agency of record, but you need to invite me to assume jurisdiction."

Paul's eyebrows rose.

"You and Oren have spent more years working together than I've been alive. Friends and colleagues. If this is indeed arson, if you can get the perp on your own, any defense attorney will use your relationship with Oren to raise doubts, no matter the evidence. He'll claim your conclusions are biased. I have a similar, but lesser, conflict of interest. Oren's my chief deputy, but we've worked together less than a year, we don't have your history. And he ran *against* me for sheriff."

Paul stared at the ruined houses and finally nodded. "I get you. I don't like it, but I get you."

"We could put a team together on this," she continued. "Should do that. Basil, of course would be the lead, and we need someone from the state expert with burn patterns, accelerants."

"I intend to help."

"We'll need your help."

"Oren might provide the best evidence," Paul added. "He might have seen something, heard something. Might have been threatened. We need to talk to Oren."

"Sure," Piper said. "*If* he can talk. *If* he recovers. But I know he's in the hospital because someone set fire to his house. Deliberate. Hate. I'm going to find out who did this."

Paul opened his mouth to say something else, but Piper edged away, turning on her flashlight and walking toward what little was left of Oren's place.

"Be careful!" Chief Wollach called to her.

Piper raised her hand to acknowledge his concern.

So very much like some of the bombed-out, burned places she'd crawled through when she was in the Army. Insurgents hid in the ruins then, rising and sniping. She'd been wounded one night, but not seriously, and she'd managed to save two of her fellow soldiers, gaining a Purple Heart for the ordeal. Where would she be right now if she'd stayed in the Army? Not newly married to Nang. Not sinking her roots ever deeper into Spencer County.

And not being so damn furious that someone had burned down Oren's home.

She noticed two firemen poking through the remains of the house next door. One of them waved both arms to catch the chief's attention.

"Body!" the fireman called.

"Two!" his companion added. "Two bodies, Chief."

Piper rushed over, slogging through the icy water, slipping and catching herself to stay upright. She heard feet pounding behind her, saw the beams of big flashlights bouncing. Stopping next to the firemen, she looked at something she didn't want to see.

Blackened twisted bodies lay in what had probably been the bedroom.

Oren's neighbors had not gone to Florida after all. Arson escalated to murder.

Piper keyed her radio and called her dispatcher.

"Send the coroner," she said.

Then Piper sank deeper into the folds of her winter jacket.

4

---

6 a.m.

The antiseptic smell clung heavy in Millie's nostrils. She hated it. She also hated the polished floors—looked like terrazzo—that gleamed dully, and the lighted monitors near the bed, and the tube that delivered oxygen from the wall, and the other thin tubes that dangled from a stand and dripped some sort of liquids into her grandfather Oren Rosenberg.

Or, rather, she hated the circumstances that had landed him in this ICU burn unit.

She hated all the bandages, too, that obscured almost everything but his mouth and closed eyes. The only thing she didn't hate was that the doctors said he'd survive this … "but it would be a challenging road to recovery."

They'd only just let her in to see him, probably tired of watching her pace in front of the nurses' station in her deputy's uniform. She knew she'd made a few of them nervous.

Millie had to don a disposable white jumpsuit that looked like something out of an old sci-fi movie. PPE they called it, Personal

Protective Equipment, intended to shield her grandfather from any contagion she might bring in.

She'd called Sheriff Blackwell a few minutes ago to relay the guarded good news, and to tell her "no flowers." Those weren't permitted in his room. Balloons were okay. Piper had told her to take the next week off with Oren, that her shift would be covered. Millie had spotted a small motel two blocks away and would book a room. Across the street from the hospital was a place called Vintage Threads, which looked to be an upscale secondhand shop; she'd stop there for a few changes of clothes. She'd get toiletries and aspirin—to fight her killer headache—from the little pharmacy on the first floor. Maybe they had Coke or Pepsi. Cold caffeine soon would be a seriously good idea.

Millie plopped in an uncomfortable high-backed green vinyl chair near the foot of the bed and set her breathing in time with Oren's, studying the rise and fall of his chest. The most important person in her life, it made her throat painfully tight seeing him like this. Sixty-six, her grandfather was a hale, powerfully-built soul, so full of life and purpose that he'd probably remain with the sheriff's department until his last breath. She shivered at that thought. He looked weak now, a few steps above death.

Liquid continued to drip down the tubes. The whisper-hiss that she heard was probably the oxygen flowing into his nose.

Millie's mother had issues with alcohol and reckless behavior. Her estranged father was a chaotic free spirit fishing somewhere in Alaska. Oren had raised her and paid for most of her college education. She'd joined the Spencer County Sheriff's Department shortly after gaining her Master's in the spring because law enforcement intrigued her and she thought it might help pay Oren back. He encouraged her to pursue a law degree, which she had put a dent in by taking online courses in her spare time.

But Millie liked being a deputy, didn't know if she remained serious about practicing law. Twenty-five, she had years to settle on something.

"Get better fast, Pops," she whispered. "Please."

Millie watched the lighted panels on the monitors, fluctuating lines and numbers, greens, blues, pale yellow. What did they mean? No alarms or shrill *beep-beep-beep* like she'd heard earlier down the hall. That was a good sign, right? All the relatively quiet dancing lights? Staring at the screens, she figured out which one monitored his heart.

Oren Rosenberg had an amazing heart.

"Amelia Isaakovitch?" The gentle voice came from a woman just beyond the doorway. She held a clipboard, and a stethoscope hung around her neck. "Amelia—"

"It's Millie." Almost everyone mispronounced the last name bestowed on her by a father she hadn't seen in well more than a dozen years. I-zack-oh-vitch.

"Millie. I'm Dr. Carla Mattingly. Let's talk out here."

Why? Oren did not look conscious. Did the doctor worry that something she would say could reach through his slumber and disturb him? Wound him as much mentally as he had been physically? Frighten him? Or maybe the doctor didn't want to bother putting on a PPE suit.

Millie was fast up and out in the hall.

"You're listed as his—"

"Next of kin. Granddaughter. His wife, soon to be his ex-, is in Alabama. I haven't called her yet. So, I'm it. I know I'm listed on some paperwork."

Dr. Mattingly tapped her clipboard. A thin, short woman, her long white jacket looked two sizes too big. The wide round glasses appeared overlarge, magnifying her blue eyes, and her spiky blonde hair had a half-inch of black at the roots. Did she try to look like a teenager on purpose? Did she think her young appearance put people at ease?

Millie was far from at ease.

From somewhere down the hall, she heard a shrill *beep-beep-beep*, followed by footsteps hurrying to address it. A cart clattered along the terrazzo.

"Mr. Rosenberg is fortunate. His transport was fast and we treated

26

him immediately on arrival," Dr. Mattingly began. "I believe the ER nurses might have mentioned that already. Fortunate."

Millie nodded. She heard soft laughter coming from the nurses' station. This wasn't the place for humor, she thought. Whatever they found funny had no right to intrude here.

"Tell me something," Millie said. "Something more than he's fortunate." Because she disagreed; there was nothing fortunate about Oren being burned in a house fire and now hooked up to all the things murmuring and spiking in the ICU room.

"While Mr. Rosenberg has extensive burns, they are limited to first and second degree. Serious second degree. And the deep tissue is not blackened, though some superficial edges are. We're looking at performing one graft on his left arm, but that won't be for three to five days to minimize the risk of infection. There will be some scars, and the healing time for the graft could be two weeks, barring complications. We'll keep him in the burn ICU for the duration of that. Perhaps a little longer." The doctor paused and appeared to consult something on the clipboard.

Millie heard the soft laughter again. She balled her hands into fists.

"Mr. Rosenberg will be kept hydrated and on pain control and infection prevention. We will restrict visitors, and they'll have to wear PPE, at least until we're happy with the wounds closing." She pointed at Millie's spacesuit.

Millie would have to let Piper know about that, as she suspected sheriff's deputies would be planning to visit. No flowers. Few people. PPE. She'd have to call Paul Blackwell, too. She rented an apartment above Paul's garage in Rockport. Paul and Oren went back decades; Paul would insist on coming to see his friend.

"How long do you think? How—" Millie searched for the way to end the sentence. The doctor seemed to understand.

"There's an unwritten formula that patients stay in the ICU on average a half-day to a day for each percent of TBSA burned."

"TBSA?"

"Oh, sorry. Total Body Surface Area burned. In your grandfather's case, he suffered burns to a little more than fifty percent."

Twenty-five to fifty days, Millie mentally translated. Serious hospital time.

"Too, he has an inhalation injury, though it is not severe enough to require intubation. The fire, heat, caused some damage to his trachea, but it is mostly smoke damage. He'll be able to talk. Like I said, fortunate."

Millie hated that word.

"Twenty-five days," she said softly. "Maybe fifty."

"Maybe," Dr. Mattingly said. "My guess is thirty, thirty-five. That's for the burn unit. Most of his burns will be healed by the time he gets out of the hospital and into a rehab facility. First degree burns will be cleared up in less than two weeks, the second degree, probably three or so." She went on. "Mr. Rosenberg will need some PT ... physical therapy ... to keep the contractures of the skin minimal, regain range of motion."

"Work," Millie said. "My grandfather will want to go back to work. It's his life."

Dr. Mattingly smiled. "Of course. Desk duty at first, light work. His skin graft site will be fragile for a while. I'd say eight to twelve weeks after his release he can return to full duty. That's my best guess, if there are no complications, given the extent of the burns."

Millie wished she would have thought to turn on the record function of her phone. She'd make notes as soon as possible to remember everything.

"And he'll have to come back after discharge for wound checks."

"Sure," Millie said. She'd drive him. Right now, she'd call Piper again, regurgitate the doctor-speak, think about calling Grandma, and definitely call Paul Blackwell. She'd also need to check in with Basil Meredith, who Piper had said was keeping her grandfather's precious cats. Oren would want to know about the cats when he woke up. Maybe she'd tell him before he woke up. The information might help him.

And she'd fight back the tears.

All the bad things had rained down on Oren in the past few months. His father had died earlier this year, then his wife moved out and filed divorce papers, and then his house burned to the ground. The year before, he'd lost the election for Spencer County Sheriff to a woman forty-two years younger and with no prior department experience. Sure, Piper was an MP in the Army, but that seemed insubstantial next to her grandfather's knowledge.

And yet, Millie liked Piper.

"I'm gonna call Sheriff Blackwell, then Paul."

But first she'd go back in the room with the tubes and blinking lights, watch her grandfather breathe, and sit in the uncomfortable green vinyl chair and let herself cry.

5

Piper glanced at her watch, leaned back in her old creaky office chair, hit the record function on the phone, and listened to Saundra Laubenstein, the woman who once owned the house next to Oren Rosenberg's.

The Laubensteins hadn't burned in the fire.

"There's nothing left of my place. Nothing. A neighbor texted me. Texted a picture. That's my life ... our lives ... the flames took." Saundra wailed, a gasping, gulping inhuman sound that sent a shiver down Piper's back. When she came up for air, she continued: "Wedding photos, Sheriff, a nice big album. And pictures of our parents and grandparents, farther back some tin types, all kept in the bureau. Easy to get at so we could take them out and look when we wanted. Aaron's baby pictures. We didn't have a digital camera then. We had a 35mm because Eldad loves taking and developing pictures, had a little darkroom. That's gone too. All of it gone."

Piper had discovered the Laubensteins' son, Aaron, worked as a pharmacist at the University of Louisville Hospital in Kentucky. She'd called him about the fire and the two bodies discovered, but not yet identified. Aaron immediately called his mother's time-share to discover his parents were indeed alive and vacationing in Miami.

"I am very sorry, Mrs. Laubenstein," Piper said. She didn't really know what else to say; words of condolence usually sounded hollow. "But I am happy you and your husband are all right." A pause. "Who was staying in your house?"

"No one! There was nobody—" Saundra's voice carried all manner of emotions: disbelief, anger, fear. She sobbed so hard Piper had to work to figure out what the woman was saying. "Eldad's violin. A watercolor by Charles Demuth. That was a gift. Our tallits; they'd been in the family forever, gone," Saundra cried. "Gone. Gone. Gone. Clothes, furniture, all those things can be replaced. But the truly precious things are gone forever, little pieces of my heart broken off."

"Vernon," Piper interrupted, finding a Vernon on her list of neighbors she'd met early this morning. "Vernon—"

"Madsen. He lives across the street. He's the one who texted me the picture. Aaron called him, got him to go over and take a picture of our house. What used to be our beautiful house. Vernon said everyone thought we'd died in the fire, that there were two bodies in the house. And a car in the garage that wasn't ours."

Who had died in the Laubenstein house?

Since it wasn't the Laubensteins. Piper's mind spun.

"We're starting back today, cancelling the rest of our vacation," Saundra said. "Where will we live? How can we start over at our age? I'm sixty-eight." A sobbing pause: "What caused the fire, Sheriff? Vernon didn't know, but said it started at Rosey's."

Rosey? A nickname for Oren Rosenberg?

"Is Rosey all right? Did he lose everything?"

"Oren Rosenberg's house also burned," Piper replied, her voice flat, her mind picturing the flames. She swore she could smell the acrid char again and her chest constricted as she thought about her chief deputy. "Oren was injured. He is in the hospital."

Saundra cried louder and Piper waited for it to subside. She wanted coffee, a big mug of Italian dark that she could wrap her fingers around and hold her nose over. Good coffee helped her get through rough spots. Its enticing scent would also help her forget the smell of the incinerated houses. She ran her thumb over the edge of the desk like it was a big worry stone.

"I don't know who was in our house. No one should have been in the house. You tell me, Sheriff, who was in our house." Saundra's voice sounded steadier now. "Aaron has keys to everything. Rosey has—" She paused, as if searching for the right words. "We gave a key to Rosey years ago. And we have a key to his place. It was so we could check when either of us went on vacation." Another pause, longer. "Did it really start at Rosey's? Electrical? He had some work done. Did he hire some cheap electrician who's to blame for all of—"

Piper took a deep breath and worked her thumb faster against the wood. "Mrs. Laubenstein, it is apparent the fire started at Oren Rosenberg's and spread to your home. We don't yet know what caused the fire. A fire inspector is coming from Indianapolis and we'll work with him to determine what happened. I promise to keep you informed."

"We lost everything." Saundra's voice was soft now; Piper strained to hear her. "Our tallits. The photographs. My beautiful Demuth. The violin. Where will we live?"

"Mrs. Laubenstein, we'll—"

"How will we start over?"

Piper waited. The silence smothered her. Again she thought about coffee and about the investigation. Zeke, her dispatcher, was combing through various social media sites looking for antisemitic posts, hate messages, threads that might point a finger to the arsonist. She wanted to go back to the scene.

"Aaron said he's coming up to the house today. What's left of the house. He's getting us hotel rooms. A thousand miles we have to drive. It usually takes us three days. Maybe we can do it in two."

Piper heard a car honking outside the window, looked and saw a Prius pull out in front of a pickup truck. The driver of the truck shook his fist, and both went on their way.

"We're insured," Saundra went on. "Eldad has insurance on every-thing. Except my watercolor, not enough on that. And insurance doesn't cover memories. Is Rosey going to be all right? You said a hospital. Which hospital? We should check on him."

Piper heard a man talking in the background. A shuffling sound. "Here, you tell her," Saundra said. "It's Sheriff Blackwell."

"Sheriff?" That must be Eldad.

"Yes," Piper said.

"Sheriff Blackwell, we never use house sitters, and Aaron has his own place in Louisville. No other kids. No grandkids. No one had permission. Nobody would have been staying in our house. Rosey is the only neighbor with a key. The only one. You tell me who those people were."

"We don't know," she replied honestly. *Yet*, she thought.

Piper glanced up to see Basil standing in her doorway. She wondered how long he'd been there; she should have put this conversation on speaker. She did that now with a touch of a button. Basil looked tired. She knew she did, too, only managing a nap before coming to the office.

"Mr. Laubenstein, the fire was late last night." And wasn't put out until early this morning, she thought. "We are investigating. It takes time." Piper nearly asked him about people in the subdivision, maybe new residents, who had made antisemitic comments or threats. For some reason she held back, wanting that to be a face-to-face conversation … one she also needed to have with Oren when he was able.

"You ask the neighbors," Eldad said. He had a firm, dry voice. "You ask the neighbors if they knew who was in my house. Some of them are nosey-posies. One of them certainly saw something. You ask the man at the gate. You ask. You figure it out." Frustrated, angry, grieving, he continued to rant.

Piper planned to "ask the man at the gate." Christmas Lake Village, a gated community, had a guard on post 24/7. She'd talked to the one on duty before she left the scene, but he was uncertain about releasing the video from the surveillance cameras, some of the residents being "private people." He wanted something official in writing before he'd hand it over, or permission from the Village board president.

33

As if reading her mind, Basil waived a signed search warrant for the surveillance footage.

"The arson investigator is meeting us at ten," Basil said. "I'll drive."

She'd made Basil lead on the case, just like she'd told her father at the fire scene.

"You find out who was staying in my house," Eldad continued. "You figure it out. And who turned it to cinders, you figure that out too, Sheriff. Someone has to pay. Someone has to pay dearly."

Two people in the Laubenstein house had already paid with their lives.

"I'll figure it out," she promised Eldad. She hoped that was a vow she could keep.

6

9 a.m.

Piper watched the sentry download video on the flash drives she provided. Security cameras dotted the gated collection of subdivisions that made up Christmas Lake Village. She was most interested in the feed from a few hours before Oren's fire, though the warrant specified two weeks' worth, which was as long as the Village stored it before deletion. They'd take it to the department for study, hopefully noting unusual activity, and run license plate numbers for suspicious cars.

She'd hoped to get a look at the two individuals from the Laubenstein house, but there were no security cameras on Sled Run. Maybe some residents on that street had doorbell cams that could help. As Eldad Laubenstein had said: "One of them certainly saw something."

Was it possible those burned souls had started the blaze at Oren's, not knowing it would spread and catch them? How long would it take for DNA or dental records to identify the two?

Piper and Basil squeezed into the tiny brick building behind the sentry at his desk, the closeness and the portable heater banished the frigid breeze that blew outside. Piper unzipped her coat and wondered briefly if maybe she and Nang should consider someplace tropical for their honeymoon.

Basil talked softly on his radio to the dispatcher; Piper caught something about a car stolen from outside the pizza place west of Rockport.

"Awful thing, that fire on Sled," the sentry, Kenny Caine, said. The post smelled of coffee and the pine sprigs that decorated his small desk. A pen holder crammed with peppermint sticks sat in front of a speaker that played George Strait's "Christmas Cookies." There was little room to move around, and no other chairs. An open narrow door revealed a toilet and an almost child-sized sink. A mini-fridge with a microwave on top of it, a coatrack, and a dog bed containing a grizzle-faced chocolate Labrador took up the rest of the meager square footage. The dog glanced at Piper and thumped its tail.

Caine looked to be roughly twenty, silver ring in his left ear, with a matching one in his nose. He had a tattoo of an orange and black fantailed goldfish on the left side of his neck. His hair was short except for a narrow hank in the back. "I just got back three days ago. Been to Portugal with my fiancé. Bette, she's looking to study music in Lisbon, the Superior Orchestra Academy, and I tagged along. Thinks she can get a scholarship. Violin, cello. She's really set on living and performing in Europe."

Caine continued to chat as he filled the four flash drives she'd provided, Piper only half-listening.

Piper looked out the window, down the main road that led into the Village. Her mind was occupied by Oren, the fire, the mysterious lawsuit her father had mentioned. Too many things jousted for prominence. Nang flitted in her thoughts. Married only one week ago and waiting until month's end so she'd have vacation days for a honeymoon. That trip could be postponed because of all of this, Oren being injured, she was down a deputy. Nang would understand. He might actually be happy to put it off, what with looking at buildings to buy so he could open a restaurant. Their lives seemed so busy, going opposite directions.

Things were less complicated during her four years in the Army. It had been challenging and at times dangerous, but not as interesting, heartbreaking, happy, taxing, and perplexing as working as a sheriff in Indiana. This job was challenging, and at times downright dangerous.

Caine raised his voice, recapturing Piper's attention.

"We spent a couple of days in Milfontes, a littlish place. The name means a thousand fountains. Supposedly it's choked with tourists from all over the world in the summer. But the first of December, it ain't crowded. The houses were small and beautiful. The coast absolutely gorgeous. I could live there, Portugal, find a security job, or maybe something in construction while Bette goes to school. Hell, maybe I'd get some college, too, do something important with my life, learn the language. I took a lot of pictures. Want to see them?"

Piper shook her head, not interested in someone else's vacation at the moment.

"The beach is a serious wow. Crap, sixty-two degrees that day we were there. Winter, but balmy compared to here. I almost dove in. I saw a guy catch a squid on the rocks. He picked it up, and the thing squirted ink all over him. He tossed it into the water, and it disappeared. He had black gunk all over his jeans. Me and Bette couldn't stop laughing."

Another tune came on, Alan Jackson singing something about his father getting drunk at Christmas, and Caine reached over and thumbed it off.

"I copied the list of scheduled deliveries for the past week, just in case you need them. You know, pizza, flowers, Amazon, UPS. A bunch of Amazon vans come in, especially from November on, people Christmas shopping I guess." Kenny passed her the drives. "If Bette gets accepted to that academy, it'd be great. Winter in Lisbon definitely beats winter in Spencer County. We'd move over sometime in the summer. Apartment rent isn't too bad, and—"

Piper impatiently tapped her belt, hoping he'd finish rambling.

Caine pulled out his cell phone and scrolled through his Lisbon pictures, angling it so Piper could see. "Look how blue the water is. Just look at it!"

37

"Nice scenery," she said, trying to be polite. Hitting record on her phone, she asked him a series of questions. He was quick to answer.

"People who live in the Village, they have cards for this gate and the two others," Kenny explained. "Only three ways in and out of the Village. But this is the only gate that's manned, and all deliveries come through here. No card, the gate ain't goin' up. And you'll see from the video I gave you ain't nobody been sneaking in through any of them. If you're not a resident, you have to be vouched for by someone who lives here to get in."

"You mentioned deliveries, UPS. Surely not all of them are scheduled."

He grinned and thumped a clipboard. "*Anyone* who comes in has to be approved. Like I said, vouched for. If it ain't on the schedule, some delivery showing up, I call the residence. The driver can't get past this gate unless he or she's okayed. If the resident ain't home, sometimes the driver leaves a package here, or comes back later. No exceptions. Not even for the almighty Amazon. Now the mail carrier, she's an exception. She drives in with that midget van with open doors so they can lean out and stuff the mailboxes."

Caine stroked his chin and frowned. "Okay, and emergency vehicles. We let the cops and fire department in, just like when Sheriff Rosenberg's house on Sled burned." He paused. "Oh, and this morning I let in some guy from the State Fire Marshal's office. He came through right before you showed up. Flashed me his badge and was pretty pushy. Fire Chief Wollach's back there, too."

"How long have you worked for the Village?"

"Little over two years, not quite three. Ain't a bad job. I sit on my ass mostly, watch the feeds, check everyone going in and out. Start at seven every morning, butt crack of dawn basically. Get off at three. Four days a week. They let me bring Rocket." He pointed to the Labrador. "I work two days at The Christmas Store."

Since they'd arrived, Piper had noticed a half-dozen cars leaving, the occupants dressed as if they were going to church or a fancy place for brunch. Caine had checked each one, naming the families as they passed.

"You know a lot of the people."

He shrugged. "More than nine hundred homes in the Village, and the families don't all use this gate. So, no. I don't know all that many, actually. I see their names, cars, recognize them that way, but I don't really *know* a lot. Not to know the names of their pets and kids, favorite TV shows, and what kind of beer they buy. No meaningful conversations. I know your deputy lives here." He looked over his shoulder at Basil. "I see you drive out early in the morning, Sundays with your wife and kids. Hard not to notice you."

Piper suspected he meant because Basil was black. Spencer County was basically lily white, though Santa Claus and Rockport had a smattering of blacks, Hispanics, and Asians. Deep in its history an entire community of black families occupied a large chunk of land, but they moved on for better job opportunities. A crumbling cemetery remained. She hoped her county would become more diverse, but it would need more industry and businesses to accomplish that.

"I ain't livin' in the Village," Caine continued. "Houses too expensive for my budget. And then there's that annual fee. I have a big apartment in Santa Claus. Nice one. Rent's good 'cause I have a roommate, Mason. He works here, too. Four days, three to eleven. They can't give us five days a week, you know, then we'd qualify for all the benefits."

"Mr. Caine, you mentioned—"

"My fiancé, Bette, she lives here in the Village," he prattled on. "Just 'cause she still lives with her parents. But that'll change when we move to Portugal. Her family has a two-story on Ornament Lane. Not far from Sled. Bette said she saw the flames from her bedroom window last night. All the sirens and stuff woke her up."

Piper tapped her belt faster and let out a deep breath.

Oblivious, he continued. "I met her my first morning on the job, a sort of love-at-first-sight thing. We got engaged at Thanksgiving." He skimmed through more photos on his cell phone. "Here. This is Bette and me outside the spy museum in Lisbon. A lot of spies were trained in some school in Portugal decades back."

39

Piper wanted to hurry this along. "Do you know the Laubensteins?"

"Not personally," he returned. "I know they live on Sled. Next to Sheriff Rosenberg. I know they're gray, retired, and that they're snowbirding in Miami. Every year they snowbird in Miami, got a condo or something, I think. They're gonna be surprised as all hell to come back and see the cinders."

Piper did not correct him. *Chief Deputy Rosenberg.*

"By the names you can tell they're Jewish. Laubenstein, Rosenberg. Sheriff Rosenberg ... oh, my bad. That would be deputy, right? He lost the election last year. Always waves to me in the morning. I heard he's in the hospital. Hope he's gonna be okay." Caine bumped his clipboard and nodded to a middle-aged woman driving a silver Volvo. The gate arm rose. "That's Laura White, lives on December 25th Lane. Single. No idea where she works. No idea where she's going today. Jeans and a sweatshirt? She's probably not going to church." He bumped the clipboard again. "And, no, I don't know who was staying in the Laubenstein house. I heard the gossip, two people burned there who weren't the Laubensteins. Can't help you there. I'd ask the families on Sled."

"Thank you, Mr. Caine," Piper said. She passed him her card. "If you can think of anything else that might—"

"Sure," he cut in. "I'll call if something else surfaces in my brain."

He thumbed the speaker on and Faith Hill crooned "Where Are You, Christmas?"

7

Looks like the fire started here, Sheriff, back of the house, right outside the kitchen window. See? Next to the AC unit." He paused. "What used to be the AC unit." The man wore navy blue pants, creased, tucked into leather boots that had thick soles and obvious steel toes. Sporting a mud-brown bomber jacket with an ivory wooly collar, he'd clipped his State Fire Marshal badge to the wide lapel.

"Richard Oster," he said, thrusting out an ungloved hand. "Rick."

Piper, wearing her driver's gloves, shook it, noting his grip was uncomfortably strong. She squeezed back. "Piper Black—"

"Sheriff Piper Blackwell. I know who you are. Something of a celebrity. You handled a couple of major drug busts in the fall. Serious pot farm, meth lab so big the Feds came in. Largest take downs in the state's history. The *Indy Star* ran stories for days. Made the national news. Pleasure to meet you."

"And Detective Basil Meredith," Piper added an introduction, indicating him with a hand. "He discovered the drug operations." *Along with Chief Deputy Oren Rosenberg, who nearly lost his life to this fire.*

41

"Pleasure." Oster shook Basil's hand.

Santa Claus Fire Chief Wollach joined them. He'd been walking around the perimeter of both properties, taking pictures, shaking his head as if in disbelief.

The wreckage looked worse this morning, the bright sun illuminated charred wood, collapsed bricks, sections of walls leaning precariously, and twisted things that had been furniture and appliances and memories. Oren's fireplace and chimney still stood, like a tall digit flipping off the neighborhood. The scene had been bad enough when she came out hours earlier while the volunteer fire department fought the blaze. The darkness and sleet muted much of the horror then. Odors of burned and melted things remained strong.

She turned on her body cam, noticing Basil was using the department camera, getting shots of the destruction, Oster, Wollach, and the neighbors perched on the sidewalk across the street.

Ten onlookers bundled in winter coats, two of them with cell phones up and recording, Piper noted. Maybe they were among the gawkers hours ago when the fire raged. Three men stood separate, near an open garage, the clouds of mist around their heads evidence of their conversation. Faces peered from windows, many of them children. Maybe someone watching knew something about the victims who'd died in the Laubenstein house. Or had seen something.

"I agree with you," Oster said to Basil, nodding. "This is arson. Clumsy, amateur, clear. I'll conduct a thorough investigation to back it up. I have two technicians with me and we'll get footage and samples." He filled the pause with a chuckle. "Well, they'll be back here in a little while. Baxter takes frequent pee breaks, and they're picking up coffees."

"You said the fire started here," Piper cut in. Wood crunched under her feet as she walked, pieces of Oren's house. "Show me."

"Show you?" Oster grinned. He had dark red hair with a white streak along his right temple; maybe there was a story behind that. His nose seemed a little too long for his face, and he had the hint of a mustache. He wore frameless oval glasses, and the creases at the corners of his blue eyes suggested he smiled a lot. She guessed him to be maybe forty-five, fifty, and clearly knowledgeable in his field. "Sure, I'll show you. I can't provide a course for you, Sheriff. But I recommend you take one, at least the basics of arson. My office holds them twice a year, open to law enforcement and volunteer firefighters. Won't make you an expert, but it'll teach you some things to look for."

Piper thought that would be a good idea. She'd invite either Basil or Diego to join her.

"Look, you'll see that all the answers are in the ashes, Sheriff. All of them. We just have to listen close enough."

"Listen?"

"Fire … even the aftermath of a fire … talks to you. It leaves behind a trace that says where it burned hottest and its likely point of origin. Sometimes you'll see lightbulbs melted like arrows, pointing toward the starting point. Sometimes you just see things like this."

For the next half hour Oster pointed to spots in the wreckage and described the fire's path. The char smell settled again in her mouth, though not as bad as hours ago. Wollach followed, keeping quiet.

"This fire doesn't just talk, Sheriff, it screams. Amateurs make my job a little easier. Amateur arsonists, careless burners, leave the best evidence. They don't know how to choreograph a fire. Don't know how to sculpt it." Oster stepped a little farther away and nodded to flat piece of melted plastic. "This used to be either a gas canister or big jug. My guess, five-gallon plastic gas canister." He pointed to a blackened strip of material, partially burned. "And that is what's left of the wick. Fire goes up fast, things get propelled away, not everything gets incinerated. Looks like maybe a thick athletic sock or a hunk of thermal shirt. They shoved it in the jug, lit it, and ran. A wick like that gives you time to get away. You need to bag it, might get some DNA from it. Skin cells, if the arsonist didn't wear gloves." He smiled. "Or if he used a sock he hadn't laundered. DNA can survive the heat of a fire."

Piper stared at the cloth, nothing she would have noticed. Definitely, she'd sign up for the next class. She watched Basil carefully bag it, then the remnant of the jug.

"There might be some other things left behind. I'll be here for another hour or so. Let you know what I come up with." Oster took off his glasses and tugged a handkerchief from his pocket. He deliberately cleaned one lens and then the other before shining the earpieces and putting the spectacles back on. "My belief ... and I'll analyze debris, gas chromatography, before I put it in a report. But my belief is that the arsonist took a full jug of gas, sat it up against the house by the air conditioner, stuck sock in it, lit it, and ran like hell. Maybe two gas jugs, judging by the burn patterns. Probably two. Likely gasoline rather than diesel. Gasoline burns better. I've seen this before. But we'll check for additional accelerants, see if he used anything else."

"You say 'he,'" Piper noted.

"Nine in ten arsonists are men," Oster explained. "I'd put your arsonist here as male, under forty, and single. An older man wouldn't have come out in the cold and sleet that late at night, not as likely anyway. An older soul would be inside where it's warm, with his family, watching TV maybe, or sound asleep. And I'd say he's white. But that's based on your county's demographics."

They walked the scene again, and Oster indicated various patterns that Piper would not have noticed, and where the wind had pushed the fire into the Laubenstein house next door.

"I'll check the data bases, looking for similar fires, histories, see if there's a pattern with houses lacking Christmas decorations getting torched. But I doubt I'll find anything. This feels like a one-off."

Piper raised her eyebrows.

"A one-and-done. Oren Rosenberg's house was the target. My report won't tell you *why* the fire was set," Oster continued. "That's for you to figure out. I get you're thinking hate crime. God knows there's plenty of hate in the world. Both households Jewish. And I see the six-pointed star painted on your deputy's garage. Maybe because he was Jewish. Maybe he pissed off someone he arrested. Maybe he did something one of the neighbors took exception to, didn't decorate his yard. No twinkling lights might have been a deal-breaking faux pas to some twisted son of a bitch."

They finished patrolling the perimeter, Oster talking into a recorder. He finally stopped and met Piper's stare. "Like I said, an arsonist always leaves something behind. But arsonists, they take something, too. Some of them rob a place first, grab a thing of value. Unless it's a contract they're fulfilling, money changing hands, usually what they take is satisfaction, pleasure, vengeance. I'll turn over what I come up with and leave any charges to you and the district attorney … provided you find the perpetrator. Let's hope for DNA. I doubt you'll find him by fingerprints. It was cold last night, sleeting. The arsonist probably wore gloves. Hell, I should be wearing gloves."

He walked toward the standing garage, Piper and Basil followed. Wollach hovered at the back of Oren's house, talking to someone on his cell phone.

"You can scour the yards for footprints, get pictures. But don't expect much from that with the firemen here earlier, tromping around, us tromping, and the water saturating the yard washing away evidence. The ground is hard now because of the cold, that makes it tough, too. I'm going to stop at some of the neighbors, see if they have doorbell cams, surveillance video. I'll get you copies of any footage I pull. And I'll drive down again if you need me." He handed her one of his cards and turned it over. "That's my personal cell number. Feel free."

Piper, in turn, passed over one of the flash drives. "From security cameras belonging to Christmas Lake Village," she explained.

"Thanks. Bet you used a warrant."

She nodded.

"That's important," Oster lectured. "I've seen court cases where footage gets thrown out because it wasn't obtained correctly. I've seen arsonists walk."

"Thank you. When we find this arsonist," Piper said, "he isn't walking anywhere but straight into prison facing murder charges."

8

Noon

See any strangers in the neighborhood last night?
Anyone walking around Oren Rosenberg's house?
Do you know who was staying at the Laubenstein's?
Where were you late yesterday?
Did Oren Rosenberg mention any threats he'd received?
Hear anything before the fire?

Basil walked door-to-door, asking the neighbors the same questions, varied in tempo and timbre and order. The answers—a mix of polite, eager, reluctant, and terse—were similar in substance. For the most part, nothing he found terribly useful.

Didn't see any strangers.
No one hanging around Oren's. Except for Police Chief Paul Black-well, who was over there around dinner time.
Don't know who was staying at Eldad's place.
I was home all night. Too nasty to be out.

No threats, never mentioned any threats.

What did I hear?

The television.
Nothing.
Christmas music.
My husband snoring.
The dog snoring.
Sleet hitting the bedroom window.
Sirens ... but that was after the fire started.

Basil watched as the burned Volkswagen Rabbit was towed away from the Laubensteins'. Production on those cars stopped almost forty years ago, 1984; he'd checked with a Google search.

He radioed Diego: "When it arrives, go through every inch of that car, video it, see what you can get from the VIN and the plates."

"Can't be too many vintage Rabbits on the road. Shouldn't take long to pin down the owner," Diego replied. "Doc says autopsies are scheduled back to back Monday afternoon. Then we can get dentals. DNA will take awhile if we have to go that route. But I'm betting between the old car and the teeth, we'll put names to the dead people."

Basil wished he'd worn his heavy winter coat over his uniform rather than his department jacket: while looking official, it wasn't enough to keep out the cold. His breath puffed away in miniature clouds as he moved to the next house on his list, Vernon Madsen's. Faintly, he heard Christmas music coming from it, sounded like Mannheim Steamroller or Transiberian Orchestra ... techy-pop stirred with traditional. Esme played stuff like that. He preferred light jazz.

"Nobody around here has a problem with Rosey or Eldad." Vernon Madsen lived across the street from the Laubensteins. Madsen was a robust man with a ring of black hair that made his bald spot stand out like an intended tonsure. He stepped onto his porch and glared across the street. "They're great neighbors. Long time on the block. Some people gripe about their lack of decorations, the only bare houses on the Run. But nobody around here gives a rat's ass that they're Jewish. I give a rat's ass about that." He gestured at the ruins. "Just look. Awful. Bet they bulldoze and sell and go somewhere else. Shame. Just a shame."

Only a few of the decorations along Sled Run were lit. People typically turned them on at dusk. That's when Basil did, brighten up the night. He'd strung lights on two pines in his yard and on rose bushes, stretched some icicle lights across the top of the garage, wanting to fit in. Rare to see a house in Christmas Lake Village without some sort of outdoor holiday décor. He and Esme walked with the kids almost every night to take it all in. Esme said she missed Marshall Fields' Christmas window displays and the elegant Walnut Room tree, but the Village after dark was almost an adequate substitute.

Madsen was right. Oren's and the Laubensteins' had stood out in this neighborhood because of their lack of decorations. And now they stood out because they were charred mounds, their burned reek still hanging in the chill air.

Only a couple houses left, then he'd meander the few blocks home, fix a salad, check on the cats, hope Esme wasn't angry that he'd passed Oren's clowder off to her … on top of her dealing with the kids and being pregnant, and on a deadline. She was a saint.

"A Rabbit, huh? I knew it was an old car in that garage. Saw it when the door was up, lots of rust. A Rabbit? That's like an antique," Anna Carpenter said. She lived one house up across the street from the Laubensteins. Mid-thirties, pencil-thin and yawning, wearing pajamas under a fuzzy blue robe despite the hour. Basil guessed he'd awakened her. "Sure, Detective Meredith, I saw lights on in Eldad's house. For at least a week. I knew he and his wife were in Florida, thought maybe they had a house-sitter, you know, whoever was driving that rusty white car was a house sitter. I saw a man at the window one night, looking out at my decorations. My sister puts a lot of work into our crèche. Couldn't tell you who he was, how old he was, didn't see him up close, you know. Just saw him looking."

Basil admitted the Carpenters had an impressive inflatable nativity display: manger, wise men, camels, sheep, a goat, practically the entire lawn covered with life-size blow-ups. No doubt whoever stayed in the Laubenstein house had looked out at it. Impossible to ignore.

He moved on, thoughts tumbling.

"Too busy to go over there, check out those people," Norma Wilkins said after he knocked on her door and introduced himself. "I think they were there since the beginning of the month, came in about the time Eldad and Saundra went south. Figured they were supposed to be there. Relatives. House-sitters. Didn't think much of it. This time of the year is busy for me." Norma lived next to Anna Carpenter and was an older woman with her white hair pulled back so tight into a bun it looked painful to Basil. Her long nose and the way she bobbed her head reminded him of a pigeon. "I volunteer with the letters for Santa project, one of Santa's Elves. Busy. Very busy. Santa's Elves are—"

Basil knew Santa Claus had the only post office in the country named for the red-suited "right jolly old elf." That post office received thousands of letters to Santa from all over the world, and the local volunteers, called Santa's Elves, replied to all the ones that had return addresses. The tradition dated to the beginning of WWI.

Norma went on. "Every year they go to Miami when December comes 'round, and they come back all nice and tanned in March. Have a condo or timeshare or something. They go down to chase the sun, looking for summer. I envy them in a way, but I wouldn't miss being a Santa's Elf for the beach. Saw groceries being delivered there twice since they've been gone. Well, it might have been more than twice. But I only *saw* it twice."

Basil thought the grocery tidbit could be followed up. Only one grocery store in Santa Claus delivered, maybe chasing that down could identify the two.

"Sheriff," Norma continued, "is Rosey okay? He's a good man, would do anything for you. He made the whole street safe just by being here. Can't imagine why anyone would set his house on fire. Certainly not because he's Jewish. Nothing wrong with being Jewish. Sheriff, do you think—"

"Detective," Basil corrected her. "I'm the department's detective. The sheriff is Piper Blackwell."

"Piper. Like in the Twelve Days of Christmas? Pipers piping. I seem to remember reading about her, and you, and some big drug bust last month. Drugs in our little county." She shuddered and scowled. "Oren was quoted in the paper, too, about all the drugs. Piper. I should've remembered the sheriff's name. I'm just so busy. Piper. Piper."

"You were asking—"

"Do you think the street is safe? That fire. This is a gated subdivision. *Gated.* Do you think we should be worried?"

It was a fair question.

Norma and her immediate neighbors all had Christmas displays in their yards. The hate had targeted homes without the decorations. That fact spun in his brain.

"I doubt you're in any danger," he answered truthfully.

"Gated," she said again.

"Thank you," he responded, and turned away.

That had been one of the things attracting Basil to the community. A *gated* subdivision—the only one in the county, 24/7 guard post, cameras in various places. Protected. A safe place for kids.

Standing on the sidewalk, he looked up and down Sled Run, stared between houses to see other homes on parallel streets that had Christmassy names. Saw children out playing in the snow.

Gated. Three roads in, all with check-points. Safe. Secure.

Bullshit.

Gated didn't mean impervious. It didn't mean there was a ten-foot high wall and razor wire surrounding the place. Basil knew that when he bought here. Gated did imply a measure of security, though.

Three roads in?

There were a lot more ways than that to get into this subdivision; you were only limited if you drove. His own kids dashed through yards to visit their friends. People could cut across land from outside the subdivision to get in. The golf course butted up against Christmas Lake Village, and that presented another opportunity. If someone wanted in badly enough, they'd find a way through the golf course. And it wouldn't be all that difficult.

"I should've been suspicious," David Halm told him, gesturing Basil to come into the living room and take a seat. The inside was all merry-merry with a large flocked tree and matching garland draped on the fireplace mantle. Basil first talked to him in the wee hours this morning, apparently a good friend of Oren's. "Lord, Oren is such a great guy. Who the hell would be mad enough to burn his house down? And the Laubensteins, good neighbors, but sort of keep to themselves. Why would they need someone watching their house in a place like this? Don't need a house-sitter unless you have a helluva lot of indoor plants to water or parakeets to feed. I should've thought something was up, the lights coming on over there at night."

Basil spent a half-hour with Halm, who'd seemed clearly concerned about the arson. "Gated," he mentioned repeatedly. "You can't just stroll into the neighborhood and set a fire. You have to come through one of the gates to get back here." He paused and rubbed his chin. "I sure hope it wasn't because Oren and the Laubensteins are Jewish. I can't see—"

"Hey, Dad—" The teenager tromping down the stairs wore black sweatpants and a purple sweatshirt with Sacred Leather on the chest, a heavy metal band out of Indy. He stopped and stared at Basil, eyes narrow and crazy-glazed, then popping wide, still all crazy. "What the hell is *he* doing in here? What the hell is that black son of a—"

Halm stood, mouth open, a mix of shock and ire on his face. "Jerome. Don't you talk like—"

"What the hell, Dad!" Jerome spat and leaped to the bottom of the steps, swung to his left, blond ponytail flailing behind him, bolting into the kitchen. "What the hell!"

It was reflexes that made Basil jump up, dodge furniture, slip past the Christmas tree, and run after him.

Dog to the Rabbit.

If the rabbit runs, the dog will chase it. If the rabbit had stood in place, the dog probably would not have bothered. It was the "black son of a bitch" that really fueled Basil.

The kitchen was large and bright, white cupboards and counters, gleaming stainless appliances, shiny tile floor, smell of bread baking in the oven, pot of soup on the stove, all of it a blur as Basil raced after Jerome out a back door that hung open in the teen's panicked wake.

There's a reason the rabbit bolted, and Basil needed to find out what that was. What did the teen know about the fire across the street? Was he involved? If he had a problem with blacks, did he have a problem with Jews?

David Halm hollered for his son to stop running, and for Basil to stop chasing him, the powerless words fading as the pursuit continued.

"Shit. Shit. Shit. Shit." Jerome cursed as he looked over his shoulder and pumped his arms in time with his stockinged feet. He angled across the backyard, seemingly oblivious to the icy-snowy lawn, sprinting over a fire pit, then over a row of low hedges and onto another property where children were building a misshapen igloo.

Basil, taller, had a long stride and was angry at what Jerome had called him, at being forced to run past the igloo-builders through one backyard and then another and another, now at a right angle as Jerome headed toward Donder Lane. Basil caught a glance at neighbors looking out of windows, one with a cell phone up. He heard David Halm somewhere behind them, still hollering.

He'd nearly closed the distance, and then Jerome pivoted around the corner of a brick ranch when he neared Donder, Basil losing sight of him for only a moment.

Basil planted his foot and whirled, following, gaining, eyes fixed on the blond ponytail whipping in the cold wind. Dodging snowmen and nutcrackers and Santa and his elves arrayed artfully and garishly.

"Stop!" Basil shouted. "Now!"

"Shit. Shit. Shit." Came the reply. Jerome dropped his right arm to his side, losing speed, gasping, slipping in his stocking feet but still not giving up.

"Stop!" Basil launched, a football-legal tackle, grabbing the teen around the waist and barreling into a plastic reindeer trio pulling a wagon filled with stuffed animals. The reindeer crunched under the impact, antlers snapping, stuffed dogs and cats and teddy bears flying. Softer: "I. Said. Stop."

Basil picked himself up and pulled Jerome with him, the teen's Sacred Leather sweatshirt covered with snow.

"You black son of a bitch!" Jerome cursed. He stood there, panting, red-faced from the cold, shivering, and shifting from one foot to the other as if that would cut the chill which must be lancing up from his stockinged feet. He glanced around like he might take off running again, eyes still crazy-glazed. Basil thought Jerome might be on something.

"Let's get you home," Basil said.

"I can find my own way back, you black son of—"

Basil pointed across the street.

Jerome glared. "My house is in the other direction. I don't need you to escort me home. And you can't just come into someone's house like you did. You can't just—just waltz in and—I'll have your badge. I'll ruin you! Hear me? I'll—"

"Your dad invited me in." Basil put cuffs on the kid and again pointed across the street. "We're going to my house first. Move. This way." Basil's department Explorer was parked in his driveway, which was closer now. He'd been hoofing it through the subdivision. He'd get the kid into the car, where at least he could get his feet warmed up, and take him back to his dad's house.

"You're arresting me? You can't do that. Take off these damn cuffs!" Jerome struggled, but Basil held him firm.

He didn't have to arrest him to put him in handcuffs. Basil was detaining the kid for questioning. Cuffs kept both Jerome and Basil safe.

Basil had nothing to charge Jerome with … not illegal to run, not illegal to call someone a black son of a bitch, freedom of speech and all. But let the kid think he was in serious trouble for a little while, might teach him some respect. Basil talked as he prodded Jerome along. Maybe the kid had seen something the night of the fire … or been involved.

- Were you at Oren Rosenberg's house last night?
- Do you know who was staying at the Laubensteins'?
- Where were you late yesterday? *Where were you?*
- Did you make any threats to Oren Rosenberg?
- Did you set the fire?

"Go to hell," Jerome spat. "I didn't set no fire. It's just pot. Pot. It's legal in Illinois. It should be legal here. It's just pot."

Basil stopped and patted the teen down, finding a baggie with a dozen joints in it.

"Just pot," Jerome grumbled.

"Shit," Basil said.

9

---

1 p.m.

Fatigue winnowed its way into her bones. A yawn and a glance in the mirror on the visor showed she had raccoon eyes. Should have taken the time to dab on a little concealer.

Piper stuck the straight end of a candy cane in her mouth. The sharp, sweet taste of peppermint jabbed her senses just enough to nudge her alert. It was a few minutes past one. She'd been driving for nearly an hour, and it would take another two to reach the hospital in Indianapolis. Her dad was with her. She'd ask him to chauffeur on the way back, take a nap then. But for now, she'd rely on the peppermint.

The heat barely on, Piper had shed her coat. She needed to be just cold enough to be uncomfortable, another tactic to keep drowsiness at bay. She'd called ahead to the hospital; Millie told her Oren had awakened and would talk about the fire, and said he was asking about his cats. She also said: "Pops is depressed as all hell."

The stretch through the Hoosier National Forest was Christmas card worthy, light snow-covered pine branches, the ground thinly blanketed. She'd picked this route, taking 64 through the woods toward Louisville, then 66 up through Scottsburg, Austin, and

Seymour. On the map it looked longer, an L-shaped course rather than the seemingly straight shot that State Roads 37 or 57 offered. But this was better for time, more lanes, fewer stops, no small-town congestion. Three hours instead of three and a half. Piper always seemed to be in a hurry.

Her dad, in the passenger seat of her department Explorer, had been passing the time talking about Oren's love of Freya, the first cat the chief deputy had acquired after previously having dogs, and regaling her with assorted stories from his and Oren's time together in the sheriff's department.

"I'm shpulling over at the next McDonald's," she announced. Her words slurred around the candy cane. "Shor Burger King, shor Dunkin's, shor whatever."

"Coffee?"

She nodded and took the candy cane out. "A big coffee. A really big one. I should have packed a thermos."

"Did you get any sleep this morning?"

"Two hours, I think. Maybe three. I'm good at the moment. I'll let you know if I'm not. I'm thinking fries, too, and a cheeseburger, no onions. Drive while I dine. I'm hungry."

"A double cheeseburger," he said.

She was glad her dad had insisted on seeing Oren so she'd have company. Piper knew they couldn't stay long, visiting restricted, but she wanted to show her concern and—more than that—quiz Oren about what he remembered. Maybe he knew who had been staying at the Laubenstein house. Maybe he'd seen something, saw who started the fire. She knew a face-to-face with him would yield more than a phone call.

"Talk to me, Dad," Piper coaxed.

"I have been talking to you."

"Tell me about this lawsuit against you and Oren." Traffic was blessedly light along this stretch, and that let Piper prod the Explorer five miles above the posted limit. She'd thought about turning on her lights and siren, cranking the speed. She was in a hurry, but that wouldn't be right, not an emergency, as Oren wasn't going anywhere.

The wintry countryside passed by, and she spotted a big Dutch barn with a steep pitched roof to the east. An old design, not many of them around anymore.

"Punkin', I really don't think—" Paul frowned. "How about some music? A little radio roulette? Spin the dial and—"

"Like I mentioned before, I have a meeting Monday with DA Scales, our regular monthly go-round. Maybe he'll tell me what's going on. You hinted my department might get sued, too. So, talk to me before I talk to Scales."

Paul let out a deep sigh that sounded like dirt blowing across a dry field. "Oh, hell. All right. It goes way back."

Paul drummed his fingers against the seatbelt clasp. He wore his Santa Claus Police Department uniform, even though this was a day off for him. "The lawsuit is because of something that happened before you were born. It was one of the first big arrests I made working for the sheriff's department."

He glanced out the side window, his breath hitting the glass and fogging it. "Remember asking me about Lefty Jay?"

Piper nodded. In November she'd noticed an older man with droopy jeans and frizzled hair walking past the department. Later, she saw him sitting on a bench in front of the hardware store. He was reading a Val McDermid paperback, holding it close to his face. Piper's path had taken her past him. She'd paused to chat, thinking he might be homeless or needed help; he had that look, rumpled clothes, dirty hands.

His ruddy face was wrinkled like a raisin, and he smelled of old sweat. He'd said: "You tell your dad that Lefty Jay said 'hey,' okay?"

"Yeah. I remember mentioning Lefty Jay to you. I still see him around town, wearing only jeans and a sweater despite the cold. No idea where he's living. Over really good pie you told me he should still be in prison."

A semi moved up in the lane behind her. It had a wreath and a big red bow tied to the grille. She half-expected it to pass her, but it hung back, maybe fearful she'd stop him for speeding. Not her county, but she could stop him or radio his license plate number to dispatch.

"Convicted of murder, shooting his brother. Lefty and Geno owned three small grocery stores in the county. Dale, Rockport, and Santa Claus. Friendly Foods. It happened at the Dale store, not a friendly place when Oren and I arrived. Apparently, the brothers had gotten into an argument, and Lefty pulled a gun and fired on Geno. Convicted, Lefty got sent away for life, no chance for parole. *For life.*"

"Thirty years ago? His murder charge—"

"An unclassified felony, he could have gotten death. Sentence recommendation was between forty-five and sixty-five years, and the court settled on the mid-point, fifty-five. Thirty? Him out in thirty? That's not close to fifty-five. Out twenty-five years early. If you look at him, you can tell he doesn't have twenty-five years left in that flimsy frame. He should have died in prison."

"But he's out."

"Hell, yes, he's out. It took more than a year after his arrest before all the court stuff wrapped up and he was sentenced and sent away. He's been out since Labor Day."

"He's the one suing you? And Oren?"

Paul's jaw jutted out and his fingers drummed faster. Then he pulled his hands into his jacket pockets.

"People were shopping at Friendly Foods that afternoon. Four customers. Two employees. Someone called us from the payphone in the parking lot, said there was an argument, that one of the brothers had a gun. Lefty Jay."

"So, you caught the call. Go on."

"At the end of it, Lefty ... Jayson Walden ... told us he'd shot his younger brother in self-defense, said he thought Geno was going to kill him."

"Brotherly love," Piper whispered.

"The brothers, they were young then, early thirties, were having money problems and announced they'd be closing the Friendly Foods in Santa Claus and Rockport before Christmas. They said the Dale store would follow six months later, profits too low to keep any of them going. Their relationship had deteriorated because of the financial struggles, and each had obtained an attorney about a year before the shooting. It was common skuttle that they were trying to split whatever assets they had left. Word was the brothers rarely talked to each other after announcing the closings, relied on postcards and had their wives relay messages."

"So, the money problems led to the murder." Piper stuck the candy cane back in her mouth and with a *crunch* bit off a piece. She passed the exit with the McDonald's sign, not wanting her desire for coffee to give her dad a reason to pause his story.

"It all boiled over when Lefty Jay sauntered into the Dale store around lunchtime and saw his brother talking to an employee. We think Lefty believed that employee was funneling financial information about the store to Geno, and that set it off. Witnesses said Lefty called Geno a bastard and told him to get out of the store. Lefty was the primary owner, sixty percent, so he figured the twenty-percent edge over Geno put him in charge."

Piper removed the candy cane again and waved it like a conductor with a baton. "Obviously, Geno didn't leave fast enough." She'd dig through the records in the office and courthouse for the official report.

"Lefty testified in court that Geno had punched him in the stomach, knocked him down, and kicked him several times. The witnesses in the store didn't corroborate that. Then Lefty claimed Geno pulled a knife. Lefty admitted he'd been carrying a pistol in his back pocket because there had been a few burglaries at the store. The burglaries part was true. Lefty drew the gun, a .357 Derringer. The witnesses did corroborate the gun."

"Lefty drawing it?"

Paul nodded. "Lefty said he shot Geno, said he feared for his life, said Geno was going to kill him with that knife." Paul pointed to an exit sign that indicated Burger King was two miles away. Piper drove past it.

"And—"

"And the witnesses testified that Lefty shot Geno in the back ... *in the back*, that Geno was running away ... right between the shoulder blades. They said Geno spun around and fell, was still alive and hollering for help. Lefty stomped up and shot him in the head to finish him off. We got there just as the shoppers and employees ran out the front door. Maybe they thought Lefty would shoot them, too. Lefty surrendered to us, screamed self-defense, and we called the coroner. Never found this supposed knife Geno was waving. Self-defense? Lefty'd stopped his brother with the first bullet to the back. Lefty didn't need to fire the second."

"No body cams, no surveillance video," Piper mused. "No cell phones to record it."

"You're going to say primitive policing," Paul grumbled.

"No. I was going to say it hinged entirely on forensic evidence and witness testimony."

Paul shrugged and stared straight ahead. "Sentenced to life, no chance of parole. But he kept appealing, and this past summer some damn fancy lawyer in Indy got some stuff from the trial thrown out, witness testimony tossed, raised questions about the jury—" He made a low huffing sound. "They cut Lefty loose, and he came back here. Like a ghost, he's been wandering around Rockport, getting noticed, haunting me and Oren and everyone else involved who's still alive. And that damn fancy lawyer has filed a suit against Oren and me for wrongful arrest and some other things. I know damn well the suit includes the Spencer County Sheriff's Department and no doubt the whole county. It all hasn't trickled out yet. Lefty's looking for millions."

Piper bit off another piece of candy cane and took the next exit. There was a sign advertising Wendy's. It would do.

"Crap," she said. "A crapstorm of bad news."

"Yeah. Crap. We did everything by the book. He's just looking for that big pot of gold, and that isn't going to happen. He's not going to get a penny. Lefty murdered his brother and doesn't have a case. But —" Paul let a slice of silence settle, then continued. "But it's a pain in the ass. I'm probably going to have to hire an attorney. A pain in the ass. Gonna cost me time and money. And Oren ... my old friend has to deal with it too, on top of him losing his house and almost losing his life."

"Crap," Piper repeated. She pulled into the drive-thru and decided their cups weren't large enough. She'd order at least two.

To Piper, Oren had the build of a linebacker ... tall, broad-shouldered, strong, physically fit. He'd always seemed far younger than his sixty-six years. But in this moment, he appeared weak and old, *truly old*, and all the lines and monitors and bandages were a gut-punch she'd wrongly thought herself ready for.

Her imagination had paled next to this rotten reality. Tours in the Middle East had largely inured her to the injuries fellow soldiers and insurgents suffered. But this was Oren stretched out and bandaged and hooked up, her chief deputy, burned in an arson fire set in a secure gated subdivision. A horror in a supposedly safe and rustic place.

She and Basil would find the arsonist.

The room smelled of antiseptic and something vaguely floral, though no flowers were present. Maybe there was a fragrance embedded in these white hazmat-looking outfits she and her dad wore to gain admission. Limited to two visitors, Millie had been consigned to the hall.

Oren's voice was sandpaper, like he'd smoked a pack a day for decades. Ten years older than her father, in this moment he could have been a hundred. She edged up to the side of the bed to better hear him. Paul stood by the door, looking out into the hall.

"Freya," Oren started.

"And your three other cats," Piper said. "Basil has all of them."

"Good man," Oren replied. "But he doesn't know cats. Told me he never had a pet."

"He's smart," Piper returned. "And I'm sure—"

"You don't know cats either."

"I have a cat. Marmalade is—"

"—an old cat you inherited with your fine house." Oren coughed and his shoulders bounced against the pillow. One of the lines on a monitor did an erratic zigzag jump before evening out again. "Cats orient to places, they have favorite spots in a house, are territorial. They don't know Basil's house. And they don't know Basil. Have Basil call me. Or I'll call him. Millie's going to get me a new cell phone. My cats need to be set up in a room to themselves, the laundry room, a spare bedroom, someplace quiet so they can get settled. And his kids … they shouldn't play with them for a while. My cats aren't used to rambunctious kids, I don't want them scratching or hissing or—"

"Basil's wife, Esme, took them to the vet's this morning, made sure they were okay." Piper noticed some color had appeared on the few parts of his face that weren't bandaged, worked up over his cats. One monitor showed an increased heart rate.

"I'll pay her for that, the vet trip. You tell her."

"Sure."

"And Basil, he can't dump them at a shelter either, understand. I need to call him."

"How about I have him call you on Millie's cell. Right now, he's investigating the fire and I don't want to interrupt him."

Oren let out a rattling breath and closed his eyes.

"No animal shelter," he said again.

"No. That won't happen," Piper promised. She meant it.

"Maybe they'll do fine. Basil has a nice house. Maybe it'll work out. Kids need pets. Maybe—"

"It's just temporary, until you're—"

"—home?" He opened his eyes. "I've no home to go to. I've lost everything."

She almost argued. His boat remained. The land the house had been on. His cats. He hadn't lost his beloved cats. "Give this time, Oren. The doctors here are good. You'll feel—"

"Feel? I don't feel anything, Sheriff Blackwell. I'm on so many painkillers I can't even feel my lips."

"When you're better, when you're home—"

"I told you I have no home," he said, voice so soft she didn't catch everything. "Not anymore. Not ever again. Thanks for the visit, Sheriff Blackwell, Paul."

"I've a big house," Paul said from the doorway. "Stay with me until—"

"No."

Piper tried. "You could—"

"—cash in my chips if I had any left to cash," Oren returned. "I just need to make sure the cats are all right, cared for. The cats are what's important. Always were. If they can get along with Basil's kids, that's—"

"That's nonsense you're talking," Paul interrupted. "You're going to get through this and—"

"—and I don't *want* to get through this, Paul. I've had enough years."

"Oren, you—"

"It was 1980, I was twenty-three." Oren glanced at Piper. "Young. I went to Niagara Falls, Baltimore, the aquarium there, then New York. Took about two weeks. I love Bette Midler. She'd a book come out, *A View From A Broad*, and she was signing copies at a store. Saw the notice in a newspaper. I stood in line four hours to buy that book and get her to sign it. Thin book, about a hundred and fifty pages, lots of photographs. She personalized it to me. Got her picture taken with me. Crystal in my mind. Only signed book I ever owned. On the top shelf with the picture of me and her. They're gone. Everything's gone. Pictures of my kids, Millie, my cats. If my cats can get along with Basil's kids—"

Piper abruptly understood Millie's comment about "Pops is depressed as all hell." She couldn't blame him; he'd been dealt one rotten blow after another, and hope was a four-letter word not in his vocabulary right now. How could one man be so tortured by life's events ... father dying, wife divorcing, house burning? A strong man, but was he strong enough to get through this?

"Millie told you the fire was intentionally set," Piper said, wanting to get to the real reason for her visit.

Oren closed his eyes again. "Yeah. She told me."

"We're going to find out who—"

"Basil's a damn fine detective. He'll figure it out."

63

Piper felt almost insulted by that. "State Fire Marshal has an arson investigator down. We're working on it. We're going to find who—"

Again, Oren cut her off. "Hope Basil does find the perp. Hope the son of a bitch gets nailed to the wall for it." He coughed, shoulders bouncing again, the lines on the monitor beeping quietly. "So, you're going to ask if I'd pissed anybody off. If any of the neighbors and me were jousting. No. I like my neighbors. Like the whole damn subdivision. Never ever had a problem with any of them. That's why I suggested Basil move there. Safe, gated. Lakes and golfing. It was perfect until last night."

"Any threats? From someone outside the subdivision?"

He tried to laugh. "Yeah, Paul and me got threatened by a lawsuit. Maybe Lefty Jay figured his suit wasn't enough. Paul ... better watch your house."

"Did you hear anything?" Piper asked. "Before the fire? Someone in your yard, someone—"

"I heard my smoke detectors go off. Was sleeping."

Piper had intended to mention the six-pointed star on his boat garage, the hate-crime angle. A nurse tapped on the doorframe and displayed her watch. Piper held up a finger. *One more question.*

"Oren, two people died in the Laubenstein house, but they weren't the Laubensteins. We're trying to figure out who they—"

"Millie told me that, too. I saw lights on in the house once in a while, thought that Eldad had set up some sort of timer to make it look like they were home. He was always paranoid like that. I had a key to his place, but I'd no reason to check inside. I didn't know anyone was there. And, no, not a clue who they were. Ask the neighbors. Some of them are busy-bodies. Someone saw something. And someone probably saw Lefty Jay lighting the match."

The nurse motioned time to leave. Paul lingered a moment, leaned over Oren's bed and said something Piper couldn't hear. Maybe something about Lefty Jay, who was now on the suspect list. Maybe he'd tell her later, but probably not.

"I'll talk to Pops some more after he's rested," Millie told Piper in the hallway. "Earlier he told me the same thing he said to you, but he never mentioned a Lefty Jay. No enemies in the neighborhood. No threats. Hadn't seen anyone skulking around. Hadn't heard anything before all hell broke loose. No clue. He signed a DNR, Do Not Resuscitate form this morning. Insisted on it."

Piper could tell she'd been crying. "He's tough, Millie. He'll get through this." But she wasn't sure that he would.

10

Diego leaned against the door jamb. "The Rabbit—the molten slag that's left of it—belongs to Howard P. Eltrovog of Chimayo, New Mexico, a bitty-burg north of Santa Fe. More than twelve hundred miles from the Laubenstein garage. Eltrovog is a retired school teacher who reported the car stolen two years ago. And since I just got off a video chat with him, I can attest that he's not one of the burned bodies."

Basil didn't say anything. He stared straight ahead at the calendar on his wall. December, the picture was a snow-covered hill with colorfully-dressed children sledding down it. The photograph looked joyful, everyone having a grand time. He'd bought two sleds at the start of the month, intending to take his kids out to a popular hill in the country. They had originally planned to go today.

"Hey, the young guy in the cell. What's he in for?"

"For being a pain in the ass."

Diego snorted. "He's got a nasty mouth. Swore at me when I looked in on him. Spit. What did he—"

"What did he do? He wasted well more than an hour of my time,"

Basil replied. "Took me away from my investigation. Not a distraction I needed. Now I have to finish the paperwork on him before I can get back out."

Diego cocked his head, looking for more information. Basil knew Diego was the curious sort, part of what made him a good deputy.

"Lives on Sled Run. I charged him with possession because of a dozen joints." Basil added.

"Not a lot of pot. Not like the mountain of it we had last month at the Carlson farm. One dozen joints?" Diego laughed, spun, and left.

Agreed, it wasn't much pot, and Basil hadn't wanted to arrest Jerome Halm for it. Couldn't look the other way today. Didn't want to. The kid had been beyond rude, truly a pain in the ass, and locking him up gave Basil some measure of satisfaction. Didn't matter that two neighboring states—Illinois and Michigan—had legalized marijuana for recreational use—for adults. Like Indiana, Kentucky across the river stood firm against it. So did Basil.

Basil didn't like pot, drugs in general, anything that impaired the senses. But it didn't matter what Basil thought about it.

Seventeen-year-old Jerome Halm had a dozen joints in his pocket.

Class B misdemeanor, a maximum penalty of half the year in jail, with a fine of up to $1,000. The charge could have been worse if Jerome had a prior conviction. The teen had no record. Basil explained to Jerome's father—who had showed up with a sack containing a pair of tennis shoes and a winter jacket, and a request to keep the boy overnight as a lesson—that the case might not have to go to trial.

Basil would talk to DA Scales about a "diversion," which could lead to an eventual dismissal of the charge. It would involve a fine and taking a substance abuse class.

In November, he, Oren Rosenberg, and Diego had shut down a massive pot-growing operation on a farm in the county. The entire family was involved, and because of the amount of pot and the interstate trafficking, the charges were serious enough the feds had stepped in. It wouldn't go to trial for a few months, but stories about it still popped up in the news.

He wondered if Jerome had gotten his marijuana from the farm operation; the teen refused to say where he'd come by it. The boy's father asked Basil to come back to the house and search to see if there were other drugs.

Basil would do that, but after he talked to a few more people in the neighborhood about the fire. Someone had to have seen *something*.

Twelve joints had delayed his search, and he wouldn't let himself get distracted again.

The arson trumped everything else right now.

"I was afraid my house was going to catch fire, too. Terrified." Beverly Parker owned the saltbox next to the Laubensteins. A petite woman in an overlarge red sweatshirt and jean leggings, she stood in the doorway holding a white-muzzled schnauzer on her hip. "Shame someone died in that house. Didn't know anyone was staying there," she told Basil. "The couple who owns the place head to beach before the first of December. Come back in the spring with golden tans. They left a few days after we had Thanksgiving dinner with them. Norma ... she lives kitty-corner across the street over there ... Norma said she saw lights in their house, but I didn't see any lights. Truth be told, I don't pay all that much attention to what goes on in the neighborhood. I'm not nosey. I'm baking cookies, snickerdoodles. Want some?"

He smelled a lot of tempting cinnamon, but he politely declined and moved to the next house on his list.

Basil had the feeling he was being watched, though he couldn't tell from where. Someone peering out a window, maybe perched between houses. Someone curious regarding what he was doing, where he was going, who he was talking to. He felt their eyes. Maybe they'd seen him chase Jerome Halm and prod the teen along in his stockinged feet. No doubt that newsy tidbit had raced through the entire Village and would be a topic around dinner tables tonight.

Maybe the eyes had seen something involving the fire at Oren Rosenberg's.

It was one of those sixth or seventh senses, knowing he was being watched. Discovered the talent in the military, fostered it in the Chicago Police Department. It resurfaced here in the Village. Right now it didn't make his spine dance; he picked up no malicious intent. Curiosity, the eyes felt like that.

Basil shrugged it off and kept walking.

"So, you think it was set, huh? Those house fires?" This from a man walking two cocker spaniels. Reynolds Barnes lived one street over and said he'd gone fishing with Oren this past summer. He had a wide face and fog-gray eyes and Basil remembered seeing him walking the dogs in front of his house a few times. "Feel awful for Oren. Helluva nice guy. Do you know what hospital he's in? I should send something."

Reynolds reached down and scratched the larger dog's ears. "Arson, eh? Bet it was someone he arrested, pissed off. That's what I'd put my money on. They should roast in hell for doing that. Hope you catch them. Wonder how they got into the neighborhood? Gated, you know. Safe. You live around here, too, right? Got a little boy who looked like Sponge Bob on Halloween? Girl dressed up as Judge Judy?"

Basil smiled at that and gave Reynolds a business card in case he remembered seeing something suspicious. "Yes, Sponge Bob and Ruth Bader Ginsberg."

"Cute kids," Reynolds continued. "I've got one, a lot older, a junior in high school. Kicker on the football team." He looked down the street and gestured. "Have to get my steps in. Supposed to be safe, this neighborhood. Arson. That's a rotten thing. Safe."

Basil would share all the recordings from his interviews with Sheriff Blackwell when she returned from Indianapolis. Hopefully she'd get something out of Oren to help the investigation. He'd drive up to the hospital Monday or Tuesday for a visit, stop at the big Lego store in Castleton Square on the way back for a little Christmas shopping for the kids.

His phone buzzed with a text. Esme saying she had cheese and broccoli soup in a pan simmering on the stove, and there would be fresh sourdough rolls for dinner ... if he wanted some. If he was coming home.

YES, he texted. *Will be there by 5. Early dinner, then a walk to see the lights?*

She texted a smiley face in reply.

Despite her encouragement to move to Spencer County last spring, he knew Esme hadn't liked it at first, this lily-white county far from the big, vibrant city they'd lived in since they'd been married. The big city with all the guns, innocent children caught in the cross-fire. One such shooting so close to their home had sent him from the Gangs and Narcotics division in search of another job in a smaller place.

He'd seen the Spencer County Sheriff's Department detective posting almost by accident, wondered if God had waived it in his face. He'd applied, for the Santa Claus Police Chief posting, too, and for a few other law enforcement openings in Tennessee, near Nashville where Esme's parents lived.

Piper's offer came through first, and he took it in part because he liked her. Young, but seemed like she knew what she was doing. And she learned fast. Too young? Too white?

The only black man in the department ... and come to find out the only black man in law enforcement in the entire county.

"Black son of a bitch," Jerome Halm had called him.

Blindingly-white place he'd landed in. Definitely a "White Christmas" county. Santa Claus was the largest town at 2,700. Not much more than a "suggestion of a place" in Chicago terms. A hair past blink and you'll miss it.

Oren had pointed him to Santa Claus and Christmas Lake Village to look for a house. Oren liked the area; said he'd never had a problem with any of his neighbors.

But someone had a problem with Oren.

Why now?

Oren had lived on Sled Run for a long while.

Why now?

What had changed?

Basil had figured the houses in the Village would have been out of his price range, but most were between two and three hundred thousand dollars, and his came in at two-seventy-five. Brick. Big yard they would fence in the spring. The kids would get a dog. For grins he and Esme had looked at a near-mansion on Tinsel Circle that listed at one-point six million. It finally sold a month or so ago.

Gated, there were rules to follow … mainly no junk cars sitting out, lawn trimmed, yearly fee that fed into street repairs and park and lakefront upkeep.

Gated.

Safe.

Thought they were safe.

More than half of Santa Claus' residents lived in the Village. Twenty-five hundred acres encompassing three lakes—Christmas Lake, Lake Holly, and Lake Noel. Oren had taken his boat out on all of them, told Basil he liked Lake Holly the best for fishing. It all nested against the Christmas Lake Golf Course.

A touch more than ninety-eight percent of Santa Claus' population was white. Basil and his family fell into the remaining less than two percent, which also included Hispanics and Asians. It mirrored the other towns in the county.

His former Chicago Police Department partner, Tug, recently moved to Spencer County to get his teenage daughter away from a particular and persistent gang and to have Basil nearby for backup. Tug ran a little tavern in Fulda, and also commented on how glistening like snow the county gleamed.

"Diversity?" Tug had said over beer and herbal tea. "I'd say there is no diversity here. Diversity is not in Spencer County's dictionary."

"We're the diversity," Basil had returned with a quick, hollow comeback. While this county would do for a while, Basil wanted his kids to experience more of a melting pot. But they hadn't seemed to notice the whiteness of this place, or at least had never mentioned it to him. They could play in the yard without the fear of stray bullets. And they were trying to enjoy Oren's cats—which Esme said constantly ran and hid from them.

71

He knew Esme found the peacefulness conducive to her writing. She claimed to get in a lot more words-per-day. Santa Claus appeared to be growing on her, but she frequently commented on how white everything was.

How long would they stay in Spencer County? How long *could* they stay?

Having Tug around helped. Having engaging work in a depart-ment where he liked the other deputies was a plus. Working with Piper Blackwell kept it interesting. She seemed good for the county.

Was he good for the county? Was he making a difference?

Basil took another circuit of what little remained of Oren's house, stopping at all the places of note Oster had pointed out. Maybe he'd sign up for that arson course with Sheriff Blackwell. He made a broader circuit, checking the property lines once more. Snowy patches remained here and there. The ground hard, he'd not noticed useful tracks, and so much of the yard had been trampled by the fire-men. Clues obliterated.

He felt the eyes on him again.

Maybe someone in the row of houses behind Oren's and the Laubensteins' watched him. Maybe they had seen something last night, had looked out their back windows, caught a glimpse of someone sneaking through the yards. He hadn't talked to everyone yet. Someone had to have seen or heard something.

Then, at the very edge of Oren's property, Basil saw *something*. He'd missed it earlier.

Tire tracks, odd ones because they lacked deep tread. Appeared to cut through from the street behind Sled Run and end at the back of Oren's yard. He took photographs, noting a place where the vehicle skidded, turning around. Not a four-wheeler. Not a car, the wheels looked only four feet apart.

The sun set at five in Spencer County in mid-December, dusk chasing it a half hour later. Full dark by six-thirty. He jogged, following the tracks as best as he could, realizing they pointed toward the golf course.

He paused to text Esme: *Sorry, I might be late for dinner.*

11

8 p.m.

Piper curled on the couch next to Nang, the only light in the room the blinking colored strands on the tree. Beautiful, she thought, noting gaps between the branches that could use some ornaments ... an excuse to visit The Christmas Store in Santa Claus, get one of those "First Christmas Together" globes.

And a small box of maple-walnut fudge.

And maybe a couple of those saucer-sized chocolate chip cookies.

She'd jog extra miles to make up for it.

Piper had stopped in the office before coming home, learning from Basil that the arsonist entered the Village on a cart that he stole from the golf course and drove to Sled Run.

The golf course was typically open year-round, as golfers braved the cold to play even in December. Except if there was snow and ice on the grounds. The greens and fairways closed those days, though the restaurant on site still served lunch and dinner. Basil reported that the greens had been closed the past three days because of the weather, and the assistant manager he'd talked to didn't expect that to change until the temperature climbed enough for the snow to melt.

And since the greens were closed, the security cameras had not been on. "Why run the cameras when there's ice and snow? When it is impossible to play golf. Never had a break-in before. Ever," the assistant manager had said.

Apparently it looked like the thief had tried several carts before finding one that still had a charge on the battery. And it was returned when the arsonist finished his work at Oren's.

Basil dusted for fingerprints ... nothing on the cart; the perpetrator was probably wearing gloves. Took pictures of boot prints in the snow, and documented the cart's route. The thief had sliced the fence between the golf course and the Village, revealing how he got into and out of the gated community. The route avoided security cameras, suggesting the man was definitely familiar with the subdivision. Wouldn't have been easy taking a golf cart over ice and snow. No deep treads to help with traction, which attested to the rather serpentine path, all the slipping and spinning.

The arsonist had been determined.

Piper wondered why he just hadn't walked into the Village. But that would have left a lot of boot prints, and it would have been tough to carry gas containers that far. The arson investigator said two gas cans were likely used, looked to be the five-gallon size. Gas is lighter than water, so that would have made each container weigh about thirty to thirty-five pounds. Slogging up to seventy pounds through the neighborhoods in the sleet would have been too onerous, hence the golf cart.

In the morning, she and Basil would to talk to people who lived against the golf course. They would interview the scattering of souls in the Village who didn't decorate for Christmas to discover if they'd had threats or golf cart tracks in their yards. See if they could find anyone with video surveillance near the golf course who might have recorded a vehicle the arsonist drove to the building.

In what remained of this night, Piper intended to study the video surveillance from the Village she'd picked up this morning, even though Basil had already looked through it and said nothing stood out.

She was just so damn tired from the long and depressing day. She'd have more focus if she rested first, just a little while. Then she'd open her laptop and plug in the flash drive.

She yawned.

Piper'd planned to take a nap on the ride back from Indy, but instead had talked to her father. She'd tried to drag more out of him about the lawsuit and Lefty Jay, but he'd ended up chatting nearly three hours about his pug.

Nang put an arm around her, pulled her close. He smelled of musk and a hint of chicken fried rice, which he'd made for dinner and offered to warm up. She passed. Too tired to eat. And not really hungry anyway. She inhaled deep and held his scents.

And yawned again.

Camaro, her elderly golden retriever, stretched out on the red velour tree skirt next to Tater, Nang's bitzer—bits of this and bits of that. The cat Marmalade hadn't made an appearance tonight.

"You are so quiet," Nang said, kissing her forehead. "How is Oren?"

"Awful." She recounted her sad conversation with the chief deputy. In that moment Piper realized how fortunate she was. A job she loved with good people surrounding her, a husband she loved even more, a fine house with plenty of shed fur on the carpet, antique vehicles in her big garage. She had no debt.

And her chief deputy had nothing except a depressed heart and uncertain future.

"He's absolutely awful."

"I will tell Oren he can live in my trailer until he decides what he wants to do." Nang had a double-wide behind the garage at his Quick Stop. Piper had been there several times. Nice furniture, well-appointed kitchen, shelves full of Marvel and DC graphic novels.

"I was going to rent the trailer," he said. "Probably to someone working for me. But letting Oren use it is a much better idea. He could keep all his cats there."

After she and Nang got married last week, he'd moved from that trailer into her house ... a big ranch with an overlarge garage, spacious fenced yard, and a convenient dog door. There'd been no question where they were going to live. Nang hadn't brought all that many boxes, seeming to live a minimalist life—sans the graphic novels and cookware. But so far he'd only unpacked his clothes. Both of them busy, there'd been little time for unboxing and rearranging, little time to settle into the marriage. This was all new.

"I will drive up and visit him tomorrow," Nang continued. "There are some restaurant supply stores open on Sunday, and I will stop in. One trip, two reasons. See if he will accept the key to my trailer."

"Restaurant supply stores? Because you settled on a building to buy?" Piper yawned and squeezed his hand. Nang had been toying with opening a Vietnamese restaurant in the county, a serious step up from the three tables at the back of his Quick Stop.

"I wanted to surprise you, but over a fancy dinner and wine." He seemed mildly disappointed he'd spilled the news. "And now I have ruined the surprise by mentioning the restaurant supply stores. I just knew I was going to ruin it."

"I am surprised," she countered. "I know you were looking at a lot of empty buildings." Rockport had the most vacant buildings to choose from, the downtown sparse. But all the little towns in the county had "empties." The big box stores across the river had played taps for so many small businesses.

"I made an offer this morning, and three hours later it was accepted." His smile reached his dark eyes.

"So—"

"I'd narrowed it to three properties. One in Dale, one in Santa Claus, and the larger one in Rockport. I almost picked the Santa Claus place because the town is bigger. But the one in Rockport is only three blocks from the sheriff's department. Walking distance. Ready for this?"

"For what?"

"Walking distance. I am going to call it Nang's Uptown Wok. So many advertising slogans can come from that. Take a Walk Uptown. Take a Walk on the Wild Rice Side. Go for a Wok." His grin widened. "It's a dream, you know, doing this."

"A Quick Stop, garage, and now a restaurant. My husband is building an empire in Spencer County."

"The three places were once grocery stores. Have been closed for decades."

Piper's breath hitched.

"They were put on the market in the early fall, and the price was reasonable because so much work will need to be done. Rewiring, making the plumbing up to code, new HVAC, not to mention taking out all the old shelves and counters, putting down new floor, painting, refrigerators, stoves. Nice size. Perfect size, parking lot right next to it. Easily customized to what I need." Nang spoke fast in his excitement. "It will take months and months and months of work. Exciting. Down the road, I could offer Vietnamese cooking classes."

He continued to talk and Piper's stomach twisted. Three grocery store buildings closed for decades. Thirty years. The ones owned by Lefty Jay and his murdered brother. Why hadn't the buildings been sold while Lefty Jay was in prison? Surely couldn't his wife—or ex—if they had divorced, sold them? Or the dead brother's widow, she probably owned shares. Why hadn't they dumped the buildings before now? Why had they hung onto property someone no doubt continued to pay taxes on? Why sell them now? Because Lefty Jay was out of prison and gave the green light? And why the hell did Nang have to put in an offer on one?

Piper knew she could stop him if she wanted, explain the situation, the lawsuit against her father and Oren, get him to back out of the deal.

"Really, this place is perfect," he said. "I thought about the one in Dale. The building was cheaper, by a lot. But I found out there was a murder there. The grocery stores all closed after the murder. Even though it had happened long ago, I didn't want to open a restaurant in a place where someone had been killed. There would be a stigma. People might not come to eat there because of the tragedy."

He paused. "Well, what do you think?"

Piper didn't want to think about it, not now. There was the arson to work with Basil, her chief deputy was in the hospital, depressed ... and now her husband wanted to buy a building from someone suing her dad.

She closed her eyes and pretended to sleep.

A moment later, she didn't have to pretend.

12

1 a.m. Sunday, December 13th

Bap.

Bap.

Paul Blackwell buried his head under the pillow.

Bap.

Wrinkles didn't sound like most other dogs, perhaps because of his short neck and smooshed-in face.

Bap.

It wasn't a loud noise, just annoying. The elderly black pug didn't do anything loud, except snore. His bark came out a muted *bap. Bap. Bap. Bap.* Like a sound effect from Donkey Kong.

Bap.

Paul tossed the pillow aside, opened one eye, and leaned over the side of the bed, picking through the shadows to see the little dog.

Bap. Bap. Bap, Wrinkles continued.

The pug stood beneath the window, agitated, prancing.

"Do you have to pee? Really? Right now?" Paul had stayed up late playing games on his computer to keep his mind off the lawsuit and Oren. He'd taken the dog out an hour ago to do his business. Maybe

Wrinkles had another UTI—urinary tract infection—if he had to go again so soon. That would entail a vet visit Monday.

"Okay, old man. I'll take you." He swung his legs off the side of the bed, toes feeling for his slippers. "But you better make it quick so I can—"

WHOOM!

The panes rattled.

Wrinkles bounced and barked furiously: *bapbapbapbapbap-bapbapbap!*

Paul was at the window in two strides, looking across at his garage. It was on fire.

WHOOM! A second explosion.

The windows in the apartment over the garage blew out. The side door to the garage burst open, flames shooting through it. Fire was everywhere, dancing across the roof.

Bapbapbapbapbap!

Paul's bedroom sat on the second floor of his saltbox, the detached garage only a dozen feet away. When he opened his window and stuck his head out, he felt heat mingled with the wintry cold, smelled the flames, charring wood, chemicals, a heavy stench.

WHOOM! This one not as loud, but heralded even more fire.

He stared. Some part of him said *Move! Do something! Get your phone!* Disbelief held his feet fast, his throat closed, and he tried to gulp in the awful air. A bad dream, right? Not real. This cannot possibly be real.

Bapbapbapbap!

Shaking off the shock, he pushed away from the window, shrugged into his robe, and spun to the dresser, snatching his cell phone and pressing 9-1-1. His gun on the nightstand, he grabbed it and shoved it in a pocket as he ran from the room toward the stairs.

Candace picked up. "9-1-1. What is the nature of your emergency?"

"Fire!" Paul shouted. "My garage is on fire. It exploded!" He rattled off his address, though he knew the dispatcher could pull that up automatically. "Hurry. Hurry!"

Bapbapbap. Wrinkles followed him.

He stumbled on the last step, phone flying from his fingers, knees slamming down on the hardwood. Chest tight, he wondered if he was having another heart attack. The old pug danced around him as he pushed himself up, fumbled for the bannister, and tugged himself to his feet.

Paul hit the light switch, though he didn't really need it. A hellish orange glow from the garage fire came through every window. He spotted his dropped phone, picked it up, and realized he'd been disconnected from Candace.

He punched 9-1-1 again as he stumbled into the kitchen and toward the side door across from the garage.

"The Rockport Fire Department is on its way," Candace told him. "Is the fire limited to—"

"My garage." Paul reached the door and put his free hand to the glass, swearing he could feel the heat. He looked down at Wrinkles. "You stay here. No." On second thought, he scooped up the pug and held him tight under his arm. If the fire leaped to the house, the pug might die. He went outside. To Candace: "It looks like just my garage. At the moment. But it's a fireball. It's all burning. The wind could chase it to my house, to the neighbors' houses. Hurry."

His chest grew tighter still, and he tried to swallow, the color of the flames so bright it was hurtful. Millie rented the apartment over the garage. If she'd been there—and not in Indianapolis with Oren— she'd be dead.

A leash. He should put Wrinkles on a leash. Paul worried if he slipped on the ice, he might drop the pug. Fire trucks coming, the fire raging, he needed to keep the pug safe. He darted back into the kitchen, half-listening to Candace. Had she given him an ETA? Couldn't tell, the fire so noisy. His heart pounding, breath coming difficult and fast. The air hot and cold and stinging.

Bapbapbap.

The pug had tried to alert him minutes ago, barking by the window, had picked something up with his selective hearing. Some- thing? Someone. Someone had set the fire, like they'd burned Oren's house. The gun in his pocket? He'd shoot the son of a bitch arsonist if he saw him.

The garage fire was not an accident. Not an accident! The words slammed through his thoughts.

From his hospital bed less than a dozen hours ago, Oren had said to him: "Maybe Lefty Jay figured his suit wasn't enough. Paul, better watch your house."

Paul dropped the cell phone into his pocket next to the gun, snapped the leash on Wrinkles' collar, and went back outside into the awful, burning, choking, icy air.

Snow soaked his terrycloth slippers and sent shivers from his toes to the top of his head as he put the dog on the porch. His teeth rattled from the cold, yet the fire seemed at the same time stifling. His bathrobe protected only his modesty from the dueling sensations.

Should never sleep in the buff in case of fire, he scolded. *Dear God where are the trucks?* It felt like he'd called ages ago. He pressed himself up against the side of his house, the open kitchen door to his left, Wrinkles to his right. The little dog leaned against Paul's leg and gave another series of *baps.*

He couldn't take his eyes off the flames. They worked quickly at his garage, devouring it. Eating his car, Millie's apartment.

Paul knew his immediate neighbors must have heard the explosions. He knew what had caused them ... propane tanks. He grilled a lot and had three in the back of his garage. Shouldn't store propane tanks in a garage, he knew, but he'd always put them there during the winter. There were a couple of full gasoline cans, too ... for the riding lawnmower and snowblower. Probably had other flammable stuff in there.

His car—a 2022 Hyundai Tucson he'd bought new, first new car in ages—was in the garage. So was Millie's car. Both gone to the fire. And now she was homeless like Oren. He'd be homeless if the trucks didn't get here fast. The fire was stretching, reaching for his home.

His police cruiser was in the driveway. He should move it, right? Before the flames reached it. Get it out of the way.

"C'mon, old man." Another time into the kitchen, where he

grabbed his keyring. One more trip outside, and he saw it between gaps in the flames on the garage. A six-pointed star in red spray paint. Paul held the keyring in his teeth and retrieved his cell phone. Candace had stopped talking, disconnected again.

That painted star.

Paul thought maybe he wasn't the arsonist's target, maybe it was Millie. The six-pointed star, like at Oren's. Millie, Jewish. Maybe Basil was spot-on about the hate crime.

Hate crime. Paul hated whoever set the fire. Paul hated the arsonist with everything he had. He'd shoot the son of a bitch.

He held up the phone and took a picture of the star. Took a half a dozen fast pictures before the flames ate the star and the entire wall. Then he hurried to his cruiser, sweating from the heat, put the pug inside, pulled himself beside the dog, and backed it out of the driveway just as he heard a multitude of sirens coming down the street. He almost turned on the police radio, but realized that was pointless. He had a front row seat to the unfortunate action.

It had taken the trucks an eternity to get here. The garage and its contents a total loss, the flames extending, stretching, teasing his house now. Best the fire crew could manage would be to put out the fire while keeping it from spreading. Good there was little wind. An eternity it had taken.

He tried to catch more breath, but couldn't. Only tiny sips of air.

Not really an eternity for them to arrive, Paul knew. Only minutes that felt like forever.

Hard to take the oxygen down to the bottom of his lungs. Impossible. Felt like an elephant stepped on his chest. He parked the car across the street a few houses down, out of the way of the trucks. Away from the fire, he was chilled now. He cranked up the heat, patted Wrinkles, and reached for his cell phone once more.

Rockport had two small volunteer fire departments, serving a population of roughly 2,400 over two square miles. His house wasn't far from one of them. Three trucks, both departments were here. Two police cars, too.

Lights were on all over the neighborhood. Christmas lights

popped on too, a blinking, twinkling, fest of color. People had their faces pressed to windows. A dozen had bundled up and come out onto the walks. Not as big an audience as at Oren's fire. Was the arsonist among them? Watching his handiwork?

"Damn!" he hissed. He'd toyed around with installing security cameras, one of those back-burner notions that would have been golden here. Maybe the neighbors had them. Maybe they'd caught a shot of the asshole who'd set the fire.

Should call Piper, he thought, glancing from his cell phone to the fiery tableau on display out the car window. The fire crew pulled hoses toward his garage, the spray of water battling the blaze, causing it to smoke.

Should call Piper.

No, she already knew. Candace would have called her, probably called Basil too. They'd be on their way. He needed Piper to watch Wrinkles for him.

9-1-1, he pressed.

"Candace, send an ambulance." Lightning pulsed up his left arm and the elephant on his chest grew heavier. "Pretty sure I'm having a heart attack." He glanced at the pug. "My daughter will take good care of you."

13

6 a.m. Monday, December 14th

Y ou're in early." Zeke stepped into Piper's office and pointed to her empty mug. "Get you a refill?"

She nodded.

"How's your dad?"

"Home. The hospital ran tests, said he'd had an anxiety attack."

"His garage destroyed. That's cause for anxiety." Zeke picked up her mug and retreated to the doorway. "Think they're related? The fires? Oren's and your dad's garage?"

Stupid question, Piper thought. "Yes."

"I think so, too. Oren and his granddaughter. Someone's got it in for the family, leave them both homeless. Hate crime, right? Some anti-Jewish thing, you think? I heard about the painted stars and—"

"You're in early, too," she returned instead of answering his questions.

Zeke scowled. "Couldn't sleep. Guy in the apartment below me wanted everyone in the building to hear his music. All night and into the morning. I suspect alcohol was involved. Did you know Twisted Sister had a Christmas album? Their take on 'Oh Come All Ye Faithful' is something I will never unhear." He sighed. "I need to move. Or find a sweet deal on a house like Teegan did. I came in early to surf rental listings and enjoy some quiet."

Zeke sported black jeans, a long-sleeved white shirt, and a red tie that tucked into a cable-knit sweater vest that hovered between taupe and beige. It was both nerdier and dressier than his usual fare and Piper wondered if Dee Snider's vocals had anything to do with it. She'd known Zeke for less than a year, hiring him in May when he graduated high school. He'd impressed her with his drive, computer skills, and desire to be a deputy, which at nineteen, he was two years shy of the required age. She knew he churned through online courses in his spare time, with the intent of getting a computer-related degree useful to law enforcement.

"Why didn't you file a noise complaint?"

Zeke shrugged.

Piper raised her eyebrows. "And why are you wearing—"

"Oh, this? I'm going out to an early dinner tonight with my mom. Colby's in Owensboro. Her favorite." He shifted back and forth on the balls of his feet. "Millie. Have you talked to her? What's she going to do? Any idea who has it out for her and Oren and—"

Zeke's eyes showed concern, curiosity, and intelligence. Piper considered him crazy-smart. Curiosity was out front at the moment.

"Talked to her a couple of times yesterday," Piper replied. "She's devastated, naturally, doesn't want Oren to know about the garage fire."

"He'll find out."

"Sure."

"Everything," Zeke said, still shifting. "Oren'll find out that she lost everything. They both lost everything."

Oren hadn't lost everything.

"He saved his cats," Piper corrected. The quartet was ensconced at Basil's, still fleeing from the children, last she'd heard. "And he still has Millie."

"Yeah. But they lost everything else."

And—more than that—two people lost their lives, Piper thought.

"Where are they going to live? If I can find a new place, my apartment will be open. But Oren might not be able to handle a third-floor walk-up for a while. Millie might want it."

Piper had a lot to do this morning and didn't want to spend time talking to her first-shift dispatcher who was way the hell too chatty right now. She had more paperwork to tackle, doorbell cam video to watch again and again, wait for the arson investigator to call with a report on her dad's garage. She should have shut her office door. Zeke never pestered her when she shut the door.

Piper gave him a weary smile. "Nang visited Oren yesterday, was in Indy for business." She wasn't going to tell Zeke about Nang's planned restaurant...that would entail even more conversation, and dredge up things she didn't want to think about. "He offered Oren the double-wide behind the Quick Stop."

"Oh, great!"

Then Piper lost the smile. Nang had relayed that Oren was so badly depressed he refused to talk about the future. "Oren turned him down. But Millie asked if she could rent it for a while."

"They lost everything," Zeke repeated. "I can't imagine that." He transferred her coffee mug to his other hand. "Well, I guess I can imagine it. But I don't have all that much stuff. Oren had a houseful. Would hate to lose my computers, you know. All my t-shirts, Loot the Castle collector cards." His eyes lost focus for a moment. "Shit. They're gonna have to buy all new clothes. All new everything. Unless they go to a second-hand store and—"

"You offered coffee," Piper interrupted.

"Oh, yeah. Right away. Maybe we should set up one of those GoFundMes for them. Not possible that insurance would cover everything."

Zeke ducked out and Piper sucked in a deep breath. Her office smelled musty with a hint of Pledge. She'd polished the top of her desk before settling behind it an hour ago. The desk was old; her father had used it for all the years he served as sheriff of Spencer County, and someone else had used it before that. The chair had considerable age, too, both were older than this building. Maybe she'd scour the budget and see if she could find some money to upgrade a few pieces. Piper wanted a chair with better back support ... not that she sat behind a desk all that many hours a day, but it would be great for the stretches requiring paperwork. If there wasn't room in the budget, she would just buy a chair herself.

A small silver-framed photo of her cat and dog leaned against her in-basket. Inches away perched a silvery-framed photo of Nang and her dancing at their wedding reception at The Thirsty Turtle—the only items of personalization she'd added to the office since she started almost a year ago. A calendar hung across from her desk, courtesy of the Chamber of Commerce; the December picture showed kids sledding on a hill. Every office in the department had the same calendar. And almost every room in the department had a smattering of Christmas decorations. Except Oren's. And hers. She would remedy the latter by picking out a poinsettia tonight at the grocery store on her way home. A real pretty one.

And the big coffee mug. That was a bit of personalization, too.

Zeke brought it back, filled to the rim with Dark Italian Roast. She could smell it above the Pledge. Piper had a spare mug in her desk in case this one broke. She considered coffee her addiction, a taste acquired during her stint in the army, and it was best consumed in thick ceramic mugs that held the heat.

"Thanks, Zeke."

He nodded, opened his mouth as if to continue the conversation, then changed his mind and disappeared.

Piper held her nose over the steam. This would be her third cup ... and no more until lunch, she vowed. The scent was sharp, rich, comforting, and she took a sip and held it on her tongue. Nang's Quick Stop carried this blend, and she'd stocked up on it. The warmth seeped from the mug into her fingers, and for just a few moments she sat still, savoring the experience.

Softly, she heard the phone ring at the dispatcher's desk. Candace was still on duty, would yield to Zeke at seven. Tangled in the muted conversation was an instrumental station; she couldn't name the piece playing.

A deep swallow of the coffee this time, feeling the blessed caffeine and warmth slide down her throat.

Oren's house gone, and him in the burn unit in Indy with a rough path ahead.

Her dad's garage—and thereby Millie's apartment—gone, thankfully no one injured.

It was the same sick soul responsible for both arsons, she knew.

Two people dead, burned in the house next to Oren's. The autopsies this afternoon, she might join Basil. The dead needed names.

And she and Basil needed to catch the son of a bitch who killed them.

And almost killed Oren and all his pets.

And could have killed Millie if she'd been home.

Had that been the intent? To kill Millie and Oren? Was the act a hate crime because they were Jewish? Or because they were a specific family—the Rosenbergs? Did Oren and Millie have a mutual enemy? Was it a coincidence that both fires had been set at the homes of sheriff's deputies? Was their badges the motive?

She'd read the statistics on hate yesterday, a report published by the FBI. Hate crimes had risen steadily the past two years, most notably against Asians and the LGBTQ communities. But the increase had been noted in every category, with a third of the crimes pegged to religious hate directed against Jews. The bulk of those crimes included assaults, vandalism, and intimidation, but there were murders, rapes, and burglaries in the mix.

Hate was definitely involved in these arsons. Religiously motivated?

Or could this possibly be about Lefty Jay's vendetta against Paul Blackwell and Oren, a lawsuit against them, arson at each property? But if her dad was the target, why not torch his house? Why the garage? Millie had lived in the apartment above the garage. Piper used to live there before she inherited her fine house in Hatfield. Had the arsonist hoped it would spread from the garage to the house? Knew there were likely accelerants stored in the garage to help it along?

The questions swirled as she took another swallow of coffee. They had some answers ... how the arsonist got into the Village and onto Sled Run via a golf cart; that he'd arrived in a pickup or SUV to her dad's. Red plastic gasoline canisters with socks for wicks found in both cases. Boot prints photographed. Using SoleMate?, Tread Typer, and a few other sources, they'd come up with size 10 Timberland Pro Waterproof Work Boots, both at her dad's and Oren's. A fairly common men's shoe available from many outlets and online. The depth of the prints in the snow, taking into account the gasoline canisters, put the arsonist between one-seventy and two hundred pounds.

The big answers were elusive. *Who* did it? *Who* was wearing the boots? *Why* did they set the fires? And could her chief deputy really recover from this?

Who was responsible for all this pain?

Piper forced herself to tackle the rest of her reports, emptying her in-basket. Then she plugged a flash drive into her laptop. It had footage provided by the neighbor across the street from her dad's. The only doorbell cam that caught anything.

And it didn't catch much.

Basil, who'd viewed this several times yesterday, was right. He'd pronounced it "close to worthless, though not entirely." Which meant he saw *something*. Piper wanted to find the *something*, too.

In the video the street was an array of shadows separated by the glow of streetlights. Most people had turned off their Christmas decorations to save on electric bills. One house had a front porch light on, but too far away to be helpful. Piper grumbled that her father should have bought the security camera he'd talked about when she'd rented from him. He lacked motion sensor lights, too, had never wanted those because he said errant bunnies would activate them, and then set Wrinkles to barking. Piper's house had security cameras ringing the property because the previous owner had been paranoid, plenty of motion sensor lights, too, and a doorbell cam that recorded exceptional images of every Amazon and UPS driver who dropped off a package.

Everything in this video looked black and gray, and the pickup truck that stopped at the edge of the camera's view was dark ... black, blue, green, brown, couldn't tell. Maybe red. Red looked black at night. Just dark, and the driver had turned the headlights off before it came into view. Couldn't be entirely sure it was a pickup either, as the camera caught only the very front part. Might have been an SUV, but it had that kind of front end that hinted pickup. Too dark to make out any features of the grille or bumper, couldn't see the license plate.

Too damn dark.

A man stepped around the front, carrying two heavy gas canisters, the five-gallon size, she could tell that by the shape. The man was tall, but she couldn't get a true measure, as he was hunched over from carrying thirty-some pounds of gas in each hand ... provided the canisters were full. And why wouldn't they be full? He was dressed in dark clothes, black, blue, green, brown ... probably black. A hoodie disguised his head.

A walking slash of charcoal against an equally inky background.

When he came back without the canisters, he stood taller. She guessed him at six feet or a little more, and on the lean side. Still, difficult to tell because of the coat. Broad shoulders. He stepped around the front of his vehicle and vanished, then backed down the street without turning on the headlights.

"Close to worthless, though not entirely." Basil had meant the indistinct video had told them the man was fit because of the speed he walked when carrying the canisters, and that he could do it with them held away from his body so they didn't jounce against his legs. Fit, strong, wearing size 10 boots with a tread that matched the one noticed at the golf course and in Oren's back yard. Purposeful. Determined.

Not entirely worthless.

"Who the hell are you?" Piper whispered over the top of her cooling coffee. "And why did you do this?"

She watched the video a few more times, her breath catching at the burst of fire, the explosions she could see, but had no sound. Piper became snared by the fire, the police car and fire trucks arriving. One of the trucks pulled directly in front of the house that had the doorbell cam, ending the show.

Piper closed her laptop, leaned back in her chair and saw it was almost eight. She had her monthly meeting across the street with DA Scales. She grabbed her coat, told Zeke where she was going, and hurried out the front door.

Across the street, sitting on a bench and looking right at her, was a stoop-shouldered man with frizzy gray hair, face ruddy and wrinkled like a raisin. He wore droopy jeans and a coat inadequate for winter.

Lefty Jay.

The coffee in her stomach turned to a lump of ice.

14

8 a.m.

The cold wind whipped hair into Piper's eyes. She tucked the strands behind her ears and stared north across the street at Lefty Jay, contemplating whether to talk to him. She wanted to, quiz him where he was when Oren's house burned, when her dad's garage caught fire, ask him why he was on that bench right now watching the sheriff's department, eyes meeting hers. Smiling.

She *should* talk to him, even though he didn't fit the profile the arson investigator painted.

Too old, not as tall as the shadowy figure spotted on her dad's property. Didn't look like he could carry two five-gallon canisters of gas and move at the speed of the man in the video. His feet? She had no clue what size shoe he wore. He could have hired someone to set the fires.

Indeed, she *would* talk to him, but not right now. She had an appointment with DA Scales.

She glanced past him at Rockport's downtown. Christmas music played from speakers, the sound echoing in the short, nearly-empty canyon. Except for a handful of businesses, the faded signs, weathered wood, and grimy brick fronts looked depressing.

The Dollar Store, lights just coming on and "open" sign going up; hardware store; a craft shop that shared space with a used books dealer; a dilapidated antique store with irregular hours ... that was it. There used to be a florist, dress shop, shoe store, hair salon, furniture mart, and diner, all gone the way of many businesses in the small towns in the county, surrendered to the big box stores across the river and the convenience of on-line shopping. The husks remained, with the Chamber of Commerce gamely and unsuccessfully trying to lure people to breathe life into them. There was a rumor a wine and cheese shop might take one of the smallest storefronts, but that had been floating around for the past year or so.

Santa Claus had fared better than Rockport, mostly because of its Christmas-themed businesses, tourism, and growing population. Nang had thought about opening his restaurant there, where it would probably attract more people. He'd opted for here.

A little more than two blocks away the hulking brown brick building used to be a grocery store, abandoned thirty years past when Lefty Jay killed his brother and their businesses shuttered. Her husband intended to turn that into Nang's Uptown Wok, was giddy about it. Thought it would brighten up Rockport, be close enough so that people who worked in the sheriff's department, courthouse, police department, and other offices could walk down the street for lunch. *Take a Walk Uptown.* A good-sized parking lot to accommodate folks from farther away cinched it. And the price.

She hadn't tried to talk him out of it.

Should she have? She probably still could. All he'd likely lose would be the deposit. Piper didn't want Lefty Jay to profit a penny.

But the restaurant could be good for Nang and Rockport, remove a scar on a blighted section of downtown, maybe encourage others to fill more of the husks. The building shouldn't just sit there empty. If Nang hadn't made an offer, someone else might have ... Lefty Jay and his wife hadn't put a big price tag on it: $50,000. It needed a lot of

THE DEAD OF SLED RUN

work, had been neglected for decades. Still, she thought they could have easily asked two or three times that amount. Maybe after thirty years Lefty's wife just wanted to unload it. Were they still together? Something else to look into.

She inhaled deep, pulling the December chill to the bottom of her lungs, picking up the faint hint of car exhaust from several vehicles heading south, maybe to work at the power plant.

One more look at Lefty Jay, who tipped his rumpled hat to her, then she spun on her heel and crossed the street to the west, jogging to the courthouse, in time with the music echoing in the buildings' canyon: "Frosty the Snowman."

S cales offered her coffee, and she declined.

"I stopped by your office late Friday afternoon," he opened. "Your dispatcher said you were patrolling."

"I do that two or three times a week." Piper took a chair across from Scales at the conference table and slipped her arms out of her coat sleeves. Comfortable chair, leather, padded. One like this would be good for her office. "You could have called my cell."

Scales placed a stack of manila file folders in front of him. He was dressed in a gray suit, pale blue shirt, and navy tie with tiny red biplanes flying in angled stripes across it. His hair was cut so short it looked shaved on the sides, not quite Basil's urban fade style, but close. He had on cologne or aftershave, something musky.

"Didn't really want to talk about the lawsuit over the phone," he said finally. "It's more of a face-to-face thing. I assume you know about it by now."

"My dad mentioned it over the weekend." Piper thought she should have accepted the coffee. "He said he and Oren were being sued. That others were no doubt on the list. My department." She rested her hands flat on the table: smooth, lacquered; it had little warmth to it.

"Heard about the fire at his house. Was anyone—"

"His garage. No one was hurt. Total loss." Piper figured he already knew that, everyone seeming to know everyone else's business in the county. She heard phones ringing beyond this room, soft chatter, somebody with hard soles *clacking* down the hallway. "It's under investigation."

"Related to Oren's fire, do you think?"

She was here for their monthly meeting, cases coming up, a contract she wanted him to look over, and concerns in the county. Arson counted as a concern.

"I'm convinced. But we don't know a lot yet."

"The lawsuit," Scales returned. "We'll hit that first."

"Lefty Jay—"

"Jayson Walden," Scales corrected.

"Is suing me, too, right?"

Scales shook his head. "Not you. The sheriff's department, my office, Dale, Rockport, the entire county, and a few individuals."

"One point five million," Piper said. "I looked it up this morning. Indiana caps wrongful incarceration at fifty thousand a year. Multiply that by thirty. This is a wrongful incarceration case, right? But he wasn't wrongfully incarcerated. My dad said Lefty Jay was guilty."

"One point five million," Scales agreed. "He's claiming wrongful imprisonment, also shoddy police work, an inadequate defense … several things."

"So he wants more than one point five."

"He might get the one point five from the state, depends how it all shakes out." Scales steepled his index fingers under his chin. "It could be a lot more from other sources." He took a deep breath, looked beyond Piper, out the window, she guessed. "About a half-dozen years ago in Elkhart a newspaper highlighted some big flaws in prosecuting a man for armed robbery. He was in prison for eight years. The city coughed up seven and a half million. Largest wrongful conviction lawsuit in the state."

"My dad and Oren arrested Lefty Jay," Piper said.

"Walden's suit claims gross negligence in their investigation."

"My father has never been negligent. He—"

"Didn't find the knife Walden claimed his brother had."

Piper growled softly. "My dad has always been thorough, careful."

Scales leaned back in his chair and dropped his hands to the file folders. "Those grocery stores sat abandoned for a lot of years, Piper. Thirty. Early this past summer Clara Walden—"

"Lefty's wife?"

A nod. "She'd always stuck by him. Anyway, early this summer she bought out her ex-sister-in-law's share of the buildings. Some used car dealer had expressed interest in the Dale place, but she couldn't sell it until she had full claim."

Piper knew Nang had looked at the Dale building, where the murder happened, so the used car dealer must have taken a pass.

"That deal fell through," Scales continued, "but not before the interior was gutted, shelves pulled out ... and a knife found."

Piper sat up straight, eyes wide.

"*The* knife Walden claimed his brother waved at him, made him in fear for his life."

Piper's voice was barely above a whisper. "I vaguely remember reading about the knife last summer. A small article. I think it was printed around the time the teenagers died at the county fair."

"Yeah, you were pretty busy with that," Scales said. "And the murder of that comic shop owner right after."

"Busy," she said. She hadn't followed the knife story then, didn't care at the time about a case from thirty years back, from before she was born. Had actually forgotten all about it until now. The news had no relevance or interest—then.

"The knife was tested, had some DNA, fingerprints still on it. That all triggered Walden getting out of prison. The knife seemed to corroborate Walden's testimony of being threatened. Now, I'd still call Walden guilty, he shot his brother multiple times, and in the back, brought a gun to a knife fight. But had the knife been part of the original case, he likely wouldn't have gotten such a stiff prison term."

"Are you going to retry him?"

"There was a motion for a new trial when the DNA evidence came back. But we realized it wasn't worth the effort. To be fair, Piper, after thirty years in prison, witnesses have either moved, died, or forgot facts. We'd gotten that proverbial pound of flesh out of him. Besides, a judge probably wouldn't send him back to prison on a retrial."

"Because he'd already served thirty years."

"Exactly."

"So he's suing everyone." Piper tried to understand it all.

"Dale and Rockport because they were part of the original investigation. The entire county because it is considered the overarching entity that controls the Sheriff's Department and the County Prosecutor. More to the point, your department and my office don't have money so to speak. We have budgets, which come from Spencer County. Spencer County has the money he's going after. Your dad and Oren are included because they were the arresting officers. You and I are *not* included because we weren't part of the case."

"Are you defending the county?"

Scales frowned. "I technically represent the county, and the sheriff's department in civil cases. But a case of this magnitude ... the county board will contract it out to a private firm, probably from Indy, who has attorneys familiar with this type of work. Fresh eyes. Out of my wheelhouse for certain, and since my department is among those being sued, I'd be representing myself. I'd be an idiot to do that. There'll be lots of discovery. It's going to take a long time to go through it."

Piper remembered her father saying no knife was found when he and Oren were called to the Dale grocery store, that Lefty Jay had killed his brother in cold blood.

"Maybe the knife was planted," Piper suggested.

Scales shook his head. "Don't think so. Where it was found, under a shelf where customers testified the argument started, it was probably kicked there, not seen by your dad and Oren. Not discovered. They didn't search for it. Not hard enough anyway."

Piper found it tough to breathe.

More phones rang beyond the conference room. Someone with hard soled shoes *clacked* by again. A door shut.

"What can I do?" Piper asked.

"Nothing." Scales' voice was flat. "Nothing you can do."

"This happened before I was born. It's my department. I have to do—"

"Nothing you can do," he repeated. "It's going to play in court. His attorney, our attorneys. It'll be a while before anything settles. A long while."

Neither said anything for several moments. Piper listened to the sounds beyond the room, pictured Lefty Jay on the bench, tipping his hat to her. If somehow he was behind the arsons, she'd put him back in prison.

"How's Oren?" Scales interrupted her thoughts.

Piper shrugged, then said, "Alive."

"Let's get on with the rest of these, okay?" Scales tapped the file folders again.

He talked about DUIs, the number one ticketed offense in the county. Piper only half paid attention, her thoughts tangled with her father and Oren being sued by Lefty Jay, who was also suing her department and the county.

If she and Nang had taken a honeymoon immediately after the wedding she might be on a beach somewhere right now, oblivious to the lawsuit and a far distance from the fires.

But Piper needed to be here for all of this, to investigate the arsons, the burned bodies, to deal with the lawsuit. Still, for a handful of minutes she contemplated digging her toes into warm, white sand and staring out at crystal blue water.

"Convictions are up," Scales continued. "Your deputies are doing everything right when they catch a drunk driver, not giving them any loopholes to avoid fines, and in the case of half a dozen last month, jail time *and* revoked licenses. I've two DUI hearings this afternoon."

The honeymoon would have to wait until the arsonist was caught. Piper wouldn't leave her county until that was resolved, and the culprit charged with the deaths of the people who were found in the Laubenstein house. And she'd have to get someone to temporarily fill Oren's position until he returned. She couldn't afford to be down a deputy with this workload.

Would Oren return?

"I've accepted a plea deal from Victoria Halliday," Scales said. He'd changed the subject and Piper forced herself to concentrate. Victoria and her sister, Danica, were arrested in November for manufacturing, possession, and distribution of meth. It was a relatively small endeavor operated out of a second-floor apartment, compared to the massive meth operation her department had uncovered elsewhere in the county that had made the national news and brought in the FBI.

"Three years," Scales said. "She'll do three years, then probation. Danica thinks she can fight the charges, but that won't happen."

"No," Piper agreed. She'd been the one to arrest them, dotted every "i" and watched as a customer showed up to buy their wares. "The evidence is concrete." A glance at her watch, an hour gone. These meetings didn't usually take this much time.

"Anything on the Carlsons?" Piper asked. That was the other drug case from November, this one a pot business run by a family of farmers in the north part of the county. Basil and Oren had found that one almost by accident, and discovered it had been operating unde-tected for years.

"Not much. It'll be months before it goes to trial. Possession, manufacture, distribution of marijuana, Level 5 penalty."

"Carries six years, right? One to six."

He laughed. "They should have picked a different state, Illinois maybe, someplace where pot is legal. Indiana is one of the toughest states on pot. And six years? Roger and Amy Carlson, and their son, Trenton, would be lucky to face six years. We're adding charges, after the FBI stepped in to further investigate. They're facing conspiracy to harvest, ship, and sell, and operating a criminal enterprise. The Feds discovered they'd carted about twenty tons of marijuana over the past few years down to Florida and up to New York, had four million dollars in a separate business account from the sales, which a handful of days ago they seized. The news will trickle out, but because it's just about pot, the media won't do much with it. The Feds are trying to seize Carlson's farm or force it into foreclosure right now. I don't have the specifics on that yet. But the Feds—or the state—can try to seize anything used in a criminal activity."

"The farm. The whole farm was a criminal activity."

"They put it up for collateral when they posted bail. I suspect they'll have to find a new place to stay before their trial ... which will start sometime this spring. Six years? They wish. If convicted, Piper, they're looking at life in prison."

"Do not pass go," she said softly.

"I've heard they're filing for bankruptcy," he added.

"Do not collect two hundred dollars." She sighed and passed over a three-page document. "It's a contract. Need a quick review on it. Oren's going to be out a few months and I can't afford to be down a deputy. I don't want a full-time hire, I want Oren back. But this'll let me get a temp deputy to help cover things for a little while. The county council meets at six tonight. I'll get them to approve it, and then I'll find someone with enough experience to slip in."

"I hope Oren comes back," Scales said. He didn't sound optimistic.

Piper wasn't optimistic either.

She checked her cell phone for messages as she left Scales' office, finding one from Zeke:

The Laubensteins made it back from Florida and said they are coming in at 1.

She leaned against the wall in the hallway and let out a low breath. That was the same time the autopsies were scheduled in Evansville.

"Shit." She would have to choose. "Just shit."

Her fingers worried at the keys, texting Basil. The lead investigator on the arson cases, she'd let him pick.

The answer came back fast.

A chat with the Laubensteins would be more pleasant, and I have some questions for them. But I'll take the autopsies. I'll leave a note on your desk.

Piper first intended to have a chat with Lefty Jay. She took the steps two at a time from the second floor of the courthouse, thoughts of Walden's lawsuit mingling with the image of Oren's burning house, the charred bodies, and her father's destroyed garage.

When she came out onto the street, the bench Lefty Jay had been sitting on was empty.

The speakers appropriately played: "I'll Have a Blue Christmas."

15

noon

B asil arrived an hour early; he'd learned from Oren that Dr. Annie Neufeld always started before the scheduled time.

Dr. Neufeld and Dr. Penny Kerr, the burn victim specialist, had already cut into the first body, chatting softly, seemingly oblivious to Basil, who settled on a stool about eight feet away. The second body was on a parallel table behind them and hadn't yet been touched.

Basil's seat was more than close enough. Vicks smeared under his nose, mask in place, he could still smell the corpses. He'd been near burned bodies before. The odor was always different and yet had the same characteristics: nauseating, sweet, putrid, a little like leather tanned over an open fire. So strong he swore he could taste it.

Forty-two minutes to drive here from Rockport, another forty-two back, plus however many hours it would take for both autopsies, Basil suspected he wouldn't be home much before dinner time.

He needed names for these victims. But he knew there'd be no IDs coming today on either body. DNA and dental records weren't instantaneous. Results could take days or weeks. Or more. The names could come faster if someone in Santa Claus knew them and came forward, or if by chance the Laubensteins might provide a clue.

Basil would like to be in two places at the same time—here and back in the department. More useful information might come from the Laubensteins, but he could find them later if needed, if Sheriff Blackwell didn't get enough from them. An autopsy? That was a one-shot opportunity to pick up important tidbits, and it was always better to take it in live rather than read the report later.

Necessary, but definitely not enjoyable.

It smelled awful. He set his teeth, determined not to gag.

"John Doe," Dr. Kerr said, raising her voice for Basil's benefit, and nodding a greeting to him. "John Doe's upper airways show smoke inhalation, soot soiling the nares and oropharynx. Soot-stained mucus lining, extensive burning of the trachea."

Dr. Neufeld added, "Maybe from external contamination because the ceiling collapsed on them."

So the victim was not dead before the fire started; Basil had wanted to know that.

Faintly, he heard Dr. Kerr's knee crack as she shifted from one leg to the other. He guessed her to be mid-forties, roughly two decades younger than Dr. Neufeld, who'd retired from her pediatrics practice before running for coroner. Dr. Neufeld was a year into her second term, and had said there wouldn't be a third. Despite the age gap, the doctors were similar in build and pale complexion, both with short hair, thin fingers, angular faces, and brown eyes. Looked like they could be related, mother, daughter, but he knew they weren't. Basil had checked Dr. Kerr's background. A Connecticut native, before moving to Evansville she'd worked at the University of Rochester Medical Center in New York, a rising star in the burn center. She'd authored a book on burn injuries and treatment and was an expert in the field. Basil thought his department was fortunate to have her help.

"How old do you think?" he ventured. Not that it mattered, dead was dead. But he wanted to know all about the trespassers who had been living in the Laubenstein house. What race, religion, were they locals? What were they doing there? What had they looked like in life?

Where did they work or go to school? Who was missing them? Someone had to be missing them.

"Age?" Dr. Neufeld shrugged, then said. "Young. Definitely young."

"Not kids, though," Dr. Kerr said.

"No, not *that* young."

"Some putrefaction because of the heat of the fire, skin slippage will interfere with getting you fingerprints," Dr. Kerr said. "Maybe impossible, fingerprints. DNA though, I can get that. Not a complete char. I can tell you this man was white or very light skinned Hispanic."

White. Like Spencer County was white.

"The teeth will help," she continued. "Not enough heat to destroy them. We'll run a chemical analysis of the tooth dentin."

"Teeth appear in a certain sequence," Dr. Neufeld explained. "This body has the third molar, putting him at least seventeen. We determined that the vertebrae that made up his sacrum were not wholly fused, which happens around twenty-three."

Dr. Kerr added, "The basal suture at the base of the skull closes between eighteen and twenty-four. Not fully closed here. My estimate … until dentals get you an ID, is that John Doe was between seventeen and twenty-two."

"Young," Dr. Neufeld repeated.

"No fillings, perfect teeth, except he had dental implants, the front two upper teeth, so he'll have records somewhere."

"Maybe from a sports injury," Dr. Neufeld suggested. "Build hints he could have been athletic."

Hockey, Basil thought. Hockey players had teeth knocked out.

The doctors continued working, taking out organs, weighing them. Basil's attention was split between watching them and wondering if the burn victims had interacted with anyone in the Village, with people he'd not yet talked to. Residents on Sled Run had caught glimpses of them, saw groceries delivered, saw the car leave and come back a few times. He'd not yet come across anyone who'd talked to them. He would go to more neighboring streets in the Village after dinner. Supposedly the pair had lived in the Laubenstein house for two weeks. Someone in the area had to have more information about them. He just had to find that someone. Two cell phones were found with the bodies, but burned beyond any use.

The phone in his pocket buzzed with a text. Basil retrieved it and saw a note from Esme.

Cat crying + gacking + pain. Going to vet. Will text later.

Basil hoped the cat … whichever one it was … would be okay and that one of the kids hadn't fed it something to cause this. Oren had enough grief going on, didn't need something bad to happen to one of his precious felines.

"He was alive at the time of the fire, I'd bet my license on that. And he suffered," Dr. Kerr said. "Fluid loss. Some bone fracturing because of the heat, skin splitting here and here from the body heating." She indicated those areas. "Skin contracts and tears. I saw photos from the scene, suspect he got trapped when the roof collapsed on him and couldn't get out. Extensive, though not total, burning, but smoke inhalation got him first."

"Fortunately smoke inhalation," Dr. Neufeld said. "If there is anything fortunate about his death." She raised her head. "I suspect the girl will show the same thing, but we'll be thorough, meticulous."

"I have a blood sample running in the hospital's bio-chem department," Dr. Kerr said. "It will back up that he was alive when the fire started, checking for CO-Hb."

"Carboxyhaemoglobin," Dr. Neufeld translated.

Dr. Kerr nodded. "A cigarette smoker's runs ten to twenty percent. If it's above fifty percent it means he was alive at the time of the fire and breathed in smoke and fumes. Soot below the vocal cords here is more evidence. I want everything covered."

"I told you she's good," Dr. Neufeld said. "The best."

Dr. Kerr shrugged. "Probably took two to ten minutes for him to pass out and die before the carbon monoxide became lethal. He suffered in those minutes."

"Hope you and Piper can catch the son of a bitch who set the fire and killed these people, put my friend Oren in the hospital." Dr. Neufeld's eyes were rimmed with tears, and she looked quickly away from Basil and back to the body. "You catch who killed John Doe here and Daphne."

Basil sat straight. "Daphne?"

Dr. Neufeld nodded. "Don't have a last name on her, haven't started cutting. But we took off her jewelry. Over there on the counter. Daphne Doe. John had a ring. It's over there, too."

Basil padded over to the counter. The effects that had been taken off the bodies were charred and few ... the *Daphne* necklace, name set with what looked to be a bunch of tiny green stones, two stud earrings, one hoop earring mostly melted, clothing fragments, five small rings he suspected had been worn by the woman, and a ring, larger and rectangular, the one Dr. Neufeld said was taken off the man. Burnt flesh and other material adhered to everything. They'd need to be cleaned up in a lab. The Indiana State Police had a good crime lab right in town.

"It looks like a class ring, but it isn't," Dr. Neufeld said. "I think it's military, which would put John Doe above age seventeen. Unless it's a relative's ring he wore. If you're going to take that stuff, you know the drill with the forms. Chain of evidence and all."

Basil hoped the cat would be okay and that Esme would be understanding. He wouldn't make it home for dinner again tonight. When the autopsies finished, he would go to the crime lab.

Not a class ring? He studied it.

It had a similar look. Dr. Neufeld could be right with her guess of a military ring.

Might be a long day.

He really hoped the cat was going to be okay.

16

I f your father was still sheriff, he'd have arrested someone by now. He would've caught the *farbrekher* that destroyed our home, and Rosey's place. Your father would have—" Saundra Laubenstein vented her anger and Piper let her. It was just noise, necessary for Saundra, hurtful for Piper, rattling the air in her office, bouncing off the walls, overriding the instrumental Christmas music playing on the street outside the window. "Joy to the World."

"That someone could so hate us because we're Jewish would ruin everything significant in our lives. All the baby pictures and keepsakes, my grandmother's antique dining table, the quilt on our bed. The quilt made by my sister, dead five years now to the cancer. That some antisemitic asshole who—"

Piper let her rant drift to the background, waiting for an important tidbit to surface or for Saundra to come up for air. She wanted to hug the woman, but that wouldn't lessen the grief or help anything.

"Fifteen hours and nineteen minutes it took to drive home ... except there was no home to drive to. Char and ashes. Looks like a war zone, our house and Rosey's. Like a bomb dropped on Sled Run.

We're in a hotel. A damn hotel with no walk-in shower and faded bedspreads with fraying thread and—"

Saundra and Eldad Laubenstein sat across from Piper, desk between them, door closed. Piper had hoped to talk to them in the spacious break room, but the whiteboard there—covered with pictures from the fire investigation—would have upped their trauma. There were printouts of Tweets and Facebook posts with antisemitic comments that Zeke had collected from his social media dive, a list of Spencer County residents who had made them. Diego had been tasked with investigating the social media posters for a link to the fires. Saundra and Eldad didn't need to see all that right now.

Easier to focus here, though Saundra's misery made Piper's small office even smaller.

"You hear it on the news, crimes are up. Hate in this country is up. Up. Up. This year? The highest it's ever been. This morning … this very morning I read the news on my phone … the ADL says four thousand crimes against us this year. Against Jewish people."

Piper knew ADL stood for Anti-Defamation League. She'd read some of the recent reports. Saundra was right. Hate was high. Hate for races, religion.

"But hate shouldn't be here. Not in Santa Claus. Especially not in the Village. Gated. Safe. For the most part safe. Never a problem before, not with that much hate. Not with any hate. We get looks sometimes. Looks because we don't decorate like the neighbors do. Got a note on our front door right before Thanksgiving, suggesting we put up Christmas lights. Rosey got one, too, just ask him. Same thing last year. Didn't come from someone on our block, I can tell you that. Good neighbors, we have. They didn't do it, burn the house, our neighbors didn't do that. Gated. It's not right."

The Laubensteins contrasted. Saundra was petite, shorter than Piper, maybe five feet, and tiny like she could shop in the children's department. Records put her at sixty-seven, though her face was smooth and tanned, and only a few wrinkles held the corners of her wide hazel eyes. Her blonde hair, with a smidgen of gray roots, was pulled back in a pony-tail that dangled between her shoulder blades, and her lilac perfume wafted overly sweet and strong. She looked youthful, wearing colorful ice-dyed jeans and a Miami Dolphins leather jacket zipped all the way up to her chin, Mickey Mouse diamond stud earrings. Tears running down her cheeks and streaking her mascara marred her otherwise pretty face. Her fists were clenched so tight the knuckles were white.

"There are cameras in the Village," Saundra continued. "Why haven't you arrested someone? I don't understand. You should have seen who did it. The cameras. Someone should have seen. The *farbrekher* should be in your jail, rotting."

Eldad was easily a foot taller, and his long black wool coat must have been a XXXL. One year older than his wife, he had a deeply weathered face like ancient tree bark, bald on top with bright white hair ringing his head. His pale blue eyes looked tired and sad, and a pair of thick-lensed sunglasses poked out of his shirt pocket.

"With the cameras, the gate security. Gated subdivision. Gated. Gated, I say. You should have someone arrested." Saundra thrust out her chin and sobbed. "All our important memories were in that house. Irreplaceable. Your father—" Her shoulders shook and Eldad reached over and clasped her arm.

"I don't mean it, you know, Sheriff Blackwell," Saundra said. "The part about your father. I don't know that he would have found who burned down our house. I'm just so pissed I'm not thinking right, and my tongue is too sharp. I don't know your father. Know *of* him, sure, that he's the Santa Claus police chief now. But I never spoke to him, not in all the years we've lived in this damn county. Not when he was sheriff. Never needed to." Her breath hitched but she kept going. "Hate. All the hate in the world did this. I've never hated anyone. Not before now. But I hate the *farbrekher* that set this fire."

Eldad leaned forward. "Maimonides wrote that 'All the evils that men cause to each other because of certain desires, or opinions or religious principles, are rooted in ignorance.' Burning the homes of Jews is pure ignorance, Sheriff Blackwell. Ignorance of the value of life." His voice was strong and clear, and Piper thought it had a comforting quality.

"My wife and I have never experienced this vitriol on our street, only amity from our neighbors, the community. So I know it was from someone outside." With his free hand he brushed at the air, as if batting away a cobweb. "We have prattled on in our frustration and sadness, and we apologize. You have questions."

Piper placed her fingers on the edge of her desk, still shiny from the furniture polish. "I do have questions." She had a list, and Basil's questions, too. She'd start with this: "About the two people in your house—"

"No one was supposed to be in our house," Saundra said. "No house sitters. I told you on the phone that we've never had house-sitters. Never in all the years we've gone to Florida in the winter. Burglars, they were. Burglars breaking in to steal something. Punished in *Gehinom* for breaking in. They burned like everything burned."

"We don't know that they were burglars," Piper said. Not only did she not have the *who done it* of the fire, but also not the *who was killed* regarding the victims. The double-mystery hung heavy. "Honestly, we don't know anything about them. But it appears they'd been living there for—"

"Always there are burglars around Hanukah, Christmas, in the Village, around the holy days. Always figured it would not happen to us, living next to Rosey. Always figured that having law enforcement next door would make us immune. Sometimes in the summer, you hear about it, the little thefts," Saundra returned. "Never caught, the thieves. Never. Despite the cameras that apparently don't see anything. Never caught. Just like the *farbrekher* that burned our home hasn't been caught. I want to know who was staying in our house, Sheriff Blackwell. I want to know if they were there to steal from us. I want to know if they set the fire and got caught in their own wicked act."

Piper drew in a deep breath, tugging Saundra's perfume far into her lungs. She made a promise she shouldn't: "Mrs. Laubenstein, we are going to find the man who destroyed two homes and put my chief deputy in the burn unit. The arsonist will be caught. And we are going to find out who was staying in your house."

Saundra leaned back in her chair, sucked in her lower lip, and then closed her eyes. She trembled, whether from rage or grief Piper couldn't tell. Eldad leaned into her.

"Ask the rest of your questions," he said.

Piper went through her list, and Eldad and Saundra responded.

- Eldad: "There were no suspicious people around Sled Run before we left for vacation. Retired, nowhere to go in the fall and winter, we stay home until we head to Miami. We would have noticed someone slinking around. It would be difficult to get through a gate and prowl the neighborhood. You need a keycard, and if you don't live here, you have to be on a list."
- Saundra: "Rosey didn't mention any enemies, but certainly he had some because of all the people he'd arrested through the years. He didn't like to talk about his work much, even though we spoke to him every day. Rosey liked to talk about his cats and his granddaughter, said she's a deputy, too, and is going to be a lawyer. Rosey is proud of her."
- Saundra: "No trouble with any of the neighbors, cordial, friendly. In fact, we're friends with all of the families on Sled Run. They've all lived on the street for years. Not much turnover in this area. People like it and stay. Our next door neighbor, Beverly Parker: you could not find a better woman. Raised Catholic, she was. But I told her she has a Jewish heart. When we celebrate Purim in March, we invite Beverly over to share the hamantashen pastries I make."
- Eldad: "I'm not aware of anyone wanting to buy Oren's double-lot property. No one had tried to buy ours either, but we will be selling, moving down to Miami full-time after this. Staying would put us in a cocoon of sadness. We need to make new memories. So, finally, there will be room for a new family on Sled Run, yes?"

- Saundra: "Honestly, I don't know of anyone in the neighborhood who has been threatened. Before this ... before this ... I'd only felt safe here. People die in the Village ... heart attacks, strokes, old age, I suppose. They don't die in arson fires. I felt safe."

Basil's questions:

- Eldad: "Our keycard for the Village gate was not missing—recently or ever. It was never lost or stolen or borrowed. The keycard had only been replaced once, and that was three years ago when the gate-reader was updated. Our son Aaron does not have a keycard. We only had two, one for me, one for Saundra. On days Aaron came up from Louisville to visit, he was put on the list for the guard to let through. We always followed the Village rules."
- Saundra: "We didn't have any suspicious phone calls before we left for vacation ... except for a persistent fellow from India wanting to extend our car's warranty. I'm sure he was some sort of scammer."
- Saundra: "David and Ricia Halm across the street ... nice people. I don't care much for their son, Jerome, but that's because he's a bit of a wild teenager, a *zhlob*. Eldad is more tolerant of him than I am. Jerome plays his music loud on the weekends and in the summer, guns the engine on his Mustang, isn't respectful enough to his parents. Jerome is not polite ... but I couldn't say that he has been outright mean."
- Eldad: "Jerome likes heavy metal. Aaron used to like that racket when he was younger. Jerome is just testing the boundaries, stretching his wings you'd call it. We're not afraid of him or worried he'd do anything to our property. He's not somebody who would burn down a house. We could have complained about all his noise to the Village board, but wouldn't think of it. We like David and Ricia and

didn't want to cause them any trouble. The music is different in Miami."

- Eldad: "Not many old cars in this part of the Village, not old beaters like the VW Rabbit you mentioned. You can't have old beaters in the Village, that's part of the rules, at least they can't be sitting out. It's not like in other places in the county where people set old cars up on cinder blocks in front yards. Thankfully the Village has standards. I will miss the place. I will miss it forever."

- Saundra: "You can't let snowmobiles in the winter sit out either. Or golf carts, even the street-legal ones. Not overnight. They have to be in a garage. Quite a few people in the Village have golf carts, usually store them in the building at the course, where Eldad keeps his. But sometimes people drive them from the course to their homes, especially if they're going back to golf again the next day. Yes, you can access the golf course without driving through a Village gate. The golf course is basically part of the Village.

- Eldad: "I think I will give my cart to Beverly. She's just learning the game. A golf cart saves you a lot of walking."

- Saundra: "We're going to stick around a week or so to deal with insurance, go out with the neighbors, drive up to see Rosey in the hospital. Then we'll be off to Louisville for a few days with Aaron before moving to Miami forever. It will be easy to move. We have nothing left to pack for the trip."

Piper circled back to something that tickled her mind.

"You mentioned thefts in the Village around the holidays."

"And sometimes in the summer," Saundra said. Her voice was even now, the tears dried up. "You see it in the paper, they talk about it in the park, sometimes on the course."

Piper read the paper to keep up on all things Spencer County. Thefts from the Village had escaped her notice.

"What was stolen?" She'd stop at the Santa Claus Police Department and ask to look through those reports. She had to go to Santa Claus anyway to take another pass through the Village.

"Never anything major, but always valuable," Eldad put in. "Never anything large, anything easy to notice missing. A fine watch, like Mike Terrell's Breitling last December. He thinks it was stolen in December, anyway. Didn't notice it gone until well after New Year's when he wanted to wear it to a company dinner."

"That woman on Rudolf Lane. Didn't she say those emerald earrings she got in the Bahamas twenty years ago were gone? Missing a few other pieces of jewelry, right?"

Eldad nodded. "I think I remember that."

"Other odds and ends. Never anything big like a flat screen or a computer. All small and valuable. Antique letter opener. Some old coins. Stamps from a collection. Things that maybe were lost, misplaced, but could have been stolen. Two years back Susan Ames said a few hundred dollars was taken from her underwear drawer, which meant it was a lot more than a few hundred, which meant she was hiding money from her husband and live-in mother-in-law. Stolen. You don't misplace that kind of money." Saundra let out a long breath. "So I was wrong, Sheriff Blackwell."

Piper cocked her head.

"About Santa Claus, about the Village. About it being gated and safe. Gated, sure. Not safe. Our house, all the significant things, ashes."

"Find him," Eldad said, his comforting voice now had an edge to it. "Find the asshole and make him pay."

Piper texted Nang after the Laubensteins left.

I'm going to the county board meeting at 6 and The Thirsty Turtle at 7. Join me? Dinner? And a drink?

The reply came a few minutes later.

Love to see how my Fulda competition is doing. Will meet you there at 7.

Through her window, music seeped in: "Here Comes Santa Claus."

Piper glanced at her empty coffee mug, got up, and grabbed her coat. "Here Comes Santa Claus indeed," she said.

17

Piper plucked a fry from her plate and studied it. Golden, with the crinkled edges she favored. She registered the crispness of it, the slight touch of warmth and oil against her fingers, seriously inviting. Taking a bite, she grinned. Just the right saltiness, and a hint of spice that she couldn't identify, a bit tangy, sweet mixed with bitter.

"Glorious. This is really really really good," Piper told Nang, who sat across from her. She'd ordered a sauerkraut-smothered hotdog and the fries, and with that first taste decided to eschew catsup. "Perfect. I can't remember when I had fries this good."

Nang gave a half-smile in return. He'd ordered a hamburger and onion rings.

"You're going to tell me this isn't good for me," Piper said, stuffing a few more fries in her mouth and then wrapping her fingers around the hotdog bun. The strong, sour scent of the sauerkraut swirled.

"I will tell you no such thing." Nang picked up the burger and took a bite, chewing thoughtfully. "Medium-rare," he decided. "Smoky barbecue sauce. The bun is toasted. There's some Worcestershire and ground pepper in the beef. Unexpected. Juicy. I like it. An improvement over what he set out at our reception. And it's way the hell better than McDonald's."

"I thought you liked McDonald's."

"I do, occasionally." He took another few bites, tried an onion ring, nodded his approval, and then reached for his glass of Zombie Dust beer.

"But you don't like that you like it." Piper happily nibbled at the hotdog.

"I'm not pleased that my competition's food is tasty and is attracting customers." Softer: "And I'm definitely not pleased that I'm jealous."

"Well, I'm pleased that these fries are so friggin' good. Maybe we'll come back again next week," Piper said. "Whatcha think?"

Nang gave a noncommittal tip of his head and took another bite of onion ring.

This late on a weekday, Piper considered The Thirsty Turtle busy for Fulda. Eight tables full of diners, a mix of men and women, mostly middle-aged, plus a half-dozen younger men at the bar. All of the customers were white, except her husband. Nang was born in America to parents who had immigrated from Vietnam. They'd emphasized their Vietnamese culture throughout his childhood and teen years, and to this day he preferred Vietnamese cuisine.

"Next time I will try the pork tenderloin," Nang said. "And the fries instead of onion rings. Not a big menu to pick from."

"Bars don't offer a lot of choices. But this is damn good bar food."

The place had been a well-established dive bar for years, operated by a retired school teacher who now sat in prison for murdering the town bigot. Under its new management and name, it no longer looked like a dive.

Tug Waters had been Basil's police partner in Chicago. Tug would still be in the Gangs and Narcotics division if his teenage daughter hadn't gotten pregnant by a gang leader who insisted she join his "family." Tug whisked the girl away, finding refuge in Spencer County. He'd told Piper it wasn't likely the gang would come looking for his daughter down here in Green Acres, and felt safer with Basil in the area. While Tug had paid for the bar, on paper it was in Basil's name ... one more effort to stay hidden from the gang.

Piper had wondered if Tug would have trouble attracting customers because of how brightly white Spencer County gleamed. But judging from how busy the Turtle was right now, and how well it did on weekends, her worries were unfounded. So far, Tug had been warmly received. Would that continue? Would the apparent hate crimes of the two recent arsons spill beyond Jews? She shook the image out of her head of the Turtle burning.

Rustically remodeled with gleaming wood surfaces everywhere, fairy lights along the ceiling, scents of alcohol and food floating, pine garlands draped artfully for the holidays, and a jukebox that was currently playing an old Boz Scaggs song, the Turtle felt inviting. She and Nang had held their wedding reception here a little more than a week ago. The atmosphere took her back to her Army days when she'd go out with the men in her unit. They favored bars a few miles beyond Fort Campbell, homey, comfortable, off the beaten path, with a great selection of beer and music, and sandwiches that were palatable.

"Honestly, I had not expected the food to be delicious. Tug was a detective, not a chef," Nang groused. He finished the onion rings, took a deep breath, then returned to his burger.

"He has someone cooking for him."

"I'd like to know who that is."

"So you can hire her or him away?" Piper laughed. "You have three little tables at the Quick Mart, and someone is *always* eating there. You are a superb chef, have more variety, which means a bigger menu, offer catering, and you don't serve alcohol. That's what these people are mostly here for. The beer."

"And the burgers and hotdogs and fries and onion rings," Nang said softly.

"He's not your competition. You don't have any." She glanced around The Thirsty Turtle, seeing a few people she knew by appearance from the Quick Stop and elsewhere in the county, but not by name. Some of the conversations were loud—about work, Christmas shopping, and yard decorations. She heard someone mention the arsons, but couldn't see where that comment came from. Tug and a bartender—a wiry-looking man with a gray beard and a mop of gray-blond hair—filled drink orders. A flocked Christmas tree with turtle ornaments stood near the pool table where two stocky men in overalls chalked cues.

"I am glad you suggested this, but I'm surprised you took time for dinner," Nang told her. "Working two fires, the people who died. I didn't think you would—"

"Stop working? I did have to eat. I was so damn hungry." Piper finished the hotdog and reached for her extra-large soda. She would have ordered a beer, or preferably a strawberry margarita, but she didn't want to muddle her senses. "I haven't stopped working. I'll be at it tonight until I crash."

"Constantly thinking about the arsons and—"

"Yeah, that. Fire seems to be all I can think about. But I'm here to—"

"Good evening, Sheriff Blackwell, Mr. Phan." With the music and conversations swirling, Piper hadn't heard Tug approach. "How's married life treating you?"

"Wonderful," Nang said.

"Can you take a few minutes?" Piper gestured to an empty chair at their table.

Tug raised an eyebrow, hesitated, then pulled out the chair and sat. Built like a linebacker, muscles strained the seams of his pale green long-sleeved shirt. His skin was the shade of polished chestnut, his head shaved, and he sported a soul patch. A quarter-sized gold cross dangled from his left ear, and his intent dark eyes told Piper he didn't miss much.

"You here to lecture me about dating your dispatcher? Tee and I have only been out a few times. And I ain't about to stop her from coming to my bar. Never turn away a paying customer, even if I don't charge them."

"I never meddle in who my staff—"

"I know that. Just yanking your chain." He looked at Nang. "Do you like the Zombie Dust? Got it in by request before the weekend and I ain't tried one yet. It's one of 3 Floyds' pale ales, out of Munster, I think."

"Citrusy. I like it. I don't drink a lot of beer, but I would order this again. It pairs well with the food."

Piper nudged her plate aside and squared her shoulders, wanting to look all-business. "Mr. Waters—"

"Oooh, *Mr.* Waters. Definitely ain't a social stop, eh?"

"I just came from the county board, which approved a temporary hire for my department. My chief deputy is in the burn unit in Indy."

"I'm aware of that," Tug said. His melodic voice sounded heavy. "News and gossip are thunder and lightning in Hooterville. I know about the arsons. Hate crimes, right? Anti-Jewish? And the bodies. And that your chief deputy almost died."

"Oren is in bad shape, going to be a few months in recovery. He will recover." She hoped. "I've given his granddaughter a leave of absence to be with him, but I expect her back to work late next week."

"This ain't going where it should," Tug said.

"Two arsons that indeed look to be hate crimes, a double-murder tagged to one of them, little thefts in the Village that may or may not be involved, and that's on top of regular patrols. I can't afford to be down deputies right now."

Tug whistled and scooted back from the table. "So you decided it was a good time to come to dinner here."

The song on the jukebox pivoted to Cyndi Lauper's "She Bop."

"The board signed off on six months, but I think I'll only need someone for three." Piper wanted Oren to come back. Oren needed to work to ease his depression, to keep busy, and she needed his experience. They didn't always get along—Oren thought he should have won the election for sheriff, and sometimes Piper thought it would have been better for the county if he had. But they complemented each other and worked well together. "If he heals like the doctors hope, he should be back in three months."

Tug whistled again. "I'm sure you can find someone else who—"

"*Temporary* hire. I don't want to mess with job postings and interviews, not for a three-month gig that will draw little interest. I want someone right now. Someone with experience who can step in tomorrow, doesn't need training, just a read through of the department handbook and—"

"Gotta be some retired cops around here."

"Maybe there are," she said. "But—"

"Angel's due in two weeks." He pointed to the ceiling. Tug and his daughter lived in the big apartment above the Turtle. "My sister's coming down from Detroit for a while to help. But Angel's going to need me."

Piper didn't reply.

"And I have this bar to look after."

Piper watched him, listened to Cyndi Lauper, and heard someone rack pool balls.

"Patrolling sparkling white Green Acres? Spend time sitting a desk? That isn't something I—"

"Basil said you were a great detective," Piper cut in.

"Sherlock said that? Well, yeah, I *was* a great detective. And now I'm a great bar owner." Tug stood and looked over his shoulder, pushed the chair against the table. "My man Wez looks like he could use some assistance. He just started Friday and doesn't know where everything is yet. Nice talking to you, Sheriff Blackwell, Mr. Phan." Tug headed away, stopping at a few tables to talk to his customers.

Piper frowned. She could hire one or two Rockport police officers for hourly overtime to increase night patrols, but she'd really hoped for a full-time temp to depend on.

Nang finished his beer while Piper put money on the table.

They got up and walked outside, zipping up their jackets. Rod Stewart's craggy voice reached through a gap in the door. The parking lot was clear of ice, evidence it had been salted. Snow clung to its edges and along the road that cut through Fulda. In the distance, Piper saw Christmas lights stretched across a barn. Her breath puffed away and she tipped her head back. The streetlights were few and not bright enough to cut the effect of myriad stars overhead. Beautiful. No clouds. Not supposed to snow for another day or two.

"Damn," Piper said. "I thought I could talk him into it."

"At least we got to eat dinner together," Nang offered.

"There was that," Piper agreed. "I really liked those fries."

18

11:30 p.m.

Mr. Razzleberry can't sleep." Shaya clutched the little cat around its middle, legs hanging limp, eyes closed like he was sound asleep right now. She stood in the center of the living room and swiveled back and forth across from Basil, who'd dozed off on the couch, open laptop in front of him. The room was lit by the multi-colored strings of the Christmas tree he'd forgotten to unplug. "Mr. Razzleberry can't sleep." This time it came out a little louder.

The cat's whiskers twitched. It opened one amber eye and glared at Basil.

"He can't sleep because you're squeezing him, sweetie." Basil yawned and stretched and set the laptop aside, thankful the cat was good natured enough to put up with his five-year-old. Razzleberry had never bitten or scratched Shaya, despite her constant pestering. Basil picked up his cell phone to note the time, also finding he hadn't missed any messages while he was snoozing. Thrusting it in his pocket, he smiled at her. "If you didn't squeeze Razzle—"

"*Mr.* Razzleberry."

"If you didn't squeeze Mr.—"

"Just holding him, Daddy." Basil thought she looked adorable in her pink and white snowflake pajamas with footies attached. "I'd never squeeze Mr. Razzleberry. That'd be mean."

"Let the kitty be and go back to bed. You got school tomorrow. I need to go to bed, too." Esme had turned in more than an hour ago after he'd promised her to only be a few more minutes reviewing his notes.

"Mr. Razzleberry can't sleep," Shaya insisted, thrusting out her chin and narrowing her eyes as if for emphasis. "He's worried about the man in our back yard."

Basil shot up from the couch.

Could be nothing. The child had an active imagination, talked to invisible cartoon characters, and worried the weeping larch at the corner of the house was haunted.

Probably nothing.

But what if it wasn't?

He was out of the living room and into the kitchen, where the spicy scents from Esme's Moroccan vegetable tagine lingered. He saw a pale glow from out the rear window. Something had tripped the motion sensor light connected to the deck railing.

"Daddy, Mr. Razzleberry—"

Basil waved his daughter's words away and looked out the window over the sink, the yard bright with snow glistening in the light from the motion sensor.

"Son of a bitch!" Basil hollered. "Son of a—"

"Daddy said bad words."

There was a man on the snow-covered deck wearing a puffy dark coat with a hood, face canted down and thereby unrecognizable, lighting something in twin gasoline containers.

Basil caught the flare of fire as he rushed to the sliding doors.

"Esme! ESME! Wake up! Son of a bitch!"

"Daddy said bad words," Shaya repeated.

"Wake your mom! Your brother!" In a panic Basil fumbled with the latch and wrenched the doors open, the shock of frigid winter air needling his face. Then he was on the deck and watched the man pivot, vault over the railing into the yard, fall, jump up, and hurriedly limp away.

Basil slid on the planks, reaching the gas containers and using both hands to pull out the wicks—flaming socks stuffed into the nozzles. He burned his hands and wrists as he tossed the socks off the railing and to the snow below. The scent of gas was strong; some had been poured on the deck by the arsonist to help fuel the fire.

Basil lived in a brick house, harder to burn. But the arsonist had attacked the vulnerable big wooden deck in the back, and the flames would have reached the soffit, the roof, and easily could have taken the whole place down. Basil knew it took too long for the volunteer fire department to respond to save a structure.

"You son of a bitch!" he hollered with all the volume he could summon.

Basil wanted to do all the things at once: call 9-1-1 to alert Candace, make sure Esme and the kids were safe, pursue the arsonist, and get the gasoline canisters off his deck. He swung around to his house first and closed the sliding door so Shaya wouldn't follow him. He didn't see her; hopefully she was rousing Esme.

Basil swung back, grabbing one canister in each hand, cursing at the sting of the handles against his burned fingers, rushing down the steps with them and setting them in the snow away from the wooden deck.

Then he ran, following the tracks of the arsonist. The disturbed snow made that easy, and he pulled the phone from his pocket. He punched 9-1-1 by feel, not wasting a second to look at the numbers.

"9-1-1 what is the nature—"

"Candace. I'm pursuing the arsonist. He tried to torch my house. Send a unit. Now! Call Sheriff Blackwell, and—" the phone slipped out of his aching fingers. "Shit."

He didn't stop to retrieve it. He'd find it later. Basil wasn't about to let the arsonist get away. But the limping man was trying to do just that.

Basil had on a pair of Eco Woods lace-up canvas tennies he'd purchased on sale after Thanksgiving from an L.L. Bean catalog. Comfortable, but not made for venturing through inches deep snow. He felt its cold and wet push over the collars of the tennies with each step. His sweatpants and his Chicago Cubs t-shirt offered no protection against the night's sub-zero bite. Teeth chattering, he picked up the pace, catching site of his target in the yard behind his.

A young man, or reasonably young, Basil could tell, but he'd injured himself in the drop from the deck and favored his left leg.

Basil stoked his rage, and started to gain on his quarry. He thought he heard Esme shouting, but he couldn't be sure. His heart and feet pounded, and there was a car horn suddenly honking.

Closer he ran, into the neighbor's yard and aiming toward the opposite street, where he saw his target limp to a golf cart idling in the middle, a car behind it honking, urging it out of the way. His quarry hopped into the passenger side of the golf cart and it sped away, skidding and almost striking a pickup parked at the curb. The car behind it stopped honking, rolled on, and turned into a driveway.

Basil kept chasing. There were two of them this time, the firebug and a driver. An arson team. There'd been only one at Paul Blackwell's.

Some part of him knew pursuing the golf cart along the Village streets was a foolish exercise, but he refused to give up. He had to give himself an edge. He pumped his legs in time with his heart, fists punching the air at his sides, lit and unlit yard decorations a blur. Someone looked out the second floor window of a cape cod. He was so damn cold, and his feet were soaked inside the tennies.

Would have been easier with a gun, Basil would have shot the son of a bitch—he was that angry. Death for the deaths and destruction caused and the terror inflicted. But his gun was in a safe in the closet, locked so the kids couldn't get to it. He would have lost too much time going after it. And even more time if he'd grabbed his keys and got the Explorer out of the garage. The arsonists would have been long gone.

His time was better spent on this chase.

Basil focused on the golf cart that was leaving him behind.

"You son of a bitch!"

The cart slowed as it passed a parked car. Residents weren't supposed to leave cars out along the curb, part of the subdivision rules. Basil gained a little. Were they playing with him, taunting him? Letting him pick up some ground before opening the distance? The golf cart went faster. Yeah, playing.

"I'll end your damn game. I'll end you!"

Basil pictured the image of the man in the puffy dark coat. Then pictured him dangling in the air, a piñata like he'd given Shaya for her fourth birthday. Basil was the stick that would whack it and send the contents all over the icy ground of Christmas Lake Village.

To break that piñata, he'd have to reach it first. And he couldn't catch the golf cart on the Village streets. He could only see its taillights now. But Basil didn't have to keep to the holiday-themed streets. He knew the subdivision, had memorized its turns and double-backs from his walks with Esme and their kids. He cut through the Cambridge's yard, tripping their motion sensor lights and setting their basset hound to baying. Running faster still, he angled through Andi Wilson's property, skirting her decorative fence festooned with icicle lights that twinkled merrily. He dashed around an inflatable manger and nearly lost his footing. Then he was through the Wright's yard and into Edgar Newsome's and passed a wooden array of wise men and elves.

So damn cold and yet he'd managed to work up a sweat, which added to the sting. His breath chugged away in cottony clouds illuminated by various Christmas decorations and street lights.

Someone came out on their front porch and hollered, but Basil didn't catch any of the words. More dogs barked.

Crossing through one more yard on his shortcut route he caught site of the golf cart, only half a block away now. It rode up over a curb, heading toward the slice in the fence of the golf course the arsonist had used the night Oren's house burned.

Basil sped across the street toward the fence, hearing Christmas music playing, someone staying up late and cranking it loud enough to spill through gaps in windows. Most of the houses were dark along this stretch, and more than half the yards had already turned their yard displays off. An inflatable Santa, roughly ten feet tall, had lost some of its air and slumped drunkenly against an igloo with penguins posed out front.

His freezing, wet feet screamed at him, like he ran across thumbtacks. Despite the pain he managed to go faster ... or thought he did. In reality the cart had slowed so the piñata in the dark puffy jacket could hop out and pull the chain links wide, allowing the driver to get through.

Basil gained treasured seconds.

"You son of a bitch!" There were other words churning in Basil's mind, but those would wait until he had the men.

The cart motored through and the rider clumsily jumped back in. It continued across the snow-covered course that faintly glowed in the starlight, the trees charcoal smudges stretching up like questing fingers.

Basil darted through the gap in the fence.

Did he hear sirens?

His imagination probably.

Though it felt like he'd been running for hours, Basil knew only a handful of minutes had passed. Not enough time for either the Santa Claus Police Department or the sheriff's department to send a car. And when one arrived, Basil wouldn't be home. Hopefully Shaya could tell them what happened, that he'd run after the culprit. They'd see his tracks, follow him, find him that way ... find that he'd managed to catch the damn arsonists.

The golf cart had opened up, cruising across the course now and putting distance between it and Basil. But it slipped and swerved, having trouble with some icy patches or dips in the ground beneath the snow. One of the men in the cart shouted. Couldn't make out the words or if they might be directed to him. They had to know they were still being pursued, had probably looked over their shoulders.

Basil's teeth ached and he felt frost forming around his mouth. His fingers and arms were numb, could hardly feel his feet. His fast pace kept some of the winter at bay, though not enough. Why the hell had he put on just a t-shirt when he got home? He had sweaters, sweatshirts, anything but this old, thin Cubs shirt he used to wear in the summer when he went to games.

So damn cold.

His breath caught when he saw the golf cart spin and rise on its two right wheels like it could tip over. *Let it happen,* he thought. *Take 'em out.* And then he'd really get the man in the puffy coat out. Get both of them.

But the cart righted itself and kept going. And Basil grabbed his aching side and tried to find a little more *oomph.* They'd have to stop wherever they'd parked their car near the clubhouse. Have to get out to change vehicles, lose a few minutes there.

He could still catch them.

"Move, dammit!" he spat. "Move. Move. Move!"

Anger and determination carried him. Then his right foot plunged deep and he fell forward, slamming into the turf and feeling something snap. He tried to pick himself up, pain suddenly racing from his ankle, sending lightning flickers of agony through his limbs that didn't want to budge. He realized he'd stepped into a cup, none of them marked with flags or visible because the snow had covered everything.

Basil tugged his foot free of the hole, his shoe staying behind, the pain blossoming brighter. He got to his hands and knees and looked ahead, seeing the taillights of the golf cart, small now, like eyes glaring mockingly. Not happening! His quarry was getting away, and Basil wasn't going to let that happen. He struggled to his feet, tottering, reached down and grabbed the shoe from the hole it had fit into so perfectly. Put it back on.

"Son of a bitch!" He tried to plow forward and fell again. "Son of a bitch!"

No chance of catching them now, but he'd get to the building where the golf carts were stored, maybe finding by a miracle that the security cameras were on. He pushed to his feet, stumbled a half dozen steps before he dropped, the ankle not supporting him. He knew he'd broken it. Maybe broke a few other things. Basil tried once more, managing another a dozen steps this time before collapsing.

He lay in the snow for a moment, the cold against his skin forcing violent shivers. So quiet, a profound silence, his breath the only thing that intruded. So angry the men had gotten away. So angry they'd tried to torch his house.

He'd been wrong when he stood outside Oren's burning house with Piper Blackwell. He'd said the blaze was an antisemitism hate crime. That notion was reinforced when Paul Blackwell's garage was torched where Millie—Oren's granddaughter—lived in an apartment upstairs. Antisemitism seemed the logical reason, Jewish stars spray painted on the houses. Basil wasn't Jewish, had Christmas decorations in the yard. A hate crime against him because he was black? Jews, blacks, anything not white or Christian? Or something else?

Hate crime, yes, but pressed against the snow, the frigid air hurtful to breathe, Basil realized suddenly the commonality was the Spencer County Sheriff's Department. Not Jewish, Not Black. Deputies. A hate crime against law enforcement. Basil had to let Sheriff Blackwell know so she could alert everyone in the department, put them on guard.

Then they'd focus their investigation on discovering who had so much hate against the deputies that they would set fires.

And kill two people in the process.

Basil tried once more to stand. He managed it, weight on his left leg, right only for balance. He turned back to face the fence and the Village beyond it. One step, two, three, a dozen, two dozen. Down again, cold and pain chasing each other through his limbs. Deep breath, sucking the icy air into his chest. Then pushing himself to his hands and knees, he crawled toward the rent in the fence.

19

11 a.m. Tuesday, December 15ᵗʰ

The driver ignored the stop sign.

"And two is four." Piper was on her way back to Christmas Lake Village and hadn't wanted to waste time dealing with a simple traffic violation. But she couldn't overlook the glimmering blue Prius cruising through the intersection, the driver apparently oblivious to her sheriff's department Explorer two car lengths behind.

She hit the flashers.

Piper would write him a warning and then they'd both be on their way.

The Prius looked new, or close to it, vanity plates that read: I LUV BEER. Decal in the back window a stylized gold P symbolic for Purdue University. She ran the plates…nothing outstanding.

"I was only going five or so miles over," the driver said as Piper approached his rolled-down window. He pushed the radio knob and Megan Thee Stallion stopped rapping. "Maybe ten miles. No more than ten over."

"What about the stop sign?" Piper studied him. Young, a mass of dark curly brown hair, short on the sides and hanging down his neck in a quasi-mullet. His maroon winter jacket was unzipped, revealing a Boilermaker sweatshirt underneath. She felt the heat from the running car float out the window and tease her face. "You went right through that stop sign."

A warning should encourage him to be more careful.

"I did? Right through it, huh? Thought I stopped. Could've sworn I stopped."

She really did just want to give him a warning. She was supposed to be picking up her father right now, heading to Christmas Lake Village. A warning would be fast.

"Well, I slowed down anyway, looked both ways. Nobody was coming." After a pause: "I really honestly thought I at least tapped the brakes. Sort of stopped. I didn't hit anything." He blew out a breath and shook his head. "I meant to stop. I'll stop next time."

The notion of giving him a warning vanished, like the car's heat was dissipating as it mingled with the twenty-degree air. *Sort of stopped? Lie to me and you'll get a real ticket.* She pulled out her book and started writing.

"Hey. Hey. I'm sorry. I wasn't going *that* fast through the stop sign."

"License and registration," she returned.

"Shit." He rose up and reached into his jeans pocket, pulled out his wallet, opened it so his license showed, and held it up for her.

"Take the license out, please."

"Shit." He passed it to her. "You know, I didn't stop completely because there's ice on the road. You stop on ice and you can skid into a ditch, you know. The car's not even two years old. Don't need it going into a ditch and getting banged up."

She knew damn well he didn't even tap the brakes, and he certainly hadn't slowed. That he kept nervously babbling was more evidence of his guilt.

"Peyton M. Wallace."

"My parents are Colts fans, named me after Peyton Manning. He was with the Colts for a while. And then he played—"

Piper caught the scent of peppermint and noticed he had a candy cane air freshener hanging from his rearview mirror—not illegal since it was too small to obstruct his windshield. According to his license, he had just turned nineteen. Not illegal to proclaim a love for beer on his license plate, just illegal for him to drink it at his age, but she hadn't caught him doing that. A glance in his passenger window … one large suitcase and a Purdue backpack on the seat. No real cause to check his trunk.

"Registration?" She handed the driver's license back and tapped her foot. She should be at Basil's house, looking over the yard again. He was still in the hospital. The dispatcher had called her about the arsonist before midnight, told her Basil was injured. She'd jumped out of bed and reached the subdivision less than a half-hour later. An ambulance was loading Basil, despite his protests that Esme could drive him to the hospital later in the morning. Although Piper spent nearly two hours going over his yard, collecting the gas canisters, tracing his route, and stopping at the golf course, she wanted to see it all again in the bright sunlight.

And Peyton M. Wallace in his glimmering blue Prius had delayed her.

"Here's the registration." He handed that to her, returned his license and wallet to his pocket. "You can just give me a warning, right? The holiday season and all? Happiness and good will."

Piper looked over the registration while he continued to chatter.

"Besides, that intersection doesn't need a stop sign. Just a little county road, hardly ever any traffic on it. Like I said, would have been dangerous to stop on the ice. I could've wrecked my car. Been injured. Should put the stop sign in front of a school or something."

The registration was in his name, a 2022 model.

"If you were so worried about sliding into a ditch, wrecking your car, why aren't you wearing a seatbelt?" Piper had noticed that as she'd approached the driver's side door.

"Oh, I forgot. I hadn't noticed I didn't put it on. In a hurry, I guess."

"A hurry, which explains why you were going over the speed limit." She watched his face color.

"Can you cut me a break? It's almost Christmas."

"Law says you have to wear a seatbelt," Piper lectured. She wondered if he'd been stopped before and had managed to talk himself out of a ticket.

"How about I promise it won't happen again?" He raised two fingers like the Boy Scout pledge.

"What won't happen again? The speeding, going through a stop sign, or not wearing a seatbelt?"

"All of it. All those things."

She returned to writing in the book.

"Just a warning, please. I can't afford a ticket."

Piper knew the Prius was not a cheap car, not that recent a model. Probably in the $30,000 to $35,000 range, depending on the bells and whistles.

"I'm a junior at Purdue, don't have money, you know. I'm on winter break, home to visit with my parents and sister. If you give me a ticket, I can't buy them Christmas presents."

"Nineteen. That's young for a junior," Piper observed.

"Left high school at sixteen, gifted track, got accepted by Purdue. Studying engineering technology."

"Good for you, young man."

"Hey, you look young, too, for a deputy." He grinned at her, as if he'd delivered a compliment.

"*Sheriff*," she corrected. "I'm the sheriff."

"Oh." The color deepened. Then his face brightened. "Hey, you look really good in that uniform. Pretty. Nice to see that a sheriff—"

"Your license is valid, registration is expired."

"I was going to do that last month, renew it. I just hadn't gotten a chance with studying and—"

"It's important to renew your registration before it expires, because the state adds a penalty. I'm going to note on the bottom of this ticket where you can renew it online."

"Ticket? I—" He touched his forehead to the steering wheel. "Is this going to cost a lot?"

Piper took a deep breath and decided to take a little pleasure in this. "Disregarding a stop sign is a fine of $105, with a $135 fee. So that charge will run you $240 total." She watched him raise his head and slam it against his head rest. "The speeding violation, $44 fine, $136 fee, for $180. Seatbelt violation is only $25. The expired registration will total $160, not counting the late fee. Math wasn't my best subject, but I think that all comes to $605."

"Shit."

"And two is four." Piper passed him the ticket and his registration. "Have a good day, Mr. Wallace."

"Shit." He punched the steering wheel, put the ticket in an empty cup holder. "I can go now, right?"

She didn't answer.

"I'm leaving."

She watched him pull away, got in her Explorer and radioed Zeke about her traffic stop, then radioed her dad she'd be late. Taking a deep breath, she set off after Peyton M. Wallace again and turned on her flashing lights.

Piper wrote him another ticket for still not wearing a seatbelt.

He made an exaggerated motion of clicking the belt in place, rolled the ticket into the cup holder, and squeezed the steering wheel so hard his knuckles blanched.

"Happy holidays, Mr. Wallace," she said.

20

---

noon

Piper picked up her father at the Santa Claus Police Department and drove to Basil's.

"Your dispatcher should have called me last night. Called my department. It's my jurisdiction. Granted, you're lead on these arsons, but—"

"Yep," Piper agreed. "You are absolutely right, Dad. You should have been called. I talked to Candace. It won't happen again. I should have called you." She sucked in a breath and tapped the lid of her coffee, which she'd taken a few sips of and pronounced too burned to drink. "I don't want any of this to happen again. I don't want one more arson call-out to Santa Claus or anywhere else in the county. I want whoever's doing this in prison." A pause. "For a long time. A very long time." She thought about the two charred bodies. "Forever."

They parked on the street in front of the house and got out, zipping their jackets. The block was festive with yard decorations, lopsided snowmen, and frosted picture windows. The air smelled fresh and carried a touch of pine. Piper turned up her collar and looked at the sky. A few clouds, but snow was not in the forecast. Just continued cold in the twenty to thirty-degree range.

"Manchester Township, New Jersey," her dad said. "Read about it yesterday while I was digging into antisemitism."

"What about Manchester?" Piper headed up the driveway, avoiding a lone patch of ice the size of a dinner plate.

"Last year a thirty-four-year-old man was charged with bias discrimination, second and third degree aggravated arson, criminal mischief, some other things I can't recall. Case is finally coming to trial this week. He vandalized fourteen homes in a subdivision, spray painted swastikas on the houses, set fires—one place down to ashes, three others damaged. Most, but not all, of the homeowners were Jewish."

"Basil isn't Jewish. His yard is all merry merry merry." Piper gestured at the lights strung on the house and trees. "Oren, Jewish. Millie, Jewish ... at least I think she is. I never asked her. I'm pretty sure Millie was the target, not you."

He set his lips in a line, as if pondering a comment.

"If you were the target, he would've burned your house, not the garage."

"Fair point," he replied.

"Basil's not Jewish," she repeated.

"Black. Could be a target because of that. Black, Jewish."

Piper approached the front door and knocked. She didn't expect to find anyone home. Esme was probably still at the hospital. Piper wanted to be at the hospital checking on Basil, too, but also needed to be in the Village. Teegan said she'd stop in to see Basil before her shift, bring flowers from the department.

Esme opened the door, surprising Piper. She was in a pale peach winter jacket, gloves on like she'd just come home or was going out. Her long hair hung in thin braids past her shoulders. She looked both gorgeous and exhausted, and she faintly smelled of vanilla and roses.

"May we come in?" Piper asked.

"No." Esme's eyes, hard and unfriendly, dug into Piper. "Not right now, you can't come in, Sheriff Blackwell. You don't need to come in my house."

"I'm here to—"

"I know why you're here. The monster was in the back yard, not in the house. You can go back there and poke around until your heart is happy. Or didn't you do that earlier?" One of Oren's cats padded into view, brushing against the back of Esme's legs.

"When it was dark. Yes. Hours ago." Piper felt bad about bothering Esme right now, as upset as the woman appeared. Still, she had to investigate this. "I'd like to ask you some—"

"Questions? You should talk to my husband. He's the one who saw the man, chased the man, ended up in the hospital because of that monster. Saved our house, though." For a moment Esme's face softened, then grew hard again. "You can talk to him later. I was in bed last night until our daughter started yelling. I got nothing to say to your questions. Ask Basil."

"I will, Mrs. Meredith. In fact, I'll—"

"Not bother me anymore today is what you'll do."

Piper pointed to the door cam.

"You can get the video later, but it doesn't have anything useful. The monster came from the back. We don't have a camera in the back." Esme squared her shoulders. "Listen, Sheriff, I just came home from the hospital so I could pick up the kids from my neighbor. Now I'm going back to get my husband. They're releasing him at three. I've errands to run first."

Jelani, also dressed in a winter jacket, stepped next to his mom and grabbed her pantleg. "Have to buy groceries," Jelani said. "And cheese before Daddy comes home."

"And milk." This came from Shaya, who was behind her brother, alternating between putting on boots and petting a cat. The little girl must have been kept out of school today. "We ran out of milk. And we have to go to the post office to mail presents to—"

"And Christmas cards," Jelani added. "We have to mail them."

"But mostly we have to buy food before Daddy comes home,"

Shaya said. "So he will have lots to eat and feel better." Finished with her boots, she put on a lavender puffy jacket.

"They're releasing Basil already? That's good to hear," Piper said. "I hope to—"

"Come back later is what you hope to do," Esme growled. "Tomorrow. The day after." She leaned against the doorframe. "Or never. I'm pissed, Sheriff Blackwell. Pissed." Piper could well tell that. "Someone tried to burn our house. *Our house.* In our safe, gated subdivision. Six and a half months we've lived here, not long enough to get in the city directory. Our address isn't common knowledge, but the asshole who burned Oren's found us, and my husband is in the hospital for it. Surgery. Pins. We left Chicago to find a safe place for the kids. Safe? This is safe? Bullshit. I don't want—"

"Mommy said bad words," Shaya cut in. "Really bad words."

"I just don't want—" Esme's anger continued to churn.

"Mrs. Meredith, we want to catch this—"

"Good for you, Sheriff. Good for my husband who wants to pin the monster's—" Esme nodded to Paul on the walk behind Piper. "Good for you, Chief Blackwell. Catch the son of a—"

"No bad words, Mommy," Shaya said, waving a scolding finger.

Esme paused her tirade, looking down at Jelani, who was fidgeting and tugging harder on her pantleg.

"Can we get candy canes?" Jelani asked softly.

"Catch the man, Sheriff Blackwell. Throw him in prison. We're leaving right now, and you're not coming in."

Esme shut the door in Piper's face. A few minutes later, Piper heard the garage door open, and Esme, Shaya, and Jelani pulled down the driveway in a silvery Nissan, backed onto the street, and drove out of sight.

Piper padded around the front of the house, boots crunching in the snow. She spotted a neighbor across the street watching out a big window. He waved to her.

"If they're letting Basil out today, surgery couldn't have taken long." Piper remembered when she broke her arm in early autumn, pins, screws, they kept her overnight. But she'd also had a concussion and had been beaten up pretty bad. Maybe Basil should have stayed through the day, too, but she pictured him insisting to go home. "I know I should have come out here hours earlier, Dad. I was just so damn tired." *And then there was Peyton Wallace and I Luv Beer.*

Piper noted the skeletons of rosebushes dusted with snow, fairy lights clinging to them. She imagined it was pretty, all the lights sparkling in the night. She turned at the corner of the house and traced a path down the side, her dad in step behind her. "After I failed to catch Basil on the phone this morning before his surgery, I checked in with my dispatcher, and then crawled back into bed. I figured if I could just get a few more hours sleep—"

"—you'd be able to tackle this better," Paul finished. "You're no good to the investigation if you're not alert enough to notice—"

"—the details." Piper stopped in front of a spray painted six-pointed star, midway up on the far corner of the house. She let out a breath that spread like a piece of lace away from her face.

Red paint, like the stars at Oren's and her dad's. Roughly the same size, same configuration.

It looked like two isosceles triangles offset and outlined atop each other, the vertex angle of one pointed up, the other pointed down. All of it formed a star with six points, resembling the Hebrew Star of David. Spray paint was difficult to work with in cold weather, went on thick, took longer to dry. Probably the artist had kept the can warm in his jacket.

Piper turned on her body cam to record it, took out her cell phone to snap a few pictures. She'd not noticed this last night, everything dark, not enough light from outdoor Christmas decorations to reach here. She'd concentrated her search on the backyard, where the gas canisters were, where all the footprints led to and from the property and the street behind Basil's.

Paul took pictures, too, stood back, and made a sour sound. "Same guy."

"Sure," Piper said. "Same guy. Same star. Three houses in a handful of days. He's not done. A serial arsonist. But maybe he'll be more careful now because Basil chased him, stopped him from setting this fire. Maybe he'll wait some time before striking again."

"Or maybe he'll just be more devious. Maybe he'd gotten sloppy last night, and now he'll be more careful."

"*They'll* be more careful. Basil told Candace there were two in the golf cart."

"One in the pickup at my place."

"But *two* here. Don't know if it was one or two at Oren's."

The lines of the star were precise, as if sprayed by a steady hand or someone had used a tool like a yardstick. The paint had been put on so thick that it dripped.

"Blood," she said softly, repeating it louder so her dad could hear. "The paint drizzling down from the lines looks like blood drops. I think that was on purpose. It was that way with the star at Oren's, and at your house. I think it is *supposed* to look like blood drops. The lines are wounds, slices, and the blood is seeping from them."

She stared at it longer, felt a chill deeper than the cold that crept past the collar of her coat.

"It's not antisemitism," she said. "This wasn't because Basil is black. Not because Oren and Millie are Jewish. This is because Basil and Oren and Millie are with the sheriff's department. That star?" She turned and faced her father, pointed to the badge on her pocket. "Your badge has a five-pointed star."

Paul's eyebrows rose in question.

"Not mine. My badge has six. That star on Basil's house, and at your place and Oren's, represents this." She tapped the badge again.

The chill grew even more intense. "Someone is hunting my deputies."

21

The back yard still smelled of gasoline. Piper and her father spent nearly an hour there, taking more pictures of boot prints and inspecting the deck.

"Diego lifted two prints off one of the canisters," she said after consulting a few lengthy texts. "He's running them now. Nothing from the half-burned socks. But—" Piper canted her head back and glanced up. More clouds had appeared since they'd come here, gray ones the shade of cold ashes against the cornflower blue sky. Maybe the forecast was wrong. Maybe snow was coming.

"But?" Paul prompted.

"Diego likes true crime," Piper replied. "Something about the gas canister and the sock struck him. He said he remembered a show he'd watched in the fall, one of those Forensic Files episodes. It was about a serial arsonist who set more than three hundred fires around Washington, D.C. before getting caught. Diego said he always used the same M.O. A canister filled with gasoline, and a sock or other piece of clothing as the wick. Maybe our culprit saw the episode, a how-to-burn-a-house thing."

"A sick SOB for sure. I've an appointment with the insurance guy day after tomorrow to talk about my garage, getting it replaced. Don't know if I want to mess with building an apartment over the top this time. Maybe depends what Millie wants to do. I don't just want to toss her out on the street."

Piper gave a grim laugh as she swore the clouds instantly darkened. "How is she not out on the street right now? Living in a motel in Indy with a few changes of clothes? Don't worry. She's going to land in Nang's double-wide over by the Quick Stop. It'll give her time to figure stuff out. As for Oren—" Her voice trailed away and the sadness hit her like a punch. Piper didn't always get along with her chief deputy. Sometimes they were like sandpaper ... old, young. He had more years in the department than she'd been breathing. Plus, there was the whole her winning the election thing.

But she felt for Oren, losing his home. Recently divorced, father died a few months ago, possessions and treasures a charred ruin ... all of it gone except his boat and his cats. Would he rebuild? Or would he give up? Millie texted last night that Oren still just wanted to die.

"I'm going to see him tomorrow, Punkin'. Want to join me?"

She shook her head. "I do, but I can't. I'm staying on this." A pause: "If you want company, ask Nang. He plans to go back up."

"I'd love Nang to join me. I'll call him in a little while." Piper knew her father preferred calls to texts, claiming the latter impersonal. "And I'll stay on this the rest of the day with you. Really, it's my jurisdiction. It'd be nice if I contributed something useful."

They stood at the back of the property looking into the yards of the houses behind Basil's. It was easy to see where the chase had led to the next street, easier to see it now in daylight. The paw prints were from Thresher, the department's Belgian Malinois; Diego had brought him out earlier. Piper followed the tracks, like she had hours ago.

"I'll take left," Piper said, standing on the sidewalk of the next street over.

"Right for me, then," Paul said. "Meet in the middle on the other side."

Piper nodded. "Someone might have seen something. Someone who's home now. Fingers crossed we get some video."

"Get something helpful anyway," Paul said. "Then let's tackle the golf course."

She'd make note of addresses where she got no response and planned to come back to them later. And she had a stack of business cards in her pocket to encourage call-backs.

"We're gonna catch a break this afternoon," Piper replied. "I can feel it."

"Can we get that lucky? A witness *and* video? You didn't get either early this morning, did you?" Paul made a huffing sound and trudged down the sidewalk, hands in his pockets, head canted forward.

"No, I didn't get either earlier," she admitted softly.

It would be warmer to do this sitting at a desk, using the city directory to access the phone numbers of neighbors, call them and ask what they saw. But Piper held that face-to-face was better. In person you could read people, nudge their memories. It was too easy for them to disconnect from a phone conversation because they didn't want to be bothered.

- Did you see a golf cart late last night?
- Two men carrying heavy-looking canisters?
- Anyone looking suspicious?
- How about on other evenings?
- Notice strangers lingering in the neighborhood?
- Do you have security cameras?
- Doorbell cameras?
- Notice any vandalism on your property?
- Anything stolen?

It seemed every house along this street had decorated, some elaborately. One of the front yards displayed a miniature carnival with elves on a merry-go-round, reindeer riding a tilt-a-whirl, Mrs. Claus and Santa in bumper cars, and Frosty manning a real snow-cone machine. Piper would have enjoyed the merriment under better circumstances.

But she couldn't shake the melancholy.

If Oren didn't mend and return, a wealth of experience would be lost from her department. If Esme was so pissed she talked Basil into moving somewhere even safer, Piper would have to surrender an amazing detective.

"Sheriff!" A man walking two cocker spaniels in Christmas sweaters and boots waved to her from a few houses away. "Sheriff! I need to talk to you."

Piper felt a spark. This might be the break she needed.

He had the dog leashes in his right hand. He thrust out his left to shake. "Reynolds Barnes," he said. "I live that way." He gestured with his head, and Piper couldn't tell if he meant one street over or a dozen.

"Piper Blackwell," she said in return.

"I voted for you." He beamed. "Figured we needed new blood. Read all about your military experience. Medals."

The dogs made snuffling noises and nosed Piper's pants, probably smelling her own dogs and cat, she thought. Their stubby tails vibrated, and she crouched to cordially pet them.

"I'm in the neighborhood investigating—"

"—what happened at Detective Meredith's house. It's all over the Village. Someone tried to burn him out, like they did to Rosey."

Piper suspected the news wasn't *all* over the Village, the subdivision so large and the event roughly only a dozen hours old. She made pleasant conversation, then asked her questions but gained nothing new.

"Was sound asleep," Barnes said. "Didn't even hear the siren from the ambulance. Wife said there was an ambulance. Is Detective—"

"Detective Meredith's okay, as far as I know." Piper sincerely hoped Basil was. "You said you wanted to talk to me."

"Well, I wanted to talk to Detective Meredith, actually. He asked me about some things the other day. But you'll do. You can deliver my information, right?" Barnes tugged gently on the leashes, the cocker spaniels trying to urge him along. "He'd asked me if I saw an old white VW Rabbit in the neighborhood. Told him no. I hadn't. Then I got to thinking last night. I had seen one, just like he'd described it, old and rusty. But I hadn't seen it *recently*. It was last summer, oh, June, I think, early or the middle of. Kids out of school. It was way the heck over on Poinsettia. Summers, I walk the dogs a lot farther. A lot. Blocks and blocks. I remembered the car was in front of a big ass house, a fine and fancy one. Out of place, that beater, that's why I noticed it. Should have remembered it earlier. Anyway, I wanted Detective Meredith to know that I'd seen that car. Doubt there are two old white VW rusty Rabbits around. Not in the Village. Probably not terribly helpful. But I wanted him to know."

Piper got an adrenalin tease. "Last June."

"Yeah."

"Do you know where on Poinsettia?"

"Nope, but the street's not all that long. Couldn't give you an address. A big fancy house. Gray and black. Two levels. Square. Not far from the big lake. I remember because we walked down to the big lake." He looked at his wiggling dogs and frowned. "Going to board my babies tomorrow. So I'm taking them on a nice jaunt today. With the sweaters and boots, they don't mind the cold. I'm going to miss them."

"Going somewhere?" Piper thought she might want to talk to him some more. "Have a cell phone number?"

"I have a card, actually." He passed her the leashes and reached into his back pocket for a wallet, took it out and dug through it, producing a card that read: Reynolds Barnes, President, STBGS Spencer Tabletop Board Game Society. Piper hadn't heard of the club, figured she'd ask Zeke about it. "That's my cell. Don't have a landline. Kept getting too many spam calls. Get practically none with my cell." He took the leashes back.

"Going somewhere?" she repeated.

"Oh, sorry. Yeah. Christmas with my brother and his wife. They live in New Richmond. Ohio. His turn to host, and he's allergic to dogs. Or says he is. I'm retired now, so we can stay longer. Going to the cardboard museum over there."

Piper tipped her head.

"It's the world's largest and only cardboard boat museum. Right on the banks of the Ohio River. Checked the website. Has a replica of the Delta Queen steamboat and lots of models from the International Cardboard Boat Regatta. You can even take classes on building cardboard boats. Ain't that a heck of a thing?"

"I suppose it is," Piper replied. But it did not interest her.

"I figure maybe that museum can teach me what to do with all the empty Amazon boxes I've saved in my garage, eh? Better quit chatting so you can go catch the bad guy. Most people around here would feel safer if you got him. But I figure after Detective Meredith's place was targeted, we're all pretty safe. Your father, the police chief ... I heard they torched his place, too. So I figure the arsonist is after cops, right?"

"Looks that way." Piper was instantly suspicious of Barnes. He'd made a connection between the arsons and attempted arson, a connection that she'd only discovered a short while ago. Maybe he was more than just a dog walker. Could he have been involved? Seemed like he certainly knew the Village, and would know where the main security cameras were.

"Got some sort of an ugly hate on, somebody did," Barnes continued. But I don't think there are any more cops living in the Village. So I think we'll be okay."

"Do you golf?" she asked.

"I pretend to. Not very good at it," he said. "My wife is much better, plays in lots of scrambles. Anything else, Sheriff?"

Piper shook her head. Nothing else at the moment, but she'd give Barnes a close look.

Stumpy tails wagging, the cocker spaniels led Barnes past her and down the sidewalk. "You have a good afternoon, Sheriff Blackwell."

22

M illie drove to North Meridian Street and chose a stall in the south parking lot at the Indianapolis Hebrew Congregation Temple. She went inside to pray.

The room was warm and wrapped her like a cocoon, chasing away the December cold that had seeped into her bones. Snowing hard outside, she wondered if Spencer County, hours to the south, was spared this storm. She hoped it would stop by morning. Didn't like to drive when it looked like Star Wars hyperspace coming at her windshield.

She selected one of the oak benches at the back, the view from here making the room seem cavernous. She thought it could accommodate a few hundred. Stone walls cut by sections of wood panels, everything looking modern, yet rustic, soft lights clung to the ceiling high overhead. Her gaze settled on the wide podium at the front.

Millie could have prayed anywhere, at the nondenominational chapel at the hospital, in her grandfather's ICU room, at the little diner on the corner that served a more than passable meatloaf and mashed potato platter and that offered a dozen different flavors of hot caffeinated tea.

She found this synagogue via Google on her phone. This was the fourth synagogue established in Indiana, tracing back to 1856 and moving around before settling on this spot about a hundred years later. She'd read about the place on its website. Claimed to be all-inclusive, but primarily Reform Judaism, not that it mattered to her.

Millie considered herself Jewish, observed the major holy days, often with her grandfather, but it had been a few years since she'd stepped into a synagogue simply to pray or attend Shabbat services. Too busy, she'd told herself; too many papers to write and topics to study, she'd claimed when she attended the University of Evansville; basically too uninterested in organized religion.

Her grandfather was devout. Shabbat services every week, prayed three times a day, regularly read from the Torah.

Would God be more likely to hear her in this holy place?

Millie was skeptical.

I need some divine intervention, mostly for my grandfather, a little bit for me would also be nice. Maybe God ... Adonia, our God, Ruler of the Universe ... would pay attention if I prayed in a synagogue. Please, hear me.

It was quiet. No one around. Just the way she wanted it.

No one to intrude on her sorrow, anger, disbelief. Her utter help-lessness to which she could not give in.

Oren Rosenberg, her grandfather who practically raised her, didn't want to live. He was hooked up to tubes and monitors, his burned skin heavily bandaged, the painkillers so abundant he claimed he couldn't even feel his lips.

He would recover, in time. But his desire to do that went up in flames with his house. Everything gone.

And then two days later they'd torched her home, too.

I have nothing, it's all gone.

Millie hadn't told her grandfather about that, not wanting him to sink even deeper into depression. All she owned consisted of a shoebox full of toiletries she'd grabbed at the drug store and three changes of clothes she'd picked up at the resale shop across from the hospital.

Hate crimes, the fires.

Sheriff Blackwell had given her this week off to stay in Indy with her grandfather. Millie had intended to do that, until the arsonist struck again, this time targeting her. She'd leave in the morning, get back to Spencer County and return to work. Help catch the son of a bitch who lit containers of gasoline intended to ruin lives.

"May the source of strength, who blessed the ones before us, help us find the courage to make our lives a blessing. And let us say: Amen," Millie recited a version of the *Mi Sheeirach* that she remembered, the Hebrew prayer for strength and healing. "Bless those in need with healing, with *r'fu-ah shleima*. The renewal of body, the renewal of spirit. And let us say: Amen. *Mi shebeirach avoteinu. M'kor habracha l'imoteinu. Mi shebeirach imoteinu. M'kor habracha la'avoteinu.*"

Maybe the words were more powerful here.

Or maybe she just needed to get away from the ICU with all the flickering lights and gentle beeps, the hiss of equipment, and the clatter of carts being wheeled across the hard terrazzo floor. Get away from the emptiness in her grandfather's eyes.

She stopped in the Sisterhood Gift Shop and purchased a parchment with the Shema prayer on it and a mahogany Mezuzah, a small narrow box inside which she placed the rolled parchment. She would hang it to the right of the door in her grandfather's hospital room. Some believed it provided protection to those residing where it hung. She bought a second to hang inside the door of Nang's trailer, where it looked like she would be living for a while.

Not that she would be spending much time there.

She wouldn't rest until the arsonist was caught. Somehow, her vow seemed stronger here.

A dorned again in PPE, Mille sat next to Oren's bed and watched the bouncing lines on the monitors. His heartbeat was steady. He slept. She wanted to talk to him, but she'd wait. It was still snowing hard outside, and she didn't especially want to go back out into it, though she was hungry and the meatloaf at the corner diner called to her.

She'd talk to him soon enough. A nurse or doctor would come in and wake him, probably draw some blood from a piece of flesh that wasn't crispy, ask how he felt. "I don't feel anything," he'd say. She didn't know if the painkillers really did shut down what must be agony. But it's what she'd heard him repeat every time he was asked.

Millie texted Sheriff Blackwell that she was coming back tomorrow morning, would get the key to Nang's trailer and be available for the second or third shift, that she'd return to Indy on the following weekend to visit Oren. Then she scrolled through the weather reports, happy to discover that Spencer County was only likely to catch one to three inches. No hyperspace driving down there.

Finished, she held the phone in her gloved hands, tipped her head back, and dozed until a cart clattered by and a shrill warning bleat echoed from somewhere down the hall. A few minutes later a doctor arrived to check on Oren, a nurse in tow to take a blood sample. Pleasantries were exchanged, and then Millie was alone with her alert grandfather.

"Hey Pops," she said, almost asking him how he was doing, but managing to stop herself. She'd heard him give the doctor his "I don't feel anything." She stood and leaned over him, touched his forehead, and looked into his empty eyes. "I'm heading back to Rockport in the morning." She didn't say home, she didn't have one. "I want to help on the arson case."

"Good for you," he croaked, his voice no clearer than it had been yesterday. He coughed, his shoulders bouncing against the pillow.

His first- and second-degree burns were extensive, lungs seared. Deep tissue damaged, grafts in his future. At least thirty days in the burn ICU. A doctor had told her it was all good news, as that fire could have claimed his life.

"Good that you're leaving." His voice was coarse, like he smoked a pack a day. She knew he'd never touched a cigarette. "Don't need you sitting around here watching me die."

Millie clenched a fist. "You're not going to die, Pops. Dr. Mattingly says it's just gonna take time to heal."

"I want to die." How many times had he said that to her? "Everything's—"

She let anger and frustration win. "Listen you damn old fool, you can get through this. You have to get through this. You are the only family I have. I need you."

He opened his mouth as if to argue, but she cut him off with a finger wave.

"My dad? I haven't seen or heard from him in years. I guess he's still fishing for crab in Alaska. Mom? She's dealing with her legal problems from that hit-and-run in Illinois. I avoid her and her drama and alcohol issues. But you … you're my family. My only real family, and you damn well better not shuffle off the coil and leave me. Are you listening? I would never forgive you, Pops." She paused, and when it looked like he was going to reply, she plowed ahead.

"Yep, you lost everything. *Almost* everything. You lost your *stuff*. You still have the land, your boat, your cats. And you have me. Rebuild if you want. Live somewhere else if you want. Just live, Oren Rosenberg. If not for you, live for me." Tears started, and she hoped he couldn't see them through her head covering.

The beeps and hisses and a clattering cart filled the silence between them. Millie wasn't sure she could take much more.

"Okay," he rasped after a while. "Okay."

Millie relaxed. "I went to a synagogue today, Pops. Got you something." She pointed to the doorframe, were she'd attached the Mezuzah, though she realized from his angle he couldn't see it.

"You, a synagogue?"

"Yeah, Pops. That's a Mezuzah there. And now I'm gonna take myself out for a meal because my stomach is screaming at me. And then I'm gonna get a good night's sleep and drive back to Rockport in the morning so I can help Sheriff Blackwell and Detective Meredith find the man who burned your house." *And my apartment.* "And I'm going to tell them that you'll be back to work as soon as you are able." She paused. "You understand?"

She wasn't sure, but it looked like Oren tried to smile. For the first time, she saw his eyes spark with interest.

"Okay," he said again. "You went to a synagogue. Good for you."

"Yeah, well … I'm heading out. Love you, Pops."

"Love you, too." Oren shifted slightly in the bed. He winced and one of the lines jumped. He coughed again. "It might not be anything. Probably isn't anything."

"What?"

"The morning before the fire, and the morning of the fire, the Halm kid was standing on the sidewalk in front of my house. Just staring at my house. I thought that odd. It was early, before school. He's in high school, but I couldn't tell you what year. Probably a junior or senior. Both times that I looked out the window, he noticed me and walked away. Probably nothing."

"Thanks, Pops." The information started her thinking as she headed out of his room.

Or maybe it is something. Her fingers brushed the Mezuzah as she left, heading for the diner.

23

3 p.m.

"My fingers are too stiff for this, Punkin.'" Piper's dad fiddled with the buttons on his cell phone. "There, sending you the last one." He puffed out a sigh of relief and leaned back in the passenger seat. "Three interviews with some mildly interesting stuff, and two friendly folks who had Christmas cookies but no information. That last one, Gary Mason, said he watched a golf cart cruising by his place late. Two men in it, he figured they were drunk. They drove up and down before stopping at the house behind Basil's. Mason didn't see anything else, said he went to bed. It's something, anyway." He shoved the cell phone in his pocket and unzipped his coat.

The Explorer heated up quickly, and Piper appreciated that. She leaned forward against the steering wheel so the vents could blow warm air across her face. She was happy her dad was along today, a little company, a lot of experience, a chance to spend some time with him. Most of her free time had been with Nang during the past several months, leaving few opportunities to get together with her dad. He looked good today, complexion ruddy. But she still worried.

154

Only fifty-six, he'd had two bouts with cancer, a heart attack, and the anxiety episode from the night his garage was torched. She needed to make more time for him.

"The firebug works late at night," Paul said.

"*Bugs*," she corrected.

"Yeah, I know. Two in the golf cart. Not a lot of people up that late, and their route … it sure looks like they know the Village, know how to avoid the big surveillance cameras near the park and intersections."

"I'm convinced they're familiar with the Village." Piper thought about Reynolds Barnes as a suspect and blew out a frustrated breath. "But Basil doesn't believe it's someone from the Village, told me his gut says it's someone from outside. He has good instincts."

"So do you," Paul said. "Excellent instincts." He tapped the window. "Enjoyed tagging along today. Not traipsing down sidewalks in the cold or the reason for being here, not enjoying that. But spending time with you. I always enjoy that."

"I'll add my collection of interviews to yours, put it together back at the office, see what we got, where to go." Piper gave him a half-smile. "Thanks for coming today. I'm a little short-staffed. And I have to keep a few people on the regular day-to-day stuff. Drunks. Accidents. Had a domestic call last night Rocco handled. A chair tossed through the Red Baron tavern's big window when a husband and wife went at it."

"Exciting time in Dale."

"Not for the guy Rocco put in our jail, or for his wife, who was taken to the ER with a concussion."

They were quiet for several minutes as she drove down Evergreen to Cupid Lane to Melchoir Drive, almost every house decorated in some fashion. Piper thought she and Nang should take a tour at night before Christmas, in the department Explorer to look all official so she could get past the gate guard, see the subdivision in all its sparkling, merry, glory. The VW Rabbit had gotten past the gate sentry at some point, too, she mused.

Piper turned south onto Poinsettia Drive, seeing Christmas Lake looming at the far end of the street.

"Good stretch from Basil's house," Paul observed. "And not how you get to the golf course."

"We're stopping on Poinsettia first," Piper said.

"Nice neighborhood." A pause. "All the Village is nice. But some of the houses here are—" He gave a long, low whistle.

"Expensive," Piper finished. "Houses in general are expensive."

"Some of these more than others," Paul put in.

"If I hadn't inherited my beautiful home, I'd still be living above your—" She stopped herself from saying garage. But that's where she'd been living when she left the Army, came back to take care of her dad when he was battling cancer the second time, and when she'd run for sheriff. She was certain she'd still be there—maybe caught in the fire—had she not been given a near-new home by an old conspiracy theorist veteran who was murdered.

"Maybe I will go ahead," Paul said. "When I have the garage rebuilt, go ahead and put a little apartment over it. Maybe for Millie. Maybe for who knows. Somebody always needs a place to stay, right? I pay a lot for insurance. I should be covered for most of it."

"No more shag carpet and avocado green appliances this time," she whispered.

Piper took it slow down Poinsettia. A mix of overlarge ranches and two-story homes, most of them with poinsettias incorporated into their outdoor holiday décor. Again she thought about riding through at night.

"That has to be it." She stopped in front of a massive gray and black foursquare, a two-and-a-half story with a wide front porch festooned with evergreen boughs and crystal snowflakes the size of garbage can lids. "That VW Rabbit at the Laubensteins' ... a man walking some dogs near Basil's said he saw the car here last summer. In this driveway."

She typed in the address, got the name of the homeowner, and did a quick search to discover no other information in the system.

"You think this is tied to the arsons? The Rabbit and this house?" Paul undid his seatbelt and zipped up his coat again.

"Not exactly," Piper returned. "But maybe the people living here will tell us who was driving the Rabbit, can help me put names to the people burned in the fire. Can tell us why the people were here in June and on Sled Run last week."

Paul got out and followed her up the drive.

"Please be home," Piper whispered. "Please be home." If they weren't, she'd have to come back. "Please be home."

"Merry Christmas!" boomed the man who opened the door. He looked too thin to be Santa Claus, but he had white hair that reached his shoulders and a curly white beard that extended halfway down his chest.

"Darren," Paul said from over Piper's shoulder. "Piper, this is Darren Forsetti, he works weekends at The Christmas Store in town. Didn't know you lived in this neighborhood, Darren."

"'Deed I do! Both. Live here and work as Santa on the weekends. Gives me something extra to do. Merry Christmas! Ho. Ho. Ho! What brings the sheriff and police chief to my front step today? Fund-raising?" His left hand held the door. His right reached for his wallet. "Toys for Kids? Turkeys for the poor? How much are you looking for? Happy to help out."

Piper guessed him to be mid-seventies, cheery face heavily-lined, hands wrinkled and age-spotted, eyes walnut brown. He looked almost gaunt, but she imagined his Santa suit had some padding. She thought she recognized him from her many trips to The Christmas Store. Santa was usually perched in a grand high-backed chair next to the fudge and cookie counter. She caught a glimpse of a white Christmas tree with gold garland and red globe ornaments behind him, next to a lit fireplace. Cinnamon scent wafted out the door, suggesting someone was baking.

"We're not fund-raising," Piper said, quickly explaining why they were there and about the investigation.

"VW Rabbit? Nope. Saw it in our driveway, huh? Don't know anyone who has one of those. And rusty? I'd remember that. Old Barnes must have the wrong house, wrong block. He doesn't usually walk all the way over here. And June, you say? We weren't here in June. Our grandson has a big trailer up in Door County, Wisconsin.

157

We go up there for all of June. Have for years. Sorry I can't help you."

"Do you have any outdoor surveillance—"

"Don't believe in attaching cameras to the house."

"Did you have someone come in and water your plants? Maybe they drove that car."

Darren shook his head. "Don't have any live plants inside, 'cept poinsettias at Christmas. Let Mother Nature water the stuff outside. Boy across the street cuts the grass, and I don't think he can drive yet."

"Pool attendant?" Paul asked. "You have a pool, right?"

"'Deed I do," Darren said, grinning. "But I don't have anyone tend it while we're gone. That'd be kinda pointless."

"Someone saw the car here in June," Piper insisted. "Maybe they were visiting a neighbor and just used your driveway."

"I suppose. You'd have to ask around." Darren shrugged, the hair on his shoulders fluttering like wisps of cotton candy. "Everybody knows we aren't here in June. I suppose someone could have just parked here." He raised his right hand to his beard and tugged on it. "Let me ask my wife. Maybe she knows something." Over his shoulder, Darren shouted: "Daphne! Sheriff wants to talk to you. She's making a list, checking it twice to find out if you've been naughty or nice!"

Daphne came to the door wearing a candy cane embroidered apron over a gray sweat suit. The apron was smudged with swaths of tan batter. She looked at least a decade younger than her husband, only a suggestion of wrinkles at the edges of her eyes, no creases on her forehead. Her hair was auburn with strands of silver, all of it in an artful up-do held in place with snowflake clips. Her friendly smile reached her blue eyes.

"Sheriff," she said, looking around Darren. "Chief. Fund-raising?"

Piper gave a brief recap of what she was looking for.

"An old Rabbit? Huh. From last summer. Huh." Daphne had a smoker's voice. Piper noticed her teeth had a yellow cast and detected a faint odor of nicotine. "I don't pay much attention to cars, Sheriff,

Chief. I don't drive. Darren chauffeurs me anywhere I want to go. When did you say last summer?"

"June."

Daphne made a sour face and looked like she was working up something to spit. Piper took a cautious step back and bumped into her dad.

"June," Daphne growled. "We were robbed in June while on vacation."

"Now, sweet—" Darren started.

"Three pieces of my good jewelry taken," Daphne continued. "I called the cops after we got back." She looked at Paul. "Nothing came of it." She huffed and ground the ball of her slippered foot against the carpet. "Necklace, ring, bracelet. I didn't lose them, Darren. Didn't misplace them, like you think. Didn't take them with me to Door County and forget them there. And the filets in the freezer were gone, too."

"We might have cooked them, sweet—"

"We hadn't cooked them," Daphne huffed, shaking her finger at him. "Maybe that car you're looking for, Sheriff, has my jewelry in the trunk. Suspect the thief ate the steaks."

"Thank you for your time," Piper said, passing over a business card. "In case you can think of anything else—"

"Merry Christmas!" Darren exclaimed. "Ho. Ho. Ho!"

24

4 p.m.

The air felt electric inside the Explorer, Piper spinning images of the Rabbit, charred bodies, and thefts like shards in a child's kaleidoscope. Turning and churning, she jittered with anxious energy, wanting to piece everything into place.

"Two neighbors confirmed the Rabbit at the Forsetti house in June." Piper saw a big snowflake hit the window, then another. "And apparently neither of them told the Forsettis. They thought the young couple was house-sitting. Like people thought the Laubensteins had house-sitters. Three weeks." That's how long the neighbors spotted the Rabbit either in the garage or on the driveway. "Lights on at night, laughter from the swimming pool."

"At least we have a description of the woman," Paul said.

"Busty redhead that looked amazing in a blue bikini. Yeah, at least there is that," Piper said. One of the neighbors admitted talking to the woman, just a casual "have a nice day," never asked her name. But "busty redhead" coupled with findings from the autopsies might help put names to the dead.

"Helluva mystery, Punkin'. Why were they at the Forsettis, if they weren't house-sitting?"

"Why were they at the Laubensteins?" Piper sucked in her lower lip. "Stealing from them? Snagging a free place to stay for a few weeks? The rusty car—stolen car—hints that they were poor or maybe down on their luck." She swatted the steering wheel. "I think they were thieves. But, even so, we need to name them, get closure for their families."

"I didn't personally take the theft report from Daphne Forsetti. I'm sure I saw it, though, sent an officer out to talk to her, check with area pawn shops. That would have been standard."

The kaleidoscope in Piper's brain continued to spin. "If the Rabbit couple were, indeed, burglars, they apparently didn't steal the Forsettis blind. A few pieces of jewelry and two filet mignons. No mention of TVs, computers, and large things missing." Though she realized there were limits what could be hauled away in a Rabbit. "Maybe they stole other things Daphne didn't notice."

"How did they move through the Village? Did they get someone's keycard for the gate? How many houses did they visit? Just the Forsettis? Just the Laubensteins? And where were they in the months between those two houses?"

"I dunno, Dad. But I will find out." Piper stopped herself from swatting the wheel again.

"No, Punkin'. *I* will find out. Santa Claus, my jurisdiction. You're lead on the arsons. I'm on the thefts. The two are not connected."

Could it be connected? Piper doubted it. Just unfortunate for the couple they picked the house next to Oren's to stay in. "I get you. The arsons for me. We'll share information."

"Deal."

The arsonists were the more pressing matter in Piper's eyes. The culprits were after her deputies, and she needed to stop them before they burned anything else, killed anyone else. All the colors of her kaleidoscope turned flame red. When she got back to the department, she'd issue a warning to the deputies and dispatchers, have everyone be super wary and careful, send those on patrol past deputies' homes at night, alert the Rockport Police Department, too.

"Drop me at my office, Punkin'. I want to dig through the Village theft reports."

"Not just the Village," Piper said. "All of Santa Claus." And she'd put one of her deputies on theft reports in the county. Maybe the Rabbit got around.

A handful of minutes later, Piper headed to the golf course. The radio crackled with a call regarding a 9-1-1 Teegan took from an angry Fulda man. Piper listened as Teegan dispatched a deputy to an address, where a porch pirate had absconded with several just-delivered Amazon packages.

"Mr. Harrison Stone says he has ring cam footage of the thief," Teegan relayed to the responding deputy. "Wish people would use the regular line for stuff like this."

Christmas, Piper thought, brought out the best and worst. People buying presents online for friends and family. Bandits taking the boxes before they could be wrapped and placed under the tree. And it apparently brought out arsonists, too.

Piper pulled into the lot, big flakes still falling lazily, sticking to her windshield.

An impressive golf course for such a rural county. It was listed as the seventh most challenging in Indiana, and one of the top seventy five public courses in the country. The course boasted tree-lined fairways, hills, valleys, and lakes, the front nine mostly flat and with only one dog leg. Piper didn't golf, but she'd joined friends for lunch at the grill, delighting in appetizers of avocado egg rolls and deviled eggs before digging into a main course of Cajun Chicken Alfredo. She wondered if Nang had eaten here, and if so, what he thought of the cuisine.

"Melinda Felder," the manager said, extending a hand when Piper entered the building. Melinda was lean and tall, with an angular face and severely cut frosted hair. Her earrings, silver golf clubs, dangled on thin chains and matched the charm on her necklace. Her dark green sweatshirt read Christmas Lake Golf Club.

Melinda pointed to security cameras inside and out. "They're on now," she said. "And will stay on. Unfortunate that we need them."

Piper nodded.

"You want to see the carts, right?" Melinda's accent sounded softly southern, maybe Georgia, Piper thought, not Southern Indiana.

"Definitely, Mrs. Felder. The carts. And I've questions."

"I spoke to your detective the other night, morning technically I guess. After that fire on Sled Run. Met him out here."

"I know, and we appreciate that. Still, I've some—"

"Questions. Sure."

Melinda led Piper to where the golf carts were stored in rows. Dozens and dozens in myriad colors—red, yellow, gray, black, blue— and different sizes. Some two-seaters with canopies, four-seaters, a few that could accommodate six to eight—though if they were full of passengers there wouldn't be room for clubs. More than half were white, several of these having Christmas Lake Golf Club logos on the side. Some had custom paint jobs, flames emblazoned on the front, paisley swirls on the sides. They were mostly electric carts, plug-ins handy for all of them. Some were gas-powered, these looking older. She saw at least a dozen street-legal models, with headlights, taillights, side and center mirrors, seatbelts, windshields, and safety reflectors. A driver's license was requisite for carts in Indiana, though not all states required that. They weren't titled or registered, and didn't have to be insured. She'd done a little research: used carts could be had for a few hundred dollars, new ones could cost more than ten thousand depending on the bells and whistles.

"This is the one from last night, this morning technically." Melinda gestured to a gray four-seater separate from the others. Smudge marks from the fingerprint powder remained. It looked pricey. "Owned by William Avery. I'll clean it up for him and park it properly when you say okay."

"I say 'okay' now," Piper said. "I got a look at it earlier when your assistant manager was here." That was more than a dozen hours ago when it was dusted for fingerprints—three separate sets found. It wasn't the same cart used at Oren's fire; that had been one of the course's carts, and had no viable prints. "Where is this usually parked?"

Melinda indicated a spot.

"Tell me about Mr. Avery."

"Willie, that's what he's known as here. Willie-A." Melinda folded her arms across her chest, the sweatshirt sleeves riding up. Piper noticed a copper cuff on her right wrist and a charm bracelet on her left that featured musical instruments and states. There was also a wedding ring—tiny diamonds on a thick silver band. "He lives on Rudolf Lane, but he and his wife are looking to move to Snowball to basically be inside the golf course. Avid golfer, and from what I understand he tried to go pro when he was young. But young for Willie-A was a good forty years ago before he lost most of his left leg in a car accident. He's got one of those prosthetics and gets around well enough to golf every day when the weather's fine."

Piper would talk to him, but he was an unlikely suspect. Avery lived inside the Village; he wouldn't need to drive his golf cart to reach Basil's house. But maybe the arsonist knew Avery, got the key, and borrowed the cart.

"The key is in it, Avery's golf cart," Piper said.

"No surprise," Melinda returned. "About half our club members just leave the keys in their carts. Until the past few days we've never had a problem with people breaking in and borrowing them. And a lot of the keys are interchangeable. Willie-A's might fit the ignition of a dozen or more carts. Just the way they're made."

"Keys," Piper's voice was flat. "Keys. Didn't notice any signs of a break-in." Piper had checked the doors and windows when she was out earlier today and after Oren's fire. Unless it was a very skilled thief with impressive lock-picking skills, the golf cart "borrower" had a key or had been let in.

"Nope." Melinda set her fists against her hips. "Nobody broke in. At least I don't see how."

Piper paced, studying Avery's golf cart, then glancing to others, taking in all of the place. The walls were grass-green, and posters of men and women golfing were scattered throughout, some listing dates and events. Two benches were near the front, and a bank of beige lockers stretched across the back. Yearly membership dues ranged from $1,600 for an individual without a golf cart to $3,500 for a family with a cart to store on the premises. Not terrible, she considered, given that the place was opened year-round and meticulously maintained.

"What sort of membership does William Avery have?"

Melinda was quick to answer. "Double, just him and his wife." A pause. "And their cart."

"So he obviously has a key to this place."

"Key*card*. If you're a member and store your cart, you have a keycard. Public course, but only members can keep their carts here and get keycards. We rent carts, too. And not all of our members are from the Village or Santa Claus."

A club member, Piper figured, who stored a cart and had a keycard, was either the culprit or had been the ticket the "borrower" used to get inside. Could also be a golf course employee. Keycard to get into the building. Keycard to get into the Village.

The arsonists had used golf carts at Oren's and Basil's in the Village, but drove a pickup to her dad's in Rockport to torch his garage. Her kaleidoscope continued to whirl. What dark soul was linked to a pickup and had access to the golf club building and carts? Someone familiar enough with the Village to avoid the surveillance cameras at the big intersections, park, and lake fronts. Someone strong enough to tote twin gasoline canisters. And above all of that, someone who hated the Spencer County Sheriff's Department and had decided to act on that hate just before Christmas. Was Lefty Jay one of the spinning shards?

"Mrs. Felder, I'll need a list of your employees and all the members who store carts here." Piper would get court documents first thing in the morning to give her access to that information. "I'll come back tomorrow for—"

"I already printed a list for you. Common knowledge who belongs to the club, so I'm not giving away any secrets. And if it's one of my employees doing this, I want to know so I can fire his ass before you arrest him." A soft growl. "Or her. Fire her ass."

Piper thanked Melinda and headed out. She had deputies to caution, patrol routes to rearrange, notes and interviews to collate, and—

Her stomach rumbled in protest. So busy, she'd had nothing but a donut this morning and half a cup of burnt coffee.

She called Nang as she drove to the department.

"Miss you," he said.

"Miss you more." Piper really did. She'd been so busy since the arson at Oren's—and he'd been busy with his Quick Stop, garage, and plans for his new restaurant—that they'd barely crossed paths in the past several days. "I have some things to do."

"You always have things to do." She could feel the smile in Nang's voice. "I always have things to do." She heard Christmas music in the background, Frank Sinatra singing "Let it Snow." It was snowing harder now than when she went into the golf club. She hoped it wouldn't come down long.

"I'll be at the office until close to seven, I'm guessing."

"I have a carburetor to install on Bailey's van that will take me about that long."

"Perfect," Piper replied. "There's this Tombstone in the freezer, pepperoni and mushrooms, and—"

"—frozen, that will keep," Nang cut back. "I made Bánh Xèo today, it's a savory pancake. Rice flour, coconut milk, with pork, bean sprouts, and shrimp. And turmeric. It's very good, I promise, and just enough left for me and you. Some soup, too, canh chua. I used star-fruit, pineapple, tomatoes in this batch. It is sweet and sour, spicy with contrasting textures."

"You spoil me," Piper said.

"Because you shine."

"See you at seven." The music behind Nang switched to Eartha Kitt's "Santa Baby." Maybe he had on an oldies station in the garage; when she'd chatted with him yesterday, she heard Burl Ives' "A Holly Jolly Christmas" and Chuck Berry's "Run Rudolph Run."

Did Nang like oldies? Or maybe just old-time holiday tunes. She'd known him for a few weeks short of a year, having met him when she'd stopped for gas in Fulda last January. She'd been investigating a murder in that tiny town, and she discovered he had a marvelous menu. They dated a few times, and then it became a regular thing. They married a little more than a week ago, and her dad called it a "whirlwind romance."

Did Nang like oldies? There was a lot she didn't know about him.

"Love you," he said, before ending the call.

"Love you more."

The wind picked up and the snow came sideways.

25

Tug held the door open and Basil entered on crutches, a little ungainly, a lot uncomfortable. His ankle throbbed, the ibuprofen not cutting the pain, but he refused to take anything stronger that might muddle his senses. His armpits ached from the crutch pads, which didn't seem padded enough. No other option, though, if he wanted out of the house.

"Where's your office, Sherlock?" Tug asked.

"Not going there yet. I want to see the whiteboard and have a mug of tea."

"Tea. Herbal tea, right? That shit ain't got any taste." Tug wrinkled his nose. "There some coffee?"

Basil nodded. "They drink a lot of it here. At least Sheriff Blackwell does. Follow me." He maneuvered past the Christmas tree and Zeke at the front desk, who was just settling in for his shift. Basil offered a quick "hello," and hobbled fast. He did not want to engage the dispatcher in a conversation about why he'd come back to work after just being released from the hospital. Didn't have the time or patience for insignificant chatter.

The doc suggested he take some days off, work from home if he had to. But Basil needed to be here with the whiteboard, evidence, no distractions from cats and kids. Not having to deal with Esme, who would insist he put his foot up and take it easy. She'd refused to drive him to the department this morning, was pissed when he called Tug for a ride. He certainly couldn't drive himself, not for at least a couple of weeks. The boot protecting his foot and ankle was too clunky.

Basil knew that deep down Esme understood. He was on an important case, finding the arsonist who tried to torch their house. Like Oren and Millie, they could have lost everything. Worse, his family could have died.

"You always get here at the ass crack of dawn?" Tug grumped as he opened the door to the break room and swept a hand to indicate Basil should go past him.

"Seven isn't the ass crack," Basil returned. "And, no, usually my hours are nine to five. I just wanted to get an early start."

"Couldn't sleep, eh?"

"Not really."

"And so you decided I shouldn't either."

There were four six-foot tables in the break room, and Basil selected the one halfway between the whiteboard and the fancy coffee machine. Red and green garland hung from the counter and stretched across the top of the cabinets. A pencil pine covered in strings of gold and silver beads stood in the far corner. Softly, instrumental Christmas music played through a speaker, and someone had sprayed a heavy dose of pine air freshener for an added holiday touch.

Basil shifted from one crutch to the other, shrugging out of his coat and draping it on the back of a chair, hopping on his good foot and sitting. He lifted his booted foot, which with all the splints, padding, and thick sole felt as heavy as a boat anchor, and placed it on the chair across from him. Following doctor's orders: twenty minutes elevated for every waking hour. He was also supposed to apply an ice pack frequently for the next two days, but that wasn't practical here. He'd pull one out of the freezer when he eventually went home.

Six weeks, he was going to have to wear this damn thing.

Could have been worse, he thought. Could have been burned to a crisp.

Basil watched Tug hang up his coat and hat, smooth a wrinkle out of his shirt. Tug looked over the spare mugs and picked two, microwaved water in one of them. "Where's your tea? Here or in your office?"

"Box on the counter."

Tug poked through it. "Lavender mint, ginger root, peppermint, hibiscus, lemongrass, butterfly pea flower. Butterfly pea. What the hell is that? Bet there's not a bit of caffeine in any of these, Sherlock. So what's the point of drinking them? No zing. No jolt."

"Tea is good for you."

"Good for you. Not good for me." Tug pulled out a lemongrass bag, retrieved the mug from the microwave, and passed both to Basil. "No sugar, right?"

"Right."

"Of course not. That wouldn't be good for you either." Tug grinned and poured some coffee from the machine. "This shit smells good." He added a heaping spoonful of sugar and brought it over to the table, sat near Basil. "Where do I get the paperwork? Do I have to wait for your boss to come in?"

"Sheriff Blackwell will be here in an hour or two. She worked late."

"I'm not donating my time here. I'm going to be paid for my brain power." He drank coffee. "And toting you around. And whatever else."

Basil turned his head. "Zeke!" He could see the dispatcher desk through the open doors of the break room. "Would you grab a one-sheet employment form please?" He turned back to Tug. "Zeke is going to be a great deputy. Wants it bad. Just too young right now. Only nineteen. He's taking some college courses online. You'll like him. He's very techie, crazy smart ... and a little pure crazy."

"Trait of your dispatchers, eh? Crazy."

"You including Teegan in that?"

"Oh, yeah." Tug took another sip and made a smacking sound. "This is good. Been out with her a few times. Most decorated date I've ever had. All the piercings and tats, plum-colored hair. Go out many more times, I might ask to see all of her body art. Crazy, but sweet."

"Don't break her heart."

"She better not break mine."

Zeke came in with a manila folder tucked under one arm and balancing a platter of sugar cookies on one hand. "Candace brought in a couple of plates, said she's been doing a lot of baking. Here, have some." He sat the plate between them. Tug looked them over and selected a snowman.

"The form?" Basil prompted.

"I brought it all. In case you need the insurance form, too." Zeke dropped the folder on the table and looked at Tug. "You coming to work for Sheriff Blackwell?"

Tug didn't answer that. "Sherlock here says you want to be a deputy."

Zeke smiled wide. "Yeah. Have to wait until I'm twenty one."

"In Indiana," Tug cut back. "In most states, you do. But not Alabama. Down there, they'll take you at nineteen. You could be a sheriff's deputy right now."

"Really?" Basil saw Zeke's eyes glimmer. "Gee, Mr. Waters, do you think—"

A call came in, and Zeke hurried back to the desk to answer it.

"Not sure I'd trust a nineteen-year-old with a squad car and a gun," Tug said. "Hell, some of the twenty-one-year-old recruits in Chicago weren't ready."

"The department needs Zeke," Basil said. "And I don't need you to encourage him to go elsewhere."

"Well, your boss seems to think the department needs me for a few months. Came out to the Turtle and offered me a temp job."

"I know. Because Oren is going to be out for months."

Tug scowled. "That's not a happy situation, burned so bad. And then there's you, busted your ankle, broke bones in your foot, cracked a rib by stepping in a hole at the golf course in the middle of the night. You're way past twenty-one, Sherlock, and I wonder if you're mature enough for this." Tug laughed hard and reached over to affectionately rub Basil's shoulder.

Basil opened the folder and pointed at the top sheet, raised his gaze and gave Tug a serious look. "You doing this?"

"Yeah, I'm taking Blackwell up on her request. I better fill this out before I change my mind. Not doing this because she asked, or because the chief deputy is laid up in the burn unit and the department is down people. I'm doing this because of you. Because someone targeted you, and I have your back like you've always had mine. My turn now."

"I appreciate this." Basil really did. Tug was one of the best cops he'd worked with in Chicago, and the best partner he ever had. "Angel going to manage with—"

"Sister's coming in tomorrow. Was coming down anyway to help Angel and the baby ... due in less than two weeks."

"Good she got vacation time—"

Tug shook his head. "Sis got laid off the first of December. Who lays people off right before Christmas? Downsizing, they told her. Detroit, I say. Anyway, she's going to help us 'cause I said I'd pay her. She needs the money and my little Turtle's turning a profit so I can afford her. Says she'll stay as long as we need her ... which is going to be the duration of this temporary gig right here."

Tug grabbed the form and started filing it out.

Basil watched him, wrapping his hands around the mug, enjoying the warmth. He sipped the tea. It was mildly sweet and minty. He'd bought a carton of mixed flavors after trying some at Nang's Quick Stop; it didn't need sugar or caffeine.

"I thought Tug was a nickname," Basil said after Tug put the pen down. "All the years we partnered, I thought Tug was just a tag. It's your real name?"

"Never needed a nickname."

"Tug. Who'd call their kid Tug?"

"Named after a river, Sherlock," Tug shot back. "Me and my twin sister, Levisa." He downed half the coffee in one long swallow. "I'll give your little department an 'A' for this Dark Italian. Beats the hell out of the sludge we had in the squad." He twisted in the chair, stared at the whiteboard while he talked.

"All the years we worked together, you never told me you were named after a river." Basil thought he'd discovered all of Tug's nooks and crannies, like they were family, no mysteries.

"I never asked why you got saddled with Basil." Tug gave a sour expression and finished his coffee. "Named after a damn herb? Had to be, right? No way in hell were you named after an old big-nosed actor that played Sherlock Holmes in the black and whites."

"A river."

"A rare river," Tug said. "One of the few in this country that flows north. I wish I was in some big northern city about now."

"Where's the river?" Basil figured it must be south of here; he'd never heard of the Tug.

"My parents lived in Lawrence County, Kentucky, until I was two. A little place, like some of the little places around here that you call dinkburgs. Big on tourism because of the river. Kayaking, fishing. The Tug Fork runs almost a hundred and sixty miles from near Virginia, along the West Virginia and Kentucky border. In Lawrence County, the Tug joins the Levisa Fork and turns into the Big Sandy River. Mom thought with a last name of Waters it was appropriate to name her kids after rivers."

Tug stood, stepped to the counter and poured another cup of coffee, returned to the table, and selected a Santa cookie. "Had a younger brother named Sandy. Conveniently, he was big to match his river. Played linebacker for NIU Huskies, drafted by the Detroit Lions in the fourth round, then blew out both knees in training camp. Double ACL tears. Repaired, but he never got to play pro."

"Knew about Levisa," Basil said. "Esme and I met her at that street party two summers back. Didn't know you had a brother."

"You didn't know 'cause I don't talk about him." Tug looked solemn. "Died when he was twenty-three. Went to a place he shouldn't have at the wrong time of night. Looking for more pain pills than the doctors would prescribe him for those knees."

Basil didn't ask more particulars.

173

"You're not coming in every day this early," Tug said, changing the subject. "I'll do nine. Hell, I'll even do eight. But we're not doing seven again."

"Fine," Basil said. He wanted to argue that point. In Chicago they worked earlier than that when necessary. But Tug was his ride because Esme made it clear she'd only be driving him to a doctor's office to see how his ankle was doing. "Eight tomorrow."

"Then let's get to work, Sherlock."

26

8 a.m.

I t was twenty-nine degrees, the sky an ash gray dome. Lefty Jay
sat on the bench across the street from the sheriff's department,
a red knit cap pulled over his ears. He wore an overlarge black
and white argyle sweater, faded blue jeans, and high-top tennis shoes.

Piper figured he had to be freezing.

Why the hell was he just sitting there? Watching the comings and
goings from the department? Taunting her? They locked gazes and he
waved.

Rather than go inside to her office as she'd intended, she followed
the crosswalk. It had snowed about three inches yesterday, and
though the streets had been plowed, small drifts clung against the
curbs and building fronts. The snow, coupled with the decorations
hanging from the light posts, brightened an otherwise dismal-looking
downtown.

She'd wanted to talk to Lefty anyway, thinking he was somehow
involved in the arsons. Initially he'd been high on her suspect list.
Lefty was too old and too short to be the man seen running from
Basil's house and her father's garage fire, doubted he could tote two

full canisters of gasoline with any speed. But maybe he'd paid someone to do it, told them to add the spray painted star for an artistic and garish touch.

Lefty Jay definitely had a grudge against her department; he was suing it. And a grudge against her father and Oren, also named in the lawsuit. Maybe his time in prison had gained him connections to arsonists. Maybe the lawsuits weren't enough reprisal.

According to her father, and the incident reports from thirty years back, Lefty Jay was wholly guilty. Murdered his brother, so not entitled to vengeance in Piper's eyes. And maybe not entitled to the freedom he currently enjoyed on that bench.

If she found he had anything to do with the fires, and the deaths of the people in the Laubenstein house, he'd go right back to prison and never get out.

"Good mornin', Sheriff Blackwell," Lefty Jay said as Piper approached. His voice had little power to it. "Lovely mornin', isn't it?"

Not lovely. It was cold, overcast, she'd stayed up late reviewing video footage and so was tired and grumpy. Short-staffed, murders and arsons to solve. Not a good morning. Not a good week. This was the time of year to be festive and jolly, parties and presents and shimmering lights and happy music. Piper was overwhelmed with misery instead of merriment.

"Join me?" Lefty patted the empty spot on the bench.

Instead, Piper stood in front of him. His right sleeve was pushed back, and she saw a big square watch hanging loose on his wrist. It looked old, far from valuable. The faceplate was scratched and the stem pulled out, locking the time at 11. Maybe it was broken, or the hour might have some significance to him. He smelled fusty, enhanced with traces of shaving lotion and old sweat.

"I'm gonna win, you know. Get me?" His voice was not much more than a coarse whisper.

"Win what?" Piper wondered if he meant the suit or burning down the homes of sheriff's deputies. The video she'd watched last night included what her own surveillance cameras had recorded from around her house and fenced yard. It had been troubling.

"Win my case, of course. Bankrupt Paul Blackwell, Oren Rosenberg, take the county and city, your department included, for a lot of money." He gestured wildly with his hands, reminding her of Donald Trump during his speeches. "Set me up for life in fine style. Get me? Not that I'm likely to have all that much life left. I'm old, and thirty years in prison made me even older. Set my wife up, though, the money would. The years have been kinder to her. Hope you have no hard feelin's about the lawsuit." He gave her a crooked half-smile.

Piper hid a shiver and didn't reply. She tossed the questions around in her mind, needing to ask him about the fires and his whereabouts. In its place: "What makes you think you'll win? You murdered your brother. What makes you think a court will find in your favor?"

Lefty smiled, displaying crooked teeth, a front one chipped. "I'm not sayin' I didn't kill my brother. Never said that, girlie. I killed him. I didn't *murder* him. There's a difference. Get me? I'll win this suit. I can't tell you why, can't give up the secrets. My attorney says I shouldn't even talk to you, talk to anyone I'm suin'. But you walked over here." He sucked in a rattling breath that sounded unhealthy. "Nothin' against you personally, girlie. You might be a fine soul, and you and your husband bought my vacant store down the street. Beholdin' to you for that."

Piper gritted her teeth at "girlie." She could tell that he had on layers, a sweater under a sweater, probably something under that, made him look meatier than he really was. His wrists bony, face sharp angles and heavy creases.

A car honked behind her, a driver yelled for someone to "move, move, move." She didn't turn around to look, kept her gaze on Lefty.

"Buildin's all dirty and faded, cobwebs thick as curtains inside. Needs a new roof. But its bones are good. Hope you and your husband make it all stylish. Shouldn't sit empty like that any longer. Too many buildin's here sitting empty. A lot of years ago, things were different. This street was busy and pretty and nothin' was empty. People visited the downtown. Lots of people. They didn't have to go across the river to do their shoppin'. You and your husband, I hope you make my building—*your* building now—all useful and invitin'. It deserves that. You do it right, hear me, girlie? Get me?"

Piper didn't reply to that, either.

"I'm gonna win," he said again. "It's a slam-dunk as they say. Sorry you have to be involved. Got no beef with you. But my attorney says I had to include everyone and everythin' involved. No hard—"

"Where were you two nights ago, late?" Piper interrupted. "Do you drive?" She found no record of him owning a car, but his wife had a decade-old Subaru Forester.

"In bed," he answered. "If you're talkin' late. I don't usually make it to the ten o'clock news. The news ain't worth much listenin' to anyway."

"Do you drive?" She raised her voice.

He shook his head. "I can. But no license. It expired while I was in prison. No use for a car in prison. Get me? It's okay. I like to walk. The exercise is good for me."

"Two nights before that," Piper started. "Where were—"

"You're askin' me about the fires." Lefty's eyes shone and he grinned, displaying his ugly teeth. He gestured wildly with his arms again and leaned back against the bench. "You think I set them!" He slapped his knee and let out a laugh. "Now why the hell would I do that? I want Blackwell and Rosenberg to lose everythin' with my lawsuit. I'd get no joy from them losin' it all before it goes to court." He slapped his knee again. "But I'm flattered you'd consider me."

He didn't blink, didn't twitch, no sign of deception.

"You could have hired someone to—"

"Look elsewhere, girlie." Lefty's eyes narrowed and his expression darkened and sent a shiver down her back. "I want your dad to suffer for what he did to me, arrestin' me, his buddy Rosenberg, too. Get me? Suffer a great deal and pay." His face relaxed and his voice grew stronger. "You? I want you and your husband to make my old building live. Maybe I'll stop by to have a good Chinese meal there after the remodelin's done."

Vietnamese. She didn't correct him.

Piper turned and retreated across the street, walked two blocks past the sheriff's department to the abandoned grocery store. She felt Lefty's eyes on her. Her reflection in the dirty glass window was depressing. Did she really look that defeated and tired? Had the circumstances of the past several days beat her down that far? Or did the window's filmy smear of age and neglect gray her appearance? The building's entrance used to be boarded up, now had a heavy chain and a lock stretched across the double doors. Nang had the key, all the papers had been signed. In front of the doors a pressure plate covered part of the sidewalk, one of those that if someone stepped on it, the contact would signal the doors to swing wide. Made it easier for shoppers back in the day to wheel grocery carts in and out. She wondered if Nang would keep the feature.

She peered through the streaked glass, in the dim light through the window seeing shelves, some of them tipped over, two check-out lanes with cash registers and conveyor belts, a line of grocery carts. A faded and torn placard proclaimed ground beef on sale today for $1.30 a pound; pork chops for $.89. The floor was littered with pages of store ads and coupons. The light fixtures were industrial fluorescent, and a mass of webs stretched between them. Could be the setting for a horror movie, she thought. They certainly could have asked more for the building if Lefty and his wife had bothered to first clean it up.

It would take a lot of work and money to turn this into a fine-dining restaurant, but Piper had no doubt that Nang could do just that. So much drive and ambition and optimism swirled around her husband. Sometimes she fed off that contagious energy. Right now she operated just on the drive part, single-mindedly focused on the fires to the point she'd been ignoring practically everything else. If she could only borrow some of Nang's optimism to add into the mixture, because she wasn't sure they'd catch the arsonists before another deputy's home burned.

She knew her house was on the list.

Piper continued to stare through the window, the ruined interior giving way in her mind to the images of the charred bodies and the remains of Oren's house and her dad's garage. It would be easier to solve if Lefty Jay was the answer, but he wasn't on her suspect list any longer. Facing him, listening to him, seeing his unwavering eyes. He really did want Oren and her dad ruined, but by the court system that had jailed him. Lefty Jay had nothing to do with the arsons.

"Guilty," Piper said. He killed his brother.

Her eyes filled with tears and she brushed them away. Why did Nang have to choose this building? And why hadn't she objected? Why had she stayed silent? Because she didn't want to intrude on Nang's dreams?

Lefty Jay profited from the sale of this husk. She prayed he wouldn't profit a penny from the lawsuit.

Zeke stood as she came in the department's front door, and gestured to the break room. She looked through the open door and saw Tug and Basil sitting in front of the whiteboard. She needed to talk to her detective.

"Is Tug—"

"Joining the department? He filled out the paperwork," Zeke told her. He handed her a file folder. Then he gave her a stack of messages. "The one on top, that's the reporter from Indy again. He's on his way down to talk to you, should be here soon."

Piper grimaced. "I don't want to talk to him, to any reporter. Not now. Too busy."

"Yeah, you're way too busy. But somebody might have to. I could if you want." Zeke shrugged in sympathy. "Says he's coming here because you don't return his phone calls. Says he has an appointment to interview DA Scales."

"Fine. Let me know when he arrives. I'll give him twenty minutes."

"Sheriff?"

"Yes, Zeke?"

"Have you ever been to Alabama?"

27

9 a.m.

The right side of the whiteboard was covered with pictures from the fires, two names in large red marker, Daphne Doe and John Doe, and a short list of their possessions in black.

Daphne necklace; two sapphire stud earrings; one gold hoop earring mostly melted; silver pinkie ring sz 4; rose gold pinkie ring with amethyst sz 4; gold ring with half-carat diamond sz 6, possibly engagement ring; gold Claddagh ring sz 6; white gold ring with blue topaz, sz 7; men's ring sz 11, (1961 West Point Military Academy lapis class ring).

Front dental implants, male.

Piper quietly edged into the break room, studying the board as she went.

Basil and Tug sat facing the board, talking in almost conspiratorial whispers and sipping from mugs. Piper listened to them, surprised and pleased that Tug had given in to her temp request. Basil had probably talked him into it. Or maybe Basil's injury had prompted it. She noticed Basil had a big boot on his right foot, crutches on the floor nearby.

"No ID yet on either?" Piper gestured to the names in red. "Just young, twenties."

"Nothing yet on DNA or dentals," Basil replied. "But I'll be checking again this afternoon in case something comes in. The implants should make the dentals easier, but it still takes time. Whoever originally owned the West Point ring would have been born between 1936 and 1940. Initials inside E.B. I've contacted the academy and requested a list of 1961 graduates whose last name starts with B."

"So you're thinking E.B. was our fire victim's grandfather."

Basil nodded.

"I doubt it. And as for Daphne Doe," Piper said.

"Daphne Someone." Basil worked a kink out of his neck and placed his mug on the table. "The necklace she had on gives us a first name, not a last."

"Daphne isn't her first name." Piper reached for her cell phone, called the Forsetti's. Five rings and she expected to leave a message, but Darren Forsetti picked up.

"Ho. Ho. Ho! Merry Christmas!" His voice carried enough to be heard without Piper pressing the "speaker" button.

"Can I speak to your wife, Mr. Forsetti?" She waited as the phone was passed over, listening to Darren: "Honey dearest sweetie, can you take a break from the batter and talk to the sheriff?"

She caught Basil's raised eyebrows. "What?" he mouthed.

Piper held up a finger. "Wait," she mouthed back. Then: "Mrs. Forsetti. Daphne. Hello. Sorry to bother you in the middle of your baking." A pause. "Well, yes, I like gingerbread, but I'm calling about —" Another pause. "No. We're fine. We have plenty of cookies here. Could you describe your necklace that was stolen while you were in Door County? In June." Piper listened. "Little emeralds? Spelling Daphne? Thanks. We have your necklace, but it will be a while before it can be returned. It's evidence in another case. I'll explain more later. Appreciate your information." Piper ended the call.

She pocketed the phone. "The young woman who burned to death in the Laubenstein house spent time in the Forsetti house this past

June. She stole the necklace out of Daphne Forsetti's jewelry box. Maybe some of the rings are also Mrs. Forsetti's. I think our burned victims spent time in other people's houses in the Village and helped themselves to a few souvenirs. The military ring was likely stolen, too."

Tug gave a dry chuckle. "So they're a pair of phroggers."

Piper cocked her head. "They're what?"

"Phroggers. People who secretly live in someone else's home without the homeowner's knowledge or permission. Phrogs, a play on leap frogging from place to place. I suppose you could call them squatters, but squatters go for unoccupied places. Phroggers go for fully furnished homes with all the amenities, the owners usually on vacation or in the hospital. Some phroggers maybe stay a night. Some might stay a year before they're caught. Some are never caught and live like nomads from house to house. Modern day hobos I guess. I read about some homeowners who had a helluva time evicting them. It's as illegal as hell. Criminal trespass, burglary, destruction of property, vandalism. All sorts of charges. Never personally dealt with phroggers in the city, though the department did. I dealt with plenty of squatters, though."

The Forsettis had been on vacation, and the Laubensteins had been on their annual winter pilgrimage. Piper would check with her dad, who was investigating other theft reports in the Village and Santa Claus. Maybe those reports coincided with vacations.

She shook her head. The couple likely only took small things that might not be missed, not wanting to draw attention. They'd been guilty of several crimes. But the worst thing they'd been guilty of was sleeping in the Laubenstein house the night of the first arson.

She looked at the left side of the whiteboard, which displayed a printout with a long list of names in 24-point type.

- Avery, William and Smith-Avery, Belinda
- Barnes, Reynolds and Barnes, Stephanie
- Carpenter, Anna and Carpenter, Lulu
- Czynski, Randall and Holland, Beatrice

- Darnold, Samuel and Darnold, Tonya
- David, Andrew
- Halm, David and Halm, Virginia
- Jackson, Bruce and Jackson, Helga
- ~~Laubenstein, Eldad and Laubenstein, Saundra~~
- <u>Lasko, Vincent, former</u>
- Madsen, Vernon
- North, Richard and North, Mary Louise, former
- White, Laura
- Wilkins, Norma
- ~~Wollach, James~~
- Ye, Thomas

Probably eighty or ninety names, she guessed without counting, the printout dangling past the board to graze the floor. But this selection was highlighted with bright yellow. The Laubensteins crossed off because they certainly would not have burned down their own house. Wollach crossed off because the volunteer fire chief was not involved either.

"Okay, so we can't do anything with our burned victims until we get IDs," Piper said. "About the arsonists—"

"Nothing matching on the fingerprints from the golf carts or the gas can from my backyard. Just means it's someone not in the system." Basil softly growled. "Worthless clues."

"Clues," Tug mused. "Still no clue about who lit the match, eh Sherlock?"

"I was close. Almost had him. I think I might have hurt him," Basil said. "If I'd caught the son of a bitch that night, if I hadn't stepped in that hole and ended up in the hospital, I think I might have ugly hurt him."

"You were always good cop to my bad," Tug returned. "You only *might* have hurt the torch. I know I *would* have. But might? I damn near *might* have killed him for threatening my family."

Piper had stopped by Basil's early this morning, getting another earful from Esme and discovering that she'd missed her detective by several minutes. He'd gone to the department, to work—despite Esme's argument that he rest, Tug providing a ride. Esme almost didn't accept the poinsettia and box of herbal tea Piper had brought as get-well gifts for Basil, she was still that upset.

"Something familiar about him," Basil continued. "Too dark, too far away. Couldn't see his face. But there was something. You know, that something that niggles at your brain. Maybe the way he moved, his build. Maybe both. Something. Damn. I needed to see the face. I needed to hear him. He didn't say a word."

Piper reached for a sugar cookie, a wreath decorated with those hard silver sugar balls that threatened to chip teeth. Candace had been regularly baking all sorts of holiday cookies and bringing in plates of them. Maybe Piper should gift her something cooking related for Christmas. Piper frowned, so busy, she hadn't yet picked up presents for the department. Looked like gift cards on the horizon.

"I'm a target," she said, interrupting them. "I'm in the arsonists' sites. My house was spared because of all my security cameras. Oren, Millie. The whole department is a target. I'm putting even more patrols going by everyone's houses starting tonight."

They swiveled to face her, Basil slow and awkward with his protective boot.

"I have surveillance cameras at my house, front door, over the front-facing windows, on the garage, along the fence. I've never bothered to check them before. Didn't have a reason to. But I went through the footage last night."

"You need cameras in your tiny neck of Hooterville?" Tug quipped.

"Hatfield," she replied. "I live in Hatfield, which used to be called Fair Fight." One of the smaller communities in Spencer County, it boasted a population of 772. "I inherited the house—beautiful house—from an old man who was paranoid. He'd put up lots of cameras." Rightly so paranoid, she thought. Someone had been out to get him—and succeeded in killing him. "I'm sure that's why my house hasn't burned yet. The cameras." She twisted her foot against the tile floor, remembering how long she'd spent reviewing video from all her cameras last night. The system only stored footage for seven days before writing over it. An Amazon driver, the neighbor's roving boxer, the dark truck and the dark man—

"Go on," Basil prompted.

"Three evenings in a row, the eighth, ninth, and tenth, a pickup cruised past my house. I should say crawled, it was that slow. A dark color, I think green. The first pass I could dismiss it as someone looking for an address, maybe even when it went past the second night. One person in the cab on the eighth, two on the next nights. Can't make out any details on the people." She handed a flash drive to Basil. "Can't read the license plate either because it was mudded over." That realization had made her frightful and angry. "The tenth, the truck stopped on the other side of my property, only the taillights visible in one of my cameras. A man got out. Dark hoodie, dark pants, can't see his face, hands in his pockets until he pulls out a cell phone and holds it up, I'm guessing taking pictures. I have motion sensor lights, and they all came on. They frequently come on … squirrels, rabbits, the boxer, whatnot. Spooked him apparently, and he ran back to the truck. After a little while he comes back, crab walking down the sidewalk, staying low. Thinks he's out of the camera range. But I have a lot of cameras, and he eventually realized it. The next night, the eleventh, Oren's house went up. Oren didn't have cameras. Neither did my dad."

"And I have no cameras facing my backyard," Basil said.

"They're cautious. Don't want to be seen. Apparently they scope out a place before striking the match. My dad's neighbor, we checked his camera from the night of the fire. I'm going back to see if he has footage from the few nights before. Maybe the arsonists cased my dad's garage first before burning it and we can find a better look at them." She took a bite of the cookie. It was good, sweet. She needed a mug of coffee to go with it. The silver balls crunched hard. "There's enough of the back of the truck showing on my flash drive that we should be able to figure out the make and model. My guess is a Ford. Go through some DMV records, get a list of names."

"It's a good lead." Basil ran a hand through his hair.

They were quiet for several moments, studying the board, thinking, Piper considering what to say. She wanted to ask Basil why he wasn't taking a few days off, but she knew the answer: there was a case to solve, arsonists to catch, bodies to identify. She wanted to ask how he was feeling, but passed on that, too. He hurt, like she'd hurt when she broke her arm in the autumn, and she'd quickly tired of people asking her how she was doing.

"Tell me about this list." Piper pointed to the highlighted names.

"People we've talked to," Basil answered. "You, me, your father, Diego. They're also people who have golf carts and keycards. The rest of the names on the list also have golf carts and keycards, but we haven't chatted them up. And not all of them are from the Village. A few are from across the river in Owensboro. We'll get to them, though."

Piper remembered seeing a lot of golf carts in the building, eighty or more. No one living near Basil or Oren would need to use a golf cart; they'd drive or walk to set the fire. So it was an outsider, like Basil first suspected. An outsider with a keycard or access to one.

Zeke crept into the room, obviously careful not to disturb the conversation. He whispered to Piper: "The reporter is here."

"Put him in my office. Tell him I might be a little while."

Zeke disappeared.

"Sherlock says someone used a card to get in and steal a golf cart, no evidence of broken doors or windows."

"And they returned the carts," Basil said. "So the thief cared about the property, maybe because he knew who the carts belonged to. Two different carts were used on two different nights."

"Neither cart belonged to the thief," Tug surmised. "But maybe the thief has a cart and just didn't want to use his own. Whoever did this knows the Village and the course. So who on the list might fit … and also have a ton of hate wallowing around in his gut?"

"It's all about the keycard," Basil said.

Zeke crept in again and whispered to Piper. "Didn't want to wait. He's going across the street to talk to DA Scales, says he'll be back."

Piper nodded, still not wanting to talk to a reporter. Maybe he'd spend the whole day interviewing Scales … she should be that lucky.

Zeke stood next to her and looked at the board, raised his hand as if in class looking for the teacher's attention.

"Uh," Zeke began. "Uh, I have an idea."

Tug and Basil returned to staring at the board.

"What's your idea?" Piper respected Zeke, had hired him in May after he graduated from high school. He'd been president of the school's computer club and was a tech geek. Zeke made it clear he wanted to be a deputy, but she could only offer a dispatcher position because of his age.

"Why not ask whoever handles security for the golf course if their keycards are coded. If they are, each has a signature, and they can check who used their card late at night."

All eyes instantly turned to the dispatcher.

"Some keycards," Zeke went on, rolling his shoulders and looking important, "have unique signatures. Like companies that use keycards for their employees. You know, the employees insert a card in the slot to get in the building. If the company wants to see who comes in early and who stays late, who isn't putting in the hours, they dig into the keycard records. Unless the golf course just uses the same card signal for everyone, which I suppose it might, they should be able to tell you who used the cards to get at the golf carts." He scowled and shook his head. "I should have been paying more attention to the board, could've mentioned the keycard thing earlier. Sorry."

"Hello Alabama," Tug rumbled.

"Damn. I should have thought of that." Basil grabbed his crutches and levered himself up.

"Where are you going?" Piper saw Basil cringe as he moved.

"To my office, track down the course security, see if we can get a name to match a keycard."

"Before you go," Piper said, "tell me about Vincent Lasko. He's underlined three times in red on the list, and it says *former*."

"This man here, Vincent Lasko," Basil said, gesturing with his head, "is a triple-hater, and so is a valid suspect."

Tug passed her Lasko's folder. "Check it out, Sheriff."

On top of a stack of printouts inside were drawings. The first, a crude rendering of a purple octopus with a black Star of David on its bulbous head, tentacles wrapped around the world. The next was more artistic, a bald eagle clutching a cobra in its talons, the cobra wearing a yarmulke. The caption read: If America is to survive, the Jewish snake must be banished.

"Lovely," Piper said. She continued paging through the contents.

"Lasko used to live in Christmas Lake Village," Basil explained. "He moved less than a year ago to Dale. And he was a member at the golf course, kept a cart there until about six months ago when he sold it. I'm thinking that's when his money ran out."

She looked at another sheet, Lasko's social media postings.

The Holocaust is Jewish propaganda.

Jews crucified Christ, time to crucify the Jews.

Stop Jewish supremacy in America.

Put Aunt Jemima back in the bottle.

There were other posts even more offensive.

"Gotta love freedom of speech," Tug said.

"So he's anti-Jew and anti-black—that's the double-hate. Used to golf, and used to live in the Village," Piper observed. "Where's the triple come in?"

"He hates cops, too," Tug said.

"I pulled records on him last night, and called him to chat," Basil said. "I was doing a little work at home while Esme and the kids wrapped presents. Lasko's thirty-eight, likes whiskey, has some DUIs, the first going back twenty years when he was too young to legally drink. One too many DUIs and lost his license last May. He used to work at the power plant, but apparently that ended about a year ago. My guess is he and his wife moved out of the Village because he couldn't afford the mortgage when unemployment ran out. They're living in a six-hundred square foot trailer on Yellowbanks in Dale. He said he hasn't been back to the Village since they moved. But I haven't had time yet to deep dive on him." A pause. "But I will. I will find enough hours in this day."

"Your dispatcher pulled Lasko's social media," Tug said after Basil had left. "Sharp dispatcher. Got us these copies." He pointed to the folder Piper held. "Lasko seems to hate Jews the most, but he's got a few black jabs in there. A couple anti-Muslim posts, too. Hates cops 'cause they took his driver's license. His cop hate is plastered all over. Zeke also gave us this." He pointed to page from a ruled legal pad, notes handwritten. "Your dispatcher dates Google in his spare time, I think."

The page listed assorted facts on Indiana hate groups, of which it appeared the FBI tracked fourteen in the past few years. The largest the White Nationalist.

"Lasko's a White Nationalist," Tug said. "But he lacks a driver's license."

Piper padded up to stand next to the whiteboard. "Just because you don't have a license doesn't mean you can't get in a car ... or a dark pickup ... load it with gasoline, and drive. I can agree with Lasko as a suspect. Ride out and talk to him after lunch. Diego will go with you, and I'll be ready to follow. If he's one of the arsonists, you need backup."

"Don't need to buy me a uniform." Tug changed the subject. "They're expensive, and I ain't planning on being here the whole six months. Figure just until you get your chief deputy back and Sherlock can get around without a chauffeur."

Piper nodded. "Galls usually has some sort of sale on uniforms, so actually not too expensive. But I agree with you. No real need for a uniform and equipment. It'd take two to three weeks to get you fully outfitted and equipped anyway. I'm fine with a nice shirt and blue jeans. Except you need a bulletproof vest. Oren's will probably come close, and you can borrow that. But I'm going to order one to fit you today, and I can get it Fed-Exed here a day or two after. I insist you have body armor. I'll have to swear you in, get you a badge and ID."

"Nothing in the paper about your new temp hire. I can't have that."

"Sure. Understood." Piper knew he moved here to get his daughter away from a big Chicago gang, didn't want them finding out the small town where Tug and Angel Waters now lived. "I have to make sure you're familiar with our SOPs and qualify you on firearms."

"That's easy," Tug said. "Suspect I already know all your standard operating procedures." He paused a beat. "And I'm a good shot. Did time in a sniper division."

"I'll have Diego take you out to the range after lunch. Just a formality. Then the two of you can head to Lasko's." She glanced away from the board and locked eyes with him. Tug's face looked chiseled, like the rest of him. Skin tight, shoulders broad, carried himself like a soldier. "Thank you for signing on," she said after a moment. "Seriously, thanks. Small population this county, but it covers a lot of land. I'll get you a car in a few days. Bids are coming in on Explorers. We lost one—Oren's—when his garage burned. Have to replace it."

"I can use whatever you assigned to Sherlock," Tug said. "He can't drive, I'm his ride. So my hours have to match his."

"Not a problem."

"It's a problem for Esme," Tug said.

Piper let out a long breath. "Yeah, she's pretty upset. Didn't say a whole lot to me when I stopped by this morning."

"Hell, she didn't say even one word to me. I'm high on her shit list because I'm toting Sherlock. She'd get like this in Chicago sometimes. Mama bear has her claws out, protects her family."

"And we need to protect ours," Piper said. "We need to find these men before they burn down another deputy's house."

"The reporter's back!" Zeke called from the doorway.

"Great." Piper's tone did not match the word. "He's got twenty minutes, and then I have a deputy to swear in."

28

10 a.m.

Quinton Kincaid." The reporter thrust out his hand and Piper shook it.

Probably five-four or five-five and in his mid-fifties, she guessed, built blocky like a Lego and smelling faintly of lime aftershave. His long black hair was thickly streaked with gray and tied in a ponytail that hung between his shoulder blades.

"Nice to meet you, Mr. Kincaid." Piper settled behind her desk.

He took off his knee-length winter coat and carefully folded and draped it on the back of the chair opposite her desk. He had on a navy suit beneath it, with a green-striped tie that he straightened, formal-looking compared to other reporters she'd dealt with.

Piper considered offering him coffee, then instantly abandoned that idea. Coffee appeared cordial, might make this interview stretch longer, and she wanted to get back to work. Twenty minutes.

He glanced around her office, eyes stopping on the poinsettia on the corner of her desk, then sat. "Call me Quin." Nice voice, melodic. He pulled out a notebook and pen, surprising her; she figured he'd record the conversation. Old school, she thought, taking a closer look at his face and placing him instead in his sixties. The back of his right hand had a few age spots. His fingers were stubby, the nails manicured.

Part of her job, dealing with the media. Most days it wasn't onerous. Spencer County had a weekly paper, and occasionally reporters from Owensboro or Evansville called for quotes on this or that. She rarely fielded more than two or three a week. There'd been exceptions. She'd gotten a lot of press in the summer when a county fair ride broke and several riders were killed, and before that when a serial killer was discovered days after she took office. The killer had posed his victims to resemble scenes on Christmas cards. She remembered the Indianapolis news headline when it was all over: "Christmas Card Killer Captured". The last time she'd dealt with the media was around Halloween. Two teenagers were murdered on their way to a costume party. Their deaths were connected to sizeable drug operations: the Carlson's marijuana farm and a separate multi-million dollar meth lab and distribution network.

Kincaid was here to talk about the drugs.

Piper knew he likely hadn't heard about their arsons; only two burned houses and a third attempted one would not catch Indianapolis notice. She prayed he wouldn't ask her about Lefty Jay's lawsuit. All she could offer up on that would be "no comment." That murder happened more years ago than she'd been breathing.

"I'm working on a seven-part series about drugs in the heartland, specifically how Indiana fits into the picture. I wrote a couple of articles last month about your big meth bust, the Feds coming in, and that spurred the idea. I talked to you and your detective back then."

Piper remembered reading through a lot of articles seeing if they'd quoted her correctly.

"My focus is on manufacturing, trafficking, and enforcing, and among other things why pot farms and drug labs thrive in rural places. I'm including a sidebar from the perspective of pot growers, like Mr. Carlson. The other side of the coin so to speak."

Twenty minutes, Piper looked at her watch. He obviously intended for this to take a lot longer than that. She wanted to go back in the break room and make another study of the whiteboard with Tug, see if they were missing anything. She heard Zeke talking to someone on the phone, something about department office hours.

"Though marijuana is legal in neighboring states, Indiana's laws are firm, some say oppressive and out-of-date. The Carlson family you arrested in November is facing perhaps life in prison. *Life*, when you can walk into a store in Illinois and legally buy all manner of marijuana products. Roger Carlson told me the federal government is trying to seize his farm, and if that fails, which isn't likely, force it into foreclosure. He's filed for bankruptcy, and he doesn't expect a ruling on that until after their trial starts come this spring. He says you've wiped him out, destroyed their lives."

"Is there a question in there, Mr. Kincaid?"

"Quin. Call me Quin."

"Is there a question?"

"Do you think Indiana's laws are archaic regarding marijuana? Given what neighboring states do? And do you think the punishments are excessive? I'm not talking about opioids, meth, the harsher drugs. We'll get to them later. But marijuana—" He bounced the pen against his notebook. "Indiana compared to other states."

Piper didn't like the questions, they felt like a trap. Easy to deal with the reporter from the little weekly. This guy was slick and experienced, and leading her. He wanted her to go on the record dissing the state's marijuana laws. Maybe he was personally pro-pot. He had talked to Roger Carlson. Maybe Carlson had swayed him.

She leaned forward. "Mr. Kincaid, states bordering us—Illinois, Michigan, and Ohio—have legalized marijuana, one way or another. And while you can legally purchase it next door, it becomes illegal when you bring it into our state. And it's definitely illegal to grow it here. The Carlsons had a major operation, the scope of which was an illegal industry that operated like organized crime. Even Illinois would not look the other way."

"Okay, so remove the Carlsons from the equation. Are the penalties too stiff for the average Joe?"

Really trying to get her on record opposing the laws, Piper

thought, an obvious bent to his article, at least on the marijuana topic. "Look, Mr. Kincaid, the penalties are stiff throughout Indiana for even possessing some for personal use."

"In Marion County—"

"I'm aware that the Marion County District Attorney is no longer prosecuting low-level marijuana possession offenses, though that does not include driving under the influence of it. And that's Marion County. In Spencer County we arrest when we see an offense, no matter the severity. Does that answer your question?"

"Not exactly." Kincaid shook his head and made a few notes. "More than a dozen marijuana bills were considered by the Indiana legislature last year, but none got to the governor's desk. Do you think that's going to change? That it will ease up for offenders here? Would you encourage legalization? The Carlsons would not be looking at life in prison if their farm had been in Illinois."

What part of the Carlsons were an organized crime outfit didn't he get? Piper wanted to shake him, be forceful with her answers, but that wouldn't help. That might only give him something to write about that she would regret. She would not fall into his trap. *Stick to the facts, not the opinions.*

"I don't write the laws, Mr. Kincaid. That's not my job, but I enforce them," Piper replied. "We arrested the Carlsons because they broke the law in Indiana. Numerous laws. We've made several marijuana-related arrests in the past year. And I'm sure we'll make more."

"I understand. I looked at the blotter while I waited for you. I see that you arrested a high school student a few days ago for a mere handful of joints he had in his pocket. A handful."

Piper gripped the edge of her desk. Part of her job, she told herself, talking to the press. One of her responsibilities. If he persisted down this line, she'd find being rude and kicking him out an added responsibility.

"I enforce the laws," she repeated after a moment. "And this department will continue to enforce them when we see people in violation. Doesn't matter what neighboring states do. And drug arrests are only one part of what we—"

"I understand. So you don't want to comment on the severity of Indiana's marijuana laws."

Piper dug her fingernails into the wood. "Mr. Kincaid—"

"Quin—"

"It doesn't matter whether I personally agree or disagree with the laws involving marijuana."

"I just wanted your opinion, Sheriff. The Carlson family is losing their farm and their freedom. Their lives will never be the same."

She looked at her watch. "I've a busy schedule today and I'll have to ask you—"

Piper saw Millie glance in her office. She was in her deputy uniform. A quick wave, and she headed down the hall.

"Okay. Okay. So you don't want to talk about the marijuana laws."

She wondered if he'd pummeled DA Scales with the same questions. "I will talk about their *enforcement*."

"Moving along." He scribbled something in the notebook. "Why do you think the drug trade thrives in rural America? In places like Spencer County?"

She heard a 9-1-1 call come in, Zeke deftly fielding it, dispatching Rockport police. She had a gem in that dispatcher. He'd make a good deputy in a few years, if that's really what he wanted.

"Spencer County covers a lot of ground and has a relatively small population. Same as rural counties everywhere. That leaves lots of land to hide in. Set up mobile home meth labs, labs in abandoned root cellars, empty barns. Easier to stay out of sight. I suppose big cities have their hiding spots, too. But open land—"

"Yeah, I get it. Same thing the FBI told me. Open land and not a lot of deputies to cover it." He scribbled faster, a type of shorthand it looked like. "So how do you patrol all that? And how often do you actively look for drug production? Do you use drones? Dogs? You have a dog, right?"

His questions went on and on for another half hour, Piper answering and wishing for a second mug of coffee and a couple more of Candace's sugar cookies to go with it. A glance at her watch. Time to end this.

"Mr. Kincaid, I have work—"

"They're sending a photographer down in the next day or so, get some shots of you in the office, the District Attorney, farmland. She's going over to Warrick, Vanderburgh, Gibson, and maybe Pike, too, then swing up to Putnam, where I'm going later this afternoon. They found a trunk full of LSD, vape pens, and marijuana during a traffic stop."

Piper had heard about that, the eighteen-year-old driver pulled over for speeding and now facing a lengthy prison sentence. Probably would have been able to sell his goods and go undetected if he'd not been so heavy on the gas pedal.

"I need to get back to work Mr. Kincaid." She'd given him nearly an hour when she'd only intended twenty minutes.

"Quin, please."

"Quin."

He smiled broadly. His teeth were bright white, perfect. Maybe veneers. He put the notebook and pen in his pocket, stood, placed his business card on her desk. "You can call me anytime if you think of something to add."

She picked up the card and felt the raised ink, placed it in her drawer.

He shook her hand again, and reached for his coat.

"Thanks for taking the time. This was much nicer than talking over the phone. Hard to catch you over the phone. You're the youngest sheriff in the state, younger than your deputies, and I wanted to get a look at you, maybe do a feature just on you down the road, when your first year is in the books. Decorated veteran. Pretty impressive. My friend Josie said she is going to be calling you in the next couple of days, call a lot of people in Spencer. She covers courts, looking into a lawsuit filed against practically all of Spencer County, your department included."

Lefty Jay.

Piper felt her stomach twist and she readied her "no comment."

"I covered courts about twenty years ago," he added. "Stuffy, boring. Not compelling like the TV dramas make it. The topics I cover now are much more interesting. I pick what I want to write, years in the business has its advantage. And I like writing series. They tend to get picked up by the wire services."

"I look forward to reading your work," Piper lied.

He put on his coat and strolled out, the whiff of lime following him.

"Zeke!"

In a heartbeat he stood in her doorway. "How was the interview, Sheriff Blackwell?"

She scowled and waved a flash drive at him. "This is video from the surveillance camera at the main gate to the Village. From the two weeks before Oren's house fire. I've been through it, Basil's been through it. I watched it again last night. I want you to take a *different* look. Don't tell me what you see. Tell me what you don't see."

"Be happy to."

She heard Basil hobbling down the hall at a faster pace than he should probably manage.

"Uh-oh, he doesn't look happy," Zeke said, and bolted.

29

10 a.m.

Basil maneuvered around his desk and plopped into the chair behind it, leaning the uncomfortable crutches against the wall. His ankle burned, leg throbbed with its own awful pulse, and he couldn't tell if he was wiggling his toes.

His pledge to avoid the pain medication was about to be broken.

Basil dipped his fingers into his front pocket, tracing circles around the cap, thinking about Esme. *May Cause Drowsiness*, the warning label said. He popped it open and shook one out onto the desk, and replaced the cap.

He stared at the tempting oval tablet.

Esme had called him stubborn, and a couple other less kind things when he didn't take a pill this morning before catching a ride with Tug. She'd wanted him to stay home and rest—the latter part of that request essentially impossible with two small children and four borrowed cats.

And his mind whirling with all the components to this arson case.

Someone had tried to burn down his house, had threatened his family. Rest wasn't going to happen. Might as well be here and accomplish something.

Besides, he could breathe easier in his office; at home it felt like he constantly hung on the edge of a cold, stuffy, sniffy, his neck itched. Esme said maybe he had an allergy to the cats. Maybe. Probably. A decade back in Chicago he dated a woman who had two Siamese. Sniffed and itched and suffered when he spent time at her apartment. The cats always rubbed up against him or sidled into his lap. The relationship didn't last long. Oren's cats had left him mostly alone, except for Mr. Razzleberry, who seemed to like attention.

He told Esme he could well put up with allergies and keep the cats until Oren got out of the hospital and came back to Spencer County. Or until Millie got herself settled in a new place and could take them. He'd promised Oren they wouldn't go to a shelter.

Esme had called him stubborn regarding the cats, too.

But Basil had never considered himself that. Driven, he would concede to that. Not stubborn. There was a difference.

Basil reached for the phone, double-checked the number, and called the golf course.

The brief conversation frustrated him.

The manager was away for a dental procedure, and the assistant manager didn't know if the keycards were coded. But he agreed to check and would call back. If Basil didn't have this boat anchor on his foot, he'd drive over there and find a way to check the keycard records himself.

And since he couldn't drive … he stared at the pill a moment more before popping it in his mouth and swallowing. He might as well hurt a little less so he could think better. If he got too drowsy he could give in to the Dark Italian caffeine in the break room. He shuddered at that thought and reached for the crutches.

No use waiting in here for the assistant manager's call. He'd go back to the whiteboard and look through everything again, watch Sheriff Blackwell swear in Tug. Basil smiled. His old partner had wanted no part of working law enforcement in Spencer County, was only here to hide his daughter from a dangerous Chicago gang. Tug was a good friend, probably his best, and though he didn't like the circumstances that brought Tug here, Basil was glad to have his old partner around.

"Detective Meredith?"

Basil looked up to see Millie standing in his doorway, dressed in uniform. She had makeup on, but it wasn't enough to conceal the dark circles nested beneath her tired eyes.

"Do you have a minute, Detective Meredith?"

He gestured her in. If Millie was back, if she had a place to stay, she could take Oren's cats. The moment after that thought tickled his brain, he scolded himself. That was a selfish idea. He'd committed to caring for the cats, and Millie had enough to deal with. Allergies be damned.

She stood in front of his desk, gaze going to the crutches.

Millie opened her mouth, surprised. "What happen—"

"You haven't heard," Basil interrupted. "The firebug went after my place night before last. He missed, and I missed catching him."

She opened her mouth again.

"It was slick outside," he said, putting an end to the issue. "How is the chief dep—"

"Not good," she answered, her face and voice tightly controlled. "Not good right now. But he'll come through this and—" She took a deep breath and sat in the only other chair in the office. "And—"

"How are *you* doing?" Basil leaned the crutches against the wall again. "Millie, talk to me."

He saw her knuckles turn snow white as she grabbed the arms of the chair. Sucked her lower lip, and chewed on it.

"Millie—"

Tears suddenly ran down her cheeks and she raised a hand and brushed at them, smearing some of her makeup. She returned her grip to the chair.

"Damn. Told myself I wasn't going to cry. Damn. Not in front of anyone here. Damn. Damn. Damn. Can't let Sheriff Blackwell see me cry. Didn't want you to see me cry."

"Millie, talk to me. Sheriff Blackwell is busy in her office. She can't see you. Talk to *me*. How are you doing?"

"Awful." She drew in a deep breath, released it. "Everything, Detective—"

"Basil," he said.

She nodded.

"Basil."

He noticed her uniform was a little rumpled. Probably the one she'd worn the night she drove up to Indy and hadn't a chance to launder it yet … and her spare uniforms were ashes. One to wear, one in the closet, one at the cleaner's was the usual rotation. Maybe she had one at the cleaner's. But she probably wasn't that lucky, he thought.

"Everything. My grandfather lost everything. But I lost everything, too. Everything I owned—though it wasn't a lot—was in that apartment above Paul Blackwell's garage." She relaxed her grip on the chair, but didn't let go of it. "Zeke told me when I came in that your house was targeted, too. Didn't tell me you got hurt."

He thought about saying something, that he'd almost had the guy, that he'd ended up in the hospital because he stepped in a hole in the golf course, but he stayed silent. Basil figured Millie just needed to talk … and needed somebody to listen.

"I have two pairs of blue jeans and three sweaters. I bought them at a secondhand shop across from the hospital. A few odds and ends in a shoebox. And Jack Carr's latest big-ass book that I'm halfway through. Bought that across from the hospital, too." She closed her eyes and kept going. "I've been taking law classes online since early summer, thought I wanted to get a law degree. Told Pops I was going to."

A silence settled, and faintly Basil heard Christmas music, probably something Zeke had on. Taylor Swift's "Christmas Tree Farm." Taylor made it through an entire verse and started in on the chorus before Millie spoke again.

"I back everything up, you know. Always did, through undergrad, grad. Overboard about it. Backup external hard drive, flash drives. Everything backed up two or three times. Can't be too safe, right?

Never used the cloud. Never liked that notion, paranoid about it. Should have liked that notion." Another deep breath. "All my course work, my papers, my notes. All my little backup gadgets. My tablet, laptop, new laser printer. All burned. All gone."

Her shoulders shook, but she kept the tears under control this time. "Clothes, shoes, those can be replaced. The photo albums, no. My silly collection of Beanie Babies, no. That antique necklace Pops got me for graduation, no. I didn't have renter's insurance, didn't think I'd need it. Why the hell didn't I get renter's insurance? Who the hell *doesn't* buy renter's insurance? Would've cost about $200. Now I have two pairs of blue jeans and three sweaters," she repeated. "All of my course work gone. And after I found out about my fire, when I'm sitting there in Pops' ICU room watching him struggle for breath, I'm thinking about me, about law school, about if I'm going to continue with classes or hang it up because I lost everything I was working on. All my course work gone. And my books. My law books are ashes. I stopped thinking about Pops and instead felt sorry for me."

"Millie, I am so—"

"Don't say 'sorry'. I know everyone's sorry this happened to me and my grandfather … almost happened to you. I know everyone means well. It's nice of you and all, but I'm not looking for sympathy. You can't solve my problems, and I don't want you to try. I just needed to tell someone about my books, my course work." Much softer: "My future. Oh, and my car. My pretty little new-to-me Mustang. It burned up, too. Paul had let me use one side of the garage. At least I had insurance for it. Comprehensive. I'm going to use Pops' truck until I get the car replaced. Which will be soon because I hate driving that clunky truck."

Taylor Swift stopped singing and Sia took over with "Candy Cane Lane."

"Where are you going to stay?" Basil had an open room, which would eventually be for the baby. Esme was due the end of May. He could offer it to her, a temporary solution. But he should probably check with Esme first.

"I'm going to stay in Nang's trailer, at his Quick Stop. I have to pick up the keys sometime today. It's good of him, says he doesn't want me to pay rent, that I have more than enough things I need to spend my money on. He's right about that. But I'm going to pay him rent."

Basil had a selfish moment again, thinking the trailer was a double-wide, meaning enough room for Millie, and for Oren's cats.

"I wanted to work first," she said. "Keep my mind off stuff. Do something. I want to help catch the asshole who torched my future, all my course work, my grandfather's house, put him in the hospital. Couldn't keep sitting in that damn room."

Basil nodded. "Sheriff Blackwell will—"

"I know. I have to talk to her, see if she wants me now or to start at three or eleven. Figure if she wants me on a regular shift I might have a couple of hours before I start to pick up the key, some groceries, maybe some more clothes, you know." She shook her head. "Gonna have to order another uniform or two. My spares were in that apartment. Everything gone."

Basil realized how serious the threat had been against his family. Losing everything was ugly to envisage. Pictures of his kids, Esme's books. Past time to get a safety deposit box for the important papers or buy a fireproof safe.

"I will talk to Sheriff Blackwell, go back to her office," Millie continued. "I looked in. She had someone there, dressed like he was going to a business meeting or a funeral. She was busy so I came here. I needed to vent to someone. I didn't mean to take so—"

"You didn't take me away from anything," Basil replied, his voice gentle, though what he'd said wasn't true. He had the whiteboard and all its information he needed to get back to. "I got broad shoulders, Millie, good to lean on, and—"

The phone rang and he grabbed it, the number showing it was the golf course.

"You do track keycards," Basil said. "Excellent. I'm looking for—" He pushed the speaker button so Millie could hear; she certainly had a vested interest in this case.

"I know what you're looking for," the assistant manager returned. "You want to know who got to the golf carts those two nights."

"Yes." Basil's heart sped.

"I looked, only one person used a card to get into the storage building on any evening this month."

"Who?"

"It's okay for me to tell you that, right? I don't need some official paper do I? A search warrant?"

Not if you just volunteer it, Basil thought. Probably should have taken an official route and got a search warrant for the information. He could still do that, call across the street to the courthouse.

"I can get a search warrant," Basil said. "I'll—"

"Well, if you're going to get a search warrant, I'll just save you the trouble. It's David Halm."

Basil's grip tightened on the phone.

"Halm," Millie whispered.

"Thank you," Basil said and disconnected.

"Halm," she repeated. Millie met Basil's narrowed eyes. "Pops said the day before his fire, the day of his fire, the Halm teenager stood on the sidewalk and stared at his house. He thought it odd, maybe the kid was looking 'cause Pops had no decorations. But Pops never decorated."

"Halm teenager. That would be Jerome Halm," Basil said. His voice was low, but it dripped with ire. "The kid I arrested for a dozen joints in his pocket." The kid that had called him a black son of a bitch.

Basil had chased two people in the golf cart the night they'd tried to burn his house. Too dark, dressed dark, one taller than the other. Two people in the pickup outside Sheriff Blackwell's. Maybe there'd been two people at Oren's too, one on foot setting the canisters and striking the match, one driving the getaway golf cart.

David Halm and Jerome Halm.

David had his own golf cart, probably hadn't wanted to use it, divert suspicion. And he lived across the street from Oren, only two blocks away from Basil's. Didn't need a golf cart, could have walked. But full gas canisters would have been heavy, and a golf cart faster than men on foot. The golf course fence cut. It pointed to someone living outside the Village behind the fires. Maybe it all had been to divert suspicion. Someone outside? Someone inside?

Someone with a lot of hate.

David Halm had seemed like a concerned neighbor, helpful, courteous. His son was the opposite. Again the "black son of a bitch" flitted in his head. Maybe the father was just a better actor.

He grabbed the crutches and maneuvered around the desk, ungainly and noisily making his way to Sheriff Blackwell's office. Millie hurried behind him.

30

***

Piper drove to Santa Claus. Big, slow falling flakes hit her windshield and melted. The temperature outside had climbed to a sultry thirty-three degrees, signaling that the snow coming down wouldn't stick, and the thin drifts on the ground wouldn't stay much longer. The morning weather forecaster predicted it would warm to the high-thirties by the weekend. Maybe hit forty.

Piper hoped the weatherman was wrong. She wanted a white Christmas with Nang.

She loved summer, but found Spencer County's winters beautiful —Christmas card worthy scenes with snow covering the gray and a plethora of decorations to brighten everything. Some years back one of those happily ever after Hallmark movies was set here—sort of. "Snowed-Inn Christmas." They'd come into town and shot angles of the Welcome to Santa Claus sign. The rest of the movie was filmed in Winnipeg, Canada. The Santa Claus in the movie looked like a vibrant, large town, many times the size of the real thing.

She turned onto the street that led into Christmas Lake Village.

Tug sat in the passenger seat of Piper's Explorer. Piper had sworn him in quickly, gave him a badge, vest, cuffs, and a gun, and said she'd take him out to the range to qualify later. His musky aftershave, while pleasant, warred with the scent of peppermint from her candy cane air freshener.

"Had a helluva time driving in here to pick up Sherlock at the ass crack of dawn," Tug grumbled. "Guard had to call his house, make sure I was kosher-to-go before he let me pass."

"Hey, Sheriff!" Kenny Caine called and waved to her from his gatepost, his greeting loud enough for her to hear through closed windows.

"You? He tips his head says 'Hey, Sheriff,' and raises the gate."

"Mr. Caine knows me," Piper said, remembering that the sentry wasted too many of her precious minutes days ago showing off photos of his Portugal vacation and recounting a tale about a squid on the beach. "I've been through here often on this case."

She rolled down her window. "Mr. Caine, this is Deputy Waters. He will be coming into the Village the next several days to help with the investigation."

"Nice to meet you," Caine replied. "Hey, Sheriff. I've loaded more pictures from my Portugal trip. I got to visit Cristo Rei in Lisbon." He turned his cell phone. "Look how high up I was."

"Nice shot," Piper said.

"I've got more, just look—"

"In a hurry today, Mr. Caine."

"Oh, sure. Again, nice to meet you Mr. Waters." He waved them through.

Originally she'd planned to send Tug with Diego to investigate Vincent Lasko, the White Nationalist who'd made all manner of hate posts and used to live in the Village. Diego was still headed to Lasko's mobile home, but with Rocco instead for backup. Piper decided to follow the new lead at the Halm house herself and wanted another deputy in tow. She'd thought about bringing Millie, but told her to go shopping for clothes and supplies, get the key from Nang, and come back for the 3-to-11 shift. Piper would ask her for an update on Oren then.

"So Jerome Halm, the teenager … Sherlock arrested him a few days ago for pot in his pocket, right? He mentioned something about that this morning. Jerome Halm. Jerry. Scary Jerry. Millie said her grandfather saw the kid outside his house."

Piper nodded.

"Sherlock chased him a couple of blocks in the snow, got personal with some big lawn decorations, up real close with Rudolf. Sherlock was pretty pissed about it, would've probably let Scary Jerry off if he hadn't called him a black son of a bitch." Tug grinned. "And now you're bringing a different black son of a bitch to arrest him again."

Piper wanted to smile at that, but kept it in. She'd brought Tug because she would be stupid not to have backup. Basil—though he insisted on going—was relegated to desk duty at the office. No way would she bring her wounded detective, who had been released from the hospital only yesterday. A man hobbling on crutches could provide no help if this turned into a physical confrontation. And maybe she was a little afraid of Esme. Too, Tug supposedly had a world of experience, and Piper wanted to observe him, see if Basil's high praise was justified.

"First day of the high school's winter break is today, so Jerome might be here," Piper said. "Hopefully here so we can talk to him. This time of the day, his parents are probably at work. But maybe we'll get lucky, find them home for lunch."

"So the firebugs are a teenager and his dad. Racists, at least the kid is, and definitely cop haters," Tug said. "Maybe the mom's got a part in it. Sherlock is gonna—"

"I don't know if we're going to arrest anyone today," Piper cut in. "We can't assume they're the arsonists. The Halm keycard was used to access the golf cart building, but maybe not used by them."

Tug raised his eyebrows.

"Have to keep an open mind," Piper went on. "They're Oren's neighbors, have known him for years."

The radio crackled, Zeke dispatching a car to St. Meinrad's, a car in the ditch in front of the monastery grounds.

"It doesn't make sense that the Halms would burn Oren's house," she added. "So we look at the possibility that maybe their keycard was stolen or borrowed and someone else used it to get to the golf carts."

"Yeah, that's what Sherlock said. Open mind. He doesn't like the kid, but likes him for the arson. Said he can't imagine why the dad would burn down Rosenberg's house. Seems like the dad and Rosenberg are friends. But something could've changed in the neighborhood, shook up that goodwill toward men."

Piper turned onto Sled Run and parked in front of the charred shell of her chief deputy's house. It still looked desolate and sad amidst all the neighboring Christmas décor.

"And while you'd like to think you're keeping an open mind about this, Sheriff, deep down you figure the Halms *are* good for it. You think they're the guys because you're here," Tug continued. "That's why you sent your deputies to Lasko's trailer. You're the sheriff, the big dog, responsible for everything. Sherlock's out of commission. Your chief deputy is in the burn unit. You take me along because you need a seasoned backup in case your gut is right. You think they're the guys. And if they are the guys, you want to be the one bringing them in."

She didn't reply. But Tug was right. Even if it didn't make sense, she indeed thought the Halms were good for it—though why the hell go to the trouble of taking a golf cart from the course into the Village? Oren's was right across the street. They could have walked. Maybe they were trying to divert suspicion.

She'd learned in the early fall on Jerusalem Ridge in Kentucky that sometimes those closest to you are at the heart of evil. One of her best friends from her Army days killed some people on the Ridge and tried to kill her. Maybe neighbors close to Oren, who'd known him for many years, were at the heart of evil too. What grudge could they have against her father and Millie to burn the garage? And against Basil?

She radioed Zeke about their arrival, turned on her body cam, and got out of the Explorer.

Tug followed, checking his holster and zipping up his jacket.

The Halm yard was a riot of color, and she knew in the evening it would look even more impressive with the decorations lit. Oren's house and the Laubensteins' place were charred ruins, marring Sled Run's otherwise festive appearance.

She stood on the porch, rang the bell, and waited. In the yard to her left an older woman, likely a grandmother, helped a toddler build a snowman. She waved to Piper and turned back to her task. The snowman won't last, Piper thought, balmy high thirties coming.

She rang the bell again.

And again.

Someone was home because she heard music when she pressed her ear to the door, staccato, banging, heavy metal, likely Jerome's.

Rang it one more time and followed it with a knock.

Finally the door opened. David Halm wore blue jeans and an ugly Christmas sweater. Dark green cable knit with a lopsided four-tiered snowman holding a pink tricycle with a bent wheel. Maybe the design had some meaning, but she wasn't going to puzzle over it.

"Mr. Halm."

"Sheriff." He nodded to her. "Still looking into the fire?"

"Yes, and—"

"Do you want to come in?"

She raised her voice to be heard over the music. "Yes, please. This is Deputy—" She turned to indicate Tug, but he wasn't there. She stepped into the entryway. Halm stood in front of her, blocking her way deeper into the house, perhaps hoping this would take only a minute.

Looking past him she noted strands of garland on the mantle, a large Christmas tree with wrapped packages beneath it, a miniature village displayed on the coffee table, the banging music incongruous. The room smelled of pine and floor polish.

"Excuse the rock," Halm said. "Jerome loves his metal, and when he's not playing it over the speakers, he's in the garage jamming with friends. Says he wants to major in music, but he's got to make it through high school first. And I'm not sure what he likes is really music."

Still no sign of Tug on the front porch.

"What can I help you with, Sheriff?" Halm had a nice smile, but the right corner of his mouth twitched.

She saw something drift across his expression, unease, nervousness. There was a hint of worry in his eyes. She heard a door slam.

"I need to speak to your son, too, Mr. Halm."

He shifted from one foot to the other and looked beyond her shoulder. "What's this about, Sheriff? I already told your detective everything I saw the night Rosey's house burned."

"Have you been to the golf course lately, Mr. Halm?"

"What? No. Not since the end of October. I thought this was about Rosey's fire. What does—"

"Let's get your son in here. We need to—"

"I have him, Sheriff!" Tug appeared behind her on the porch, Jerome with him, handcuffed, a churlish expression on his face. "I caught him running out the back, just like he did when Sherlock was here before. Didn't have to chase him this time."

"You black son of a—"

"Jerome!" Halm shouted. Then he fixed narrowed eyes on Piper and his voice took an acid cast. "What the hell is this about? There's no more pot here. We've met with the DA, the charges are being dropped. Everything's fine."

"The golf course," Piper repeated. She realized Tug had disappeared to cover the back and stopped Jerome from bolting. Innocent people don't run, not in Spencer County. She turned to Jerome and stepped back outside onto the front porch. "Did you use the family's keycard at the golf course the night of the fire and—"

"I have the right to remain silent!" Jerome spat. "I want an attorney."

"Jerome!" Halm edged out, the small porch uncomfortably crowded. "Jerome! Answer the sheriff. Did you go to the course? Did you take a golf cart and—"

Jerome struggled against Tug, trying to get away, but the new deputy held him firm. The teenager quit fighting.

"All I did was open the door, Dad. I didn't do anything wrong. I just opened the damn door. And that's not a crime. I didn't burn down any house."

"You have the right to remain silent and refuse to answer questions," Piper said. "If you give up that right, anything you say can and will be used against you in a court of law." Her body cam recorded her reading the Miranda to him, and she'd repeat it at the station.

At her side, David Halm sputtered, a mix of profanity, disbelief. In his voice she could tell he was on the verge of tears.

"What did you do, Jerome? Dear God, what did you do?"

"I only opened the door, Dad. Used the card to open the door. I didn't do anything wrong. I opened the door and that was about it. I came home and put the card back in the drawer when we were done."

"And now you're going to jail," Tug said.

"Please get him a coat and some shoes," Piper told Halm.

Jerome was in his stocking feet, like he'd been the afternoon Basil had chased him. She watched the father shuffle back inside and head up the stairs. "Give me a moment," he said. Louder: "I'm calling your attorney, Jerome."

"Who did you let into the golf cart building?" Piper asked.

"Remaining silent," Jerome sneered. "I didn't do anything wrong. Not illegal to use our card. It's *our* card. Not illegal to use it. You can't arrest me for that. I'll sue you. False arrest. Profiling. Whatever. I'll have your badge. I'll sue you for everything you got."

"Not much goodwill toward men on this block," Tug observed. To Piper: "So Sherlock was right about Scary Jerry."

When Halm returned with a winter jacket and boots, he passed them to Piper.

"I called Corcoran's office. She's in court, but should be over this afternoon."

"Get your coat, Mr. Halm. We're bringing you in for questioning, too." Her gut said the father wasn't a part of this, saw nothing but innocence, grief, and incredulity on his face. But she needed to be sure. Maybe he was a good actor. "You have the right to remain silent," she began again.

"Lawyer!" Jerome spat. "I'll have your badge!"

"We'll get to the shooting range tomorrow," she told Tug as they turned off Sled Run with two suspects in the back seat. An unnecessary, but necessary trip to meet the requirements. She figured her temporary deputy could probably outshoot her.

31

---

2 p.m.

P iper smelled something delicious coming into the department.

"I brought Pho." Nang placed a thermos on Piper's desk then added a carton with a half-dozen spring rolls and dipping sauce. "The soup has bone broth today, good for winter. Rice noodles, green onions, chicken, bean sprouts. There's a tray of spring rolls on the table in the other room for everyone else." He produced a metal spoon wrapped in a cloth napkin.

Then he plopped into the chair opposite her desk and unzipped his coat. He didn't take it off, a signal he wasn't staying.

"I love you," Piper said, salivating. "I am so hungry. So busy, we didn't stop for lunch. But you didn't need to go out of your way."

Zeke fielded another phone call and turned down the volume on the Christmas music, someone singing "Up on the Housetop," a song more than one hundred and fifty years old. Not Zeke's usual style.

Nang's smile was gentle. "It wasn't out of my way. I need to visit our new building down the street, take some measurements to order a walk-in fridge. You were on my way."

215

"Thank you." Piper screwed off the thermos cap and used it as a bowl, pouring the steaming soup into it. She held her nose over it and inhaled, the spices and savory broth pleasantly drowning her senses. "This smells so damn good." She grabbed the spoon and started eating.

"Millie is in my trailer, the heat is turned on. I told her no charge for rent, but she disagreed and we settled on two hundred a month."

Piper picked up a spring roll, smiled, then dipped it in the sauce and feasted. The slivered carrots inside were crisp and sweet.

"She asked if she could have cats. I said yes. She wants to take care of Oren's cats until he is back. She can move them in as soon as she has time. I like cats. We have a good cat." Nang paused, apparently getting lost in thought.

An old cat, Marmalade, came with her house. She liked that Nang considered the cat his, too.

Piper continued to eat. The spring roll was delicious, filled with pork, shrimp, rice vermicelli and vegetables. She dipped another in peanut sauce and thought that his opening a restaurant in Rockport was a grand idea no matter the building it would inhabit. *Their* building, he'd called it.

"The double-wide has two bedrooms," Nang continued. "Perhaps Oren will stay there too until—" He shrugged. "I am not using the trailer, and it should be used."

"You're being generous," Piper said as she sipped more soup and reached for another spring roll. "That's cheap rent."

Nang shrugged again. "I hadn't wanted to charge her anything. But Millie says she has to pay me because she doesn't want charity." He made a huffing sound. "I told her she has to get renter's insurance this time."

"I love you."

"You shine." He got up, leaned across the desk, and kissed her forehead. "I love you more. I'm going to measure for that fridge. Then I'm going home, feed our furry friends and give Tater his pills, take him for a walk. I have to work late. My night manager called in sick. But first I have to go shopping, buy all the things for the Friday Christmas party I am catering for the Suttons."

"I might work late, too."

"Catch the bad guys." He waved and disappeared.

Zeke turned up the music. Bing Crosby singing "White Christmas." He must have chosen an oldies station.

Piper finished her lunch, intending to save some of the spring rolls, but instead eating all of them. She did save the rest of the soup for later. Then she dove into past arrest reports and complaints, looking for the Halms.

The music stopped sometime later. Piper rose, her search yielding no records for either father or son beyond a parking violation for David. She stretched and padded out to the dispatcher's desk, where Teegan had come on shift. Her spiced plum hair matched the color of her sweater, which was embellished with sequined snowflakes. She had snowflake earrings too and a charm bracelet with snowmen, angels, wreaths, and trees. Since Teegan had been dating Tug, Piper noticed she dressed a little less flamboyantly. And her pierced nose, eyebrow, and lip had small studs. Conservative for her.

"Sheriff, are all of Candace's Christmas cookies gone?"

"Yep. Should have saved you a few. Sorry."

"Maybe she'll bring more when she comes in tonight. She's been baking a lot." Teegan pulled a face. "But I was hoping for something sweet now. I'll order pizza later. You working late? I can get us a large."

"Yes, but not in the office. I'm going out on patrol after dark." Because someone in addition to than Jerome Halm was involved in the arsons and is still out there. "No pizza for me, but thanks. I have leftover Pho."

In the break room Tug and Basil were still at it. A section of the whiteboard listed Jerome Halm and David Halm, with bulleted points underneath including memberships and social media links. She noticed the spring roll tray was empty, wondered if Basil had been hungry enough to slide from his usual vegetarian fare.

"You've been here since seven." A glance at the clock: it read 3:15. "Go home. Halm's attorney isn't here yet."

"I want to question them," Basil said.

"I agree. I think you should," Piper returned. "But you're supposed to be on light duty, already put in eight hours, and Tug is driving you home. I'll keep you posted, record everything if the attorney shows up. She's still in court, so we might not have her until tomorrow. And they're not talking without her."

"Probably smart of them," Tug said.

"I have two off-duty Rockport officers on four-hour shifts tonight helping patrol, extra eyes out there, cruising by everyone's homes. So get out of here. Put your foot up. I'll keep you updated on Lasko, too. Get some good sleep."

Piper knew she would be lucky to catch a couple hours. Too busy, too jangled, too damn determined to get to the bottom of this. Too worried that another of her deputies would be targeted tonight, tomorrow, soon.

Three people sat in Piper's small jail: Jerome and David Halm, and Vincent Lasko. The latter had an alibi for the nights Oren's house was torched and her dad's garage burned; he was seen by at least a dozen people at a bar in Rockport. But he'd been arrested nonetheless because he grabbed an aluminum baseball bat when Diego and Rocco showed up to question him. He slugged Diego, hard enough to send the deputy to urgent care. They arrested Lasko for assault and put him in a cell.

Piper strolled back to check on them. Halm and his son sat in the other cell together, heads down.

"Mr. Halm, you and I could talk," she suggested.

"I'll wait for our attorney."

"I'm going to sue you for everything, bitch," Jerome snarled.

Pleasant young man, Piper thought. He's good for it. Whatever did Oren Rosenberg do to the teenager to gain his ire? And why also burn her father's garage? What had painted the target on her deputies? And herself? She remembered the pickup stopping outside her house, the man crab-walking to get close.

"I'm going to sue you! Word is you're already being sued, the whole county is. I'm going to shut you down!"

David Halm put his head in his hands.

"I want my phone call," Jerome said. He jumped to his feet and shook his fist between the bars. "I'm entitled to my phone call, and I want it now!"

Piper came near the bars and studied him. His eyes were rimmed with red; he'd been crying. Spittle bubbled from the right corner of his mouth. Where did such anger come from?

"Of course you can have a phone call," she said, her tone mild. "A person's right to a post-booking phone call is protected by the Fourteenth Amendment. Denying your phone call would be a violation of your civil rights."

"So give me my damn phone call!" He shook his fist again.

"Who do you want to call?" Piper was curious.

"None of your damn business. I want my phone call."

"The right to a phone call comes in after you're taken before a judge or magistrate to be arraigned," Piper went on. "And that won't happen until sometime tomorrow. You wanted to wait for your attorney, remember?"

"I'll sue you for everything, you black-loving bitch!" Jerome howled.

David Halm hung his head lower.

32

5 p.m.

J asper called itself "the wood capital of the world," perched a forty-five minute drive in the county to the north. That's where the Halms' attorney came from. She strolled into the department with her head tipped back, pointed chin leading. She stopped at the dispatcher's desk.

"I'm here to see my clients, David Halm and Jerome."

"I'll take you back." Piper had been in the break room at the white-board and saw her come in. Everything about the woman screamed attorney.

Brown pencil skirt, tweed suit jacket, cream colored blouse with a high collar, buttoned to the top. Polished leather shoes with only a slight heel, briefcase in one hand, designer purse slung over her other shoulder. Her hair was so blonde at first glance it appeared white, probably mid-length, but it was pulled tight in a bun, slicked straight back. Rimless glasses, small lenses, delicate birdlike features. Pretty, but severe. Looked to be in her early thirties. No coat, she must have left it in her car.

"Rita Corcoran," she said, extending a thin-fingered hand and raising her shoulder to keep the purse from sliding down her arm. "And you are obviously Sheriff Blackwell." Corcoran gave Piper an up-down, as if appraising her.

Piper shook her cool hand and detected a faint floral perfume, likely something expensive. Smooth skin, lacquered nails, a simple gold bracelet, no rings visible. She had earrings, three in each ear, the lowest small gold hoops, the rest diamond studs.

"Follow me."

"I want to talk to my clients alone, Sheriff, before you question them. I won't be long. It's already been quite a day. Feels like a day and a half. And you've no reason to hold the young man. A juvenile. I specialize in juvenile law and you can't hold him unless—"

"He was arrested on charges of burglary, theft, arson, and murder."

Corcoran inhaled sharply.

"David Halm hasn't been charged with anything—yet. I brought him here for questioning. He insisted on waiting for you."

Piper took her to a small room with four chairs and a wood table. She mused that maybe the furniture came from Jasper. Maybe her desk had, too. A moment later, she brought in David and Jerome, who she had put in handcuffs. "Let me know when you're ready." Then she left and closed the door and waited down and across the hall from it. The interview room wasn't like the ones in *Law & Order*; there wasn't a mirror that was a window she could observe through. That was the stuff of larger departments with more personnel and bigger budgets. But it had a video setup, and she'd turn it on during the interrogation.

Piper hadn't found a juvenile record on Jerome, sealed or other-wise, but she had an inkling something was there. Corcoran said she specialized in juvenile law, and the senior Halm had called her their attorney. They'd used her before. Maybe Jerome had been arrested and the charges dropped, hence no record. Or maybe a record had been expunged. *Something* was there.

Two deputies were in the department tonight. Millie was set to patrol in an hour. Piper called to her. They leaned against the wall shoulder-to-shoulder, waiting for a signal from Corcoran that she'd finished her consult.

"How's Oren?" Piper had meant to ask Millie earlier.

"Not good. Still not good. But there's some improvement, and he's not suicidal right now. That's something, right?"

"I need to visit him again, but that's not going to happen until we catch the—"

"That's why I came back," Millie said. They kept their voices low, even though the department walls were thick and it wasn't likely Corcoran and her clients could hear them. "Up there, sitting in his room, I felt helpless all the way around. Here, I can do something."

"You settled in the trailer?"

She nodded. "I went to Wal-Mart for some clothes, groceries. Nang's trailer is nice. Real nice. I hadn't expected it to be that nice. The little kitchen is a serious wow. I got some cat food and stuff, too, because he said I could have Pops' cats there. I need to pick them up from Detective Meredith tomorrow. I'm not a cat person, but Pops loves them. They're beautiful creatures. Always considered them aloof, though, except to him. They adore him."

Piper listened to her soft chatter. When Millie came up for air: "How are *you* doing?"

Millie tipped her head from side to side. "I'm doing. This is rough. This stinks. I really want someone to pay for all of this grief. My grief. Pops' grief. What that fire did to him, what *they* did to him, took from him. Took from me. They need to pay. The people you have in that room ... they need to pay."

Piper agreed, at least regarding Jerome.

"Not a word when we go in there," Piper admonished. "You understand. You're a witness, not a participant. You can't let your anger color anything in there."

"I watched the old *Star Trek* reruns with my grandfather while I was growing up." Millie nodded and almost smiled. "I can be Mr. Spock."

The other deputy in the office tonight was Isaac Zimmerman, Izzy, most called him. Nearly four years with the department, but Piper thought Millie's presence was the better call because she was a law student. Millie was a year older than Piper and had bachelor's and master's degrees. Piper had joined the Army right out of high school and wondered now if she should at least take a few on-line college courses. Zeke was committed to doing just that, wanting some sort of tech degree. After the holidays she'd chat with Millie and Zeke about some possibilities.

Millie was still discussing the various *Star Trek* series when the door opened.

Corcoran stood there, a sour look marring her perfectly made-up face.

"We're ready for you," Corcoran said.

Piper talked to David Halm first and solidified her belief that he had no part in the golf cart theft or the arsons. He considered Oren Rosenberg a friend, and tried to explain that his son was merely young and misguided, but Corcoran cut him off. Piper said David was free to go.

"As a courtesy, you can stay while I question your son," Piper said, as she turned on the video equipment. "It's not a right, and you can't interfere or I'll send you out."

She and Millie sat on one side of the table, Corcoran and Jerome on the other. David Halm stood in the corner behind his son, hands clasped in front of him as if he were praying.

One more time, she read Jerome the Miranda warning.

"You admitted to using your family's keycard to access the golf carts," Piper began.

Corcoran laid a hand on Jerome's arm. He didn't say anything.

"A golf cart was loaded with gasoline canisters and driven to Oren Rosenberg's house on Friday, December 11th, and—"

"I didn't drive the golf cart that night," Jerome said.

Piper saw Corcoran's hand tighten on the teen's arm.

"But you drove a cart three nights later, Monday, December 14th, to Detective Basil Meredith's house."

Jerome didn't say anything and Piper let the silence hang. She heard Millie breathe deep, like she was going to say something, but wisely stayed quiet.

"Who did you drive to Detective Meredith's house that night? The night of the fourteenth?" Piper pressed, figuring his silence indicated she'd guessed correctly, Jerome was behind the golf cart wheel then. "And why did you drive that night and not the night Oren Rosenberg's house was targeted?"

Jerome's lips were a thin line, crooked downward.

"Answer the sheriff," David Halm scolded. "Just answer the damn questions."

Piper had warned Halm to be quiet, but she was grateful for his outburst. It nudged the teenager to reply.

"He didn't know where the black guy lived," Jerome cut back. "I knew where he lived, so I drove. All I did was drive."

Corcoran tightened her grip.

Jerome slammed back against his chair, almost losing his balance.

David Halm's mouth dropped open.

"I didn't do anything illegal," Jerome sputtered. "I opened the door, okay? At the golf course. And I drove one night."

"Jerome!" A sharp warning from Corcoran.

"I didn't light a match. I didn't burn anything down. I didn't kill those people. Let me out of here. I want to go home. I don't understand why I'm here," Jerome fumed. "I didn't do anything bad."

"The golf carts weren't yours," Piper said evenly. "That's theft."

Jerome shrugged. "I'm not the one who stole them. I just opened the door with the keycard, drove the one night. I didn't kill anyone, or burn anything."

"Whoever was with you lit the match, completely destroyed Oren Rosenberg's house," Piper said. "Chief Deputy Rosenberg has been in the hospital with first and second degree burns over most of his body. And that fire spread next door and killed two people. Under Indiana law you are as guilty as the man who started the fire. Burglary, theft, arson, murder."

Jerome's eyes widened. Piper thought the teenager finally realized he was in deep trouble. She wondered if he'd been in the pickup the night her dad's garage burned, if he'd driven then or lit the match. And who was with him? Who was behind this? Why had they set the fires? What had motivated everything? Those were more questions she wanted to address.

"Why the fires, Jerome? Why were the fires set?"

He shook his head, defiant.

She tried something else: "Who was with you? At Detective Meredith's house, and who went to Chief Deputy Oren Rosenberg's?"

Corcoran leaned over the table. "We want immunity if my client gives up any names."

Names. More than one. Piper felt the heat rise in her face. It wasn't her call, immunity, but she could voice her opinion to the DA. No way in hell should this young man get immunity. All his youthful years should melt away in a prison yard.

"I don't have the authority to give you immunity. That's up to the DA. Give me a name, Jerome." Piper didn't want the DA to give the teen any concessions.

"Jerome, keep your mouth shut," Corcoran warned, her voice brittle. "Not another word. Do. You. Understand?"

Jerome nodded.

"My client will wait for the arraignment, Sheriff Blackwell. We're done here," Corcoran pronounced as she headed toward the door. To Jerome: "Not another word. Not one."

Millie took Jerome back to his cell.

David Halm shuffled out in quiet disbelief.

Piper sat alone in the room, fingers tracing a grain whorl in the tabletop that might have come from Jasper, Indiana.

33

7 p.m.

Piper drove around the block twice before pulling in the driveway. She hadn't noticed anyone watching her house, and no dark pickups were parked on the street. About half of the neighbors had their outside decorations lit, simple compared to the extravagant displays in the Village. The Hensons, Smiths, and Endicotts had icicle lights strung across the front of their houses and garages. Farther down the block were a couple of inflatables, Santa, a big snow globe, and something blue and green that had deflated and looked like an indiscernible blob. Next year she'd get some lighted reindeer. Her garage was big enough to store a herd of them. At least she'd managed to put a wreath on the front door. It was a pretty wreath, large with a red bow, and from a few feet away you could smell the pine.

She really loved Christmastime. It was also a big deal to her father, who used to always put up at least two elaborately decorated trees in the house and one in the sheriff's department, in addition to all the strands of pine garland and wintry figurines. He was about all things merry merry, and he instilled that in her, named her after day eleven in the *Twelve Days of Christmas*. She couldn't count the times they'd visited the Christmas store in Santa Claus and come away with new ornaments, and a few varieties of fudge that were usually consumed before they made it back home.

Piper wasn't in the spirit this year, the arsonists had squelched that. Good thing she'd done her Christmas shopping for Nang and her dad right before Thanksgiving, when she was feeling festive and singing along with the stores' holiday tunes. She wanted to get a little something for her fourteen deputies and the dispatchers, a tradition that her father had started when he was sheriff. She was running out of time to shop, and she was far from in the mood for it. Her dad always gave big fruitcakes to everyone in the sheriff's department, wrapped in shiny cellophane and topped with red and green bows that had overlarge candy canes threaded through them. More than a month ago he had handed her a mail-order catalog, announcing that the men and women of the Santa Claus Police Department would be getting pumpkin pie-spiced fruitcake this year, available on page twenty-one, and that she better put in an order soon for her deputies.

Her dad loved fruitcake.

Piper barely tolerated it. No way would she go that route. Some sort of food thing wasn't a bad idea, though, nothing that would take up space—for long—in anyone's home.

She'd be back to patrolling the county in a little while, could maybe come up with some ideas while she drove. Maybe something along the route would inspire her. But it was hard to think about Christmas and Hanukkah with her mind wrapped up in arsonists, two unidentified bodies, and Lefty Jay's lawsuit.

Nothing yet on dental records and DNA. She knew it took a while. It was never as fast as what the cop shows and *CSI* made it appear. It could take weeks to months, which was a considerable improvement from a decade past. Basil told her that in Chicago the average DNA wait time recently dropped from seven to four months, but he recalled a murder case from a few years ago where they had to wait eighteen months, and then it had turned up inconclusive.

She wanted to put names to the people burned in the Laubenstein house. That's what she wanted for Christmas. She also wanted the names of the arsonists Jerome Halm was involved with, but she wanted those now. Maybe DA Scales would cut a deal with the teen to get the information. She didn't like that idea, but she wanted them caught before they burned another deputy's house.

Nang said he'd fed the dogs and the cat, then walked Tater. The big ugly dog was the first to greet her when she came in. Camaro, her old golden retriever, was stretched out under the Christmas tree on his favorite place, the red skirt. He raised his head and wagged his tail, but didn't budge. Marmalade sashayed down the hall with only a casual glance her way. She didn't have to let them out; there was a doggy door in the kitchen allowing them access to the fenced back yard as they pleased. They pleased more often in warm weather.

She padded through the house, checking the windows and the surveillance cameras, and turning on a few lights to make it look like someone was home. She turned on the Christmas tree, too, and set everything on a timer. Let it go dark at 3 a.m. She knew Nang would stay at the Quick Stop until at least midnight, and he could disengage the timer earlier if he wanted.

She intended to stay out on patrol as long as she could stay awake, worried that the arsonists would strike again, wishing that Jerome Halm would have given her a name, and that the attorney would have encouraged him to talk rather than shut him down.

She stepped into the dining room. A beautiful poinsettia sat in the middle of the table; Nang's doing. One of the walls was adorned with photographs from the previous house owner's life, almost all of them military. The old man, Mark the Shark, had been in the Navy. She touched the photo of him standing on the bridge of a ship. All of the pictures would stay as long as she kept the house. There was a grand-father clock, stately and old. She'd had it serviced a few months ago, professionally deep-cleaned, leveled, the weights checked and mecha-nisms oiled. The repairman said it was a Lancaster County Pennsyl-vania tall-case, narrow-waisted style, with an unusual sweep second hand and an eight-day recoil escapement movement. The bell struck only on the hour. It had a hand-painted dial and a moon phase dial.

Probably two hundred and fifty years old, worth at least ten thousand dollars. He said to let him know if she ever wanted to sell it, he had clients who would be interested.

Piper wouldn't sell it. Like the photographs, it would stay. She listened to the clock, the tick-tick-tick sounding loud and seeming to echo in her head. Marking time. Life seemed to pass so quickly, things came in a blur ... her leaving the military, running for sheriff and being elected, meeting Nang, inheriting this house, getting married. Tick-tick-tick. Yet it wasn't going fast enough; she wanted it fast-forwarded to where she shoved the arsonists in her jail and threw the key into an impossibly hot fire.

She grabbed a can of Coke out of the fridge and went back into the living room, stood in front of the tree. It was perfect; of course it was perfectly shaped—artificial. Pine cones on the branches. Lots of ornaments, though not as chock-full as her father's. And candy canes! Those were new. A couple dozen red and white candy canes had been hung sometime while she was out. Nang knew she loved peppermint, and she plucked one off the tree and put it in her pocket. There were new ornaments, too, evidence he'd been to the Christmas store. A small saucer that looked like a cameo, a carved ivory man and woman in old-fashioned garb skating against a dark orange background. "First Christmas Together," was scrawled in silver in the ice at their feet. A little jar of marmalade, a miniature Camaro, and a ceramic Mr. Potato Head representing their cat and two dogs.

Piper smiled. First time she'd done that today, and it felt good. On her next trip to Santa Claus she'd stop at the Christmas store and find a coffee mug ornament, have them paint *Nang's Uptown Wok* on it.

She did one more walk-through, again checking windows and doors, thinking the house was much better with two people and another dog in it. She used to live in this expansive place with just Marmalade and Camaro. Another pass by the clock. Tick-tick-tick. Camaro was snoring under the tree; Tater had sprawled on the couch, his feet twitching in a dream.

Two people, two dogs, and a cat, a good house. Marmalade poked her head around the corner and meowed softly as Piper locked up and left.

She drove around the block two more times, still no sign of anyone watching her place, no dark pickup. The inflatable Santa had started to lose air and tilted sideways, its hand up as if waving to her. She headed out of Hatfield, north through Richland, and then toward Chrisney, a dinkburg with a population of about five hundred. One of her deputies lived there. The place used to have a high school, but that closed in the early seventies. Still had a grade school, and a small library. Several houses on her route were decorated, and down one street she noticed a group of children and adults caroling. She slowed, pulled over and rolled down her window. They were singing "It's Beginning to Look a Lot Like Christmas."

The colors and music melded into an idyllic scene, but it wasn't enough to lift Piper's mood. Who had been in the golf cart with Jerome? Whoever it was … were they out in the county right now, taking aim at another home to torch? Or had Jerome's capture cooled their plans?

She listened to the radio chatter of her deputies and the two Rockport officers patrolling. The dispatcher cut in and directed Millie to the Red Baron Tavern where a table of customers were getting a little too merry.

The carolers started "God Rest Ye Merry Gentlemen," one of the world's oldest Christmas songs. Piper rolled up her window and drove on, heading to Grandview on the riverbank, where Diego and Izzy lived.

Her cell phone buzzed: Zeke. Piper took it on hands-free.

"Hope I'm not interrupting anything, Sheriff Blackwell."

"Just driving, Zeke. Patrolling tonight."

Zeke made a crunching sound. He was eating something. A slurp. "I went through all that video."

"You didn't have to do that on your own time," Piper said, though she'd known he would and was glad for that.

"Eh, that's okay. Wasn't going anywhere tonight." More crunching.

Zeke was making her hungry. She pulled the candy cane out of her pocket, ripped off the cellophane, and stuck the straight end in her mouth.

"I figured out what you meant by 'seeing what wasn't there.'" Another slurp. "I had to look close, run it through a few times, check the tracking and shadows, all sorts of things. Got the idea from watching *Chicago PD*. Anyway, there are several gaps in the video."

"Gaps?" Piper pulled over so she could concentrate. She bit off a piece of the cane and chewed, the sharp taste of peppermint welcome. "Like what?"

"Well, I obviously can't tell you *what* is missing in those two weeks' worth of video 'cause it's not there. Maybe an orangutan in a Santa suit. Maybe speeding golf carts. Or maybe an old Volkswagen Rabbit tooling around. Anyway, I figured out that all totaled an hour or two of video got cut, all in little snippets. You can see it from tiny jumps in the video, shadows that don't match." Zeke chewed on some more of whatever he was eating. "I suppose it could have been an accident, the deletions. But I doubt it. There are so many, it has to be deliberate, right? I mean, Oren Rosenberg's house toasted, Detective Meredith's almost toasted. And the Rabbit. Most of the gaps are during the morning and afternoon. Actually, all of them from what I could tell. Now, if you had some big expert from a crime lab, he or she—"

Zeke rambled, and Piper let him as the information soaked in. One of the gate sentries at Christmas Lake Village had altered the video presented to her. Morning and afternoon? That was Kenny Caine's hours, though admittedly anyone with access to the Village cameras and equipment could have done it and just worked with that time range.

"Probably can't ever get back what was originally there," Zeke kept going. "The master's probably been written over by now. Probably no way to pick up the missing bits."

Piper didn't need the missing parts. Just knowing there were sections cut told her enough.

"Thanks, Zeke. You've been incredibly helpful."

"So, I helped you. Would you put in a good word for me, Sheriff Blackwell?"

"Of course, Zeke. A good word for what?" She chomped on another piece of candy cane, the peppermint giving her another tasty zing of energy.

"Tuscaloosa and Morgan counties in Alabama have openings for sheriff deputies and I'm going to apply. I only have to be nineteen in Alabama."

The candy was instantly bitter. "Sure, Zeke, if that's what you want."

"Thanks, Sheriff Blackwell. I really appreciate it." He took a long slurp of whatever he was drinking, the hollow sucking sound indicating he was at the bottom of the cup. Then he disconnected.

"Shit and two is four." Piper pulled away from the curb.

On another night she could have enjoyed the rest of her ride, all the decorations, the snow cover hanging on against the threat of warmer temperatures, the carolers. But the arsonists, Lefty Jay, Oren, and now Zeke had eradicated even a hint of merry merry.

34

10 p.m.

Etta James sang "Merry Christmas Baby" as Teegan finished filing invoices. Edgy and sultry, the dispatcher cranked up the volume and rocked her head back. James had become one of her favorite in-the-grave artists. Next on the track would be a soulful rendition of "Jingle Bells" by still-breathing guitarist Mark Whitfield, backed by soft brass and snare brushes. Her appreciation for jazz had soared since buying her old house in Santa Claus. Included with all the trash and treasure had been an extensive vinyl collection with a heavy emphasis on jazz and blues. She sold all the real valuable stuff, which paid off her mortgage and then some. But that left a still-sizable selection of LPs, including a dozen James, three of which had been recorded live.

An emergency call came in and she muted the music.

"9-1-1, what is the nature of your—"

Teegan listened and dispatched Rockport police to the corner of Fifth and Sycamore, where a disagreement had spilled out of a bar and onto the sidewalk.

"Merry Christmas!" the caller yelled as Teegan reported officers would be there in a handful of minutes. She waited on the line until the first cruiser pulled up.

Another call, this on the non-emergency line.

"Spencer County Sheriff's Department." She heard childish giggles. "Yes, our refrigerator is running, and no, I'm not going to chase it." At least they'd had a smattering of sense not to use 9-1-1. Hadn't the kids realized the department had caller ID? She thought about calling them back and scolding them, asking for a parent. Instead, she considered painting her fingernails. She had a couple of bottles in the drawer, Luscious Lavender or Marvelous Mocha. Another call nixed that.

"Spencer County Sheriff's Department, what can I— Oh, hi Mr. Halm." David Halm had called two hours ago to check on his son. "Sure, I'll go look in on him again. I'll call you back." She eased up from the chair, unmuted her music. Louis Armstrong sang "'Zat You, Santa Claus." His sharp trumpet wailed and a sinister beat tickled her feet through the floor. Not a festive song, but who didn't love Louis? Her grandfather told her that when he was a young man he'd snuck into Black Storyville in New Orleans and stood in the back of Funky Butt Hall, where Louis played one night. Only white man in the place, which sat in a red-light district. Her grandfather said he stayed until it closed because he thought the music was better in that part of the city.

"'Zat You, Santa Claus?" Teegan echoed as she hurried down the hall, hoping no calls came in while she was away from the desk. The jail was near the rear of the building, past a couple of offices and restrooms and just before the file room and storage. "'Zat you, Jerome Halm?" she asked, peering into the cell.

He flipped her the finger.

"Nice," she replied. "Need anything? A cup of coffee?"

He flipped her the finger again. "You're gonna burn, you purple-haired freak. Roger's gonna set your ass on fire!"

"I'll take that as 'no,' you don't want coffee." She spun on her heels and returned to the desk, placed a quick call to David Halm. "Your son's fine, just ducky. No, you already asked me that. No belt, no shoelaces. He can't hang himself. He's just angry, not suicidal. You have a good night, Mr.— Sure, you're welcome to call again."

The Louis Armstrong song was short. Next up, Ella Fitzgerald's "Frosty the Snowman."

Teegan settled back, listened to the radio chatter about the fight outside the bar on Fifth and Sycamore. A second Rockport car had arrived, and the participants had grown from two to eight. Emotions bubbled over at the holidays. She dispatched an ambulance.

Got to love this shift. She smiled.

E leven o'clock, Candace was late. She always showed up at least ten minutes early, dressed better than she needed to for the overnight shift and made up in photo shoot fashion. Teegan envied the dispatcher's appearance. Not that she'd try to emulate her; Teegan embraced her Goth side and assorted quirks. She'd just been turning it down a few notches since she'd had some dates with Tug Waters. Still, she couldn't nix the silver skull nose stud.

When Teegan had put on her purple Christmas sweater this morning with snowflake earrings, she'd planned on going to Tug's bar when she finished her shift. Listen to the music, snack on those splendid fries he served, and maybe play a game of pool with him if the Turtle wasn't too busy, perhaps dance. He was a good dancer. But when she found out he came in this morning and accepted Piper's offer ... or was that a plea? ... for a temp deputy job, those plans crashed.

Tug had worked a full shift and would be in again early tomorrow morning. She doubted he would be closing the Turtle tonight. That would be for his new hire, Wez, the Australian transplant. Teegan liked Tug a lot more than she wanted to. He was forty, five years younger than her. She didn't date younger men ... well, *hadn't* dated younger men. And she *hadn't* intended to find anyone, thinking she would go the solo route for the rest of her life. Selfish. Uncomplicated. Simple. Goth. Nothing might come of this Tug fling, and she still might live uncomplicated. But she hoped for it.

She truly enjoyed the Chicagoan's company. Liked everything about him. At least everything she'd discovered so far. And he'd mentioned that he wanted to see all of her tattoos. She would happily show them to him.

If he stuck with the day shift for however many months he worked here, maybe she'd ask Zeke and Piper about switching her own shift for a while, going dayside. Teegan gritted her teeth. She loved the three to eleven; it was when the interesting stuff happened, the drunks doing weird shit, domestic fights, and even the occasional slippy slide into the ditch could be lively depending on who was involved and where they slipped … and most of those happened before dinner because people were in a hurry to get home. If a pizza place was going to be robbed, it would be on her shift. Gasoline drive-offs, most often during her hours. Murders? Those had been discovered at night, her shift. But the arsons? The fires had been set later, after she passed the baton to Candace. She would've liked to have dispatched for those. Teegan didn't think she had a grisly or macabre bent, despite the attire she sometimes wore, the tats, and the piercings. She just enjoyed dispatching when her adrenalin rose. The calls Zeke handled tended to be pretty mundane. Candace's for the most part, too, except for the arsons.

Maybe someone would set another fire tonight. Sheriff Blackwell anticipated it. Teegan knew a couple of off-duty Rockport police were getting paid to patrol tonight, tomorrow, the night after that. All on-duty deputies were out driving. She was here by her lonesome. Her and the two guys in jail—Jerome and the White Nationalist—dudes with 'tudes, she called them. Even Sheriff Blackwell was out on the road.

Who the hell was burning houses?

She knew Jerome was one of the suspects, and wondered when his father would call again to check on him. Maybe when she walked back the next time Jerome would flip her double fingers and again warn that his buddy would set her ass on fire. That bothered her a little. Had he really threatened her? Or was he just flinging hateful words? He certainly wasn't going to do anything from inside a jail cell.

"He's just ducky, Jerome is," Teegan said. *A real charmer and a half.*

11:15. Where the hell is Candace?

Teegan wondered if she'd be putting in a double shift. That would be a pain, but she had leftover pizza to nibble on, plenty of caffeinated soda in the fridge, and she'd get to see Tug when he and Basil came in the next morning.

And there would be overtime pay, convenient as she still had a little Christmas shopping to do.

A radio call came in from Piper.

"Hi Sheriff Blackwell," Teegan answered. "Yeah, I'm still here. Candace is late. If she's not here in another dozen minutes or so, I'll call to check on her." She paused: "Or dispatch someone to her house. Yes, I can take a double if you need me to." An ugly thought flickered. The firebug had been targeting deputies' houses, could Candace also be on the list? She'd send a unit by her house now. An even uglier thought arose... could Teegan's own wonderful and huge fixer-upper be a target? Would Jerome's buddy Roger light the match?

"Didn't catch anyone? No more fires?" Teegan asked, as she sent a car to Candace's. "Nope, boss. No one else has reported anything suspicious. A fun little bar fight, though, and I heard Rockport cops made four arrests, one man taken to urgent care with beer bottle shards in his scalp. When you coming back? You're still gonna drive for a while? Don't you need to get some sleep?"

The reply was scratchy, Christmas music mixed in. The sheriff was playing a country station.

"Prisoners are good. Well, they're not good. They're both nasty pieces o' work and Spencer County is better off with them behind bars. The teenager has a mouth on him. Likes to flip the finger, and he called me a purple-haired freak. Said his buddy is going to set me on fire. I'll be glad when he—

"Yeah, he put a name to his buddy. Roger. It was Roger, yes I'm sure." Teegan was on hands-free and she suddenly gripped the edge of the desk at Piper's reply. "What? The kid never mentioned this Roger guy to you? No, he didn't say Roger-who. Didn't mention a last name. I could ask him."

Piper talked fast, and Teegan didn't catch it all. "Don't ask ... question. Can't be interro... without his... Corcoran."

"You think you know this Roger? Roger. Oh shit, Roger Carlson? The pot farmer. Dear, God, do you think—"

Piper's voice came over clear and slower this time. "I'm at the north end of the county, but I'm heading to the office now. Pull up Roger Carlson's files. I need to know if he employed Jerome Halm as a summer corn detassler."

"See you when you get here." Teegan signed off and took a call that came in on the non-emergency number. "Spencer County Sheriff's Department." She listened to the caller. "Sheriff Blackwell is not here, but she's on her way in. Will be here in a few minutes." How many minutes depended on how far north the sheriff was in the county and how fast she drove. "Do you want to leave a—okay, be rude and hang up. Pretty much everyone is rude tonight." Teegan clicked the laptop keys, trying to find Roger Carlson. Ah, there were some folders. She picked the earliest dated one and opened it.

"Sorry! Sorry!" Candace's shoes clacked against the tile floor. Tall and willowy, she came down the hall from the back entrance, clothes swishing with each step, three large shirt boxes balanced in her hands. "Grab these, will you?"

Teegan stood and took the boxes, a little heft to them, the aroma of sugar and cinnamon rolling through the cracks.

Cookies?

"I lost track of time," Candace babbled as she shrugged out of her puffy jacket and hung it on a hook behind the desk, fluffed out her long, curly hair. I was decorating cookies, been baking since I got up this afternoon and I didn't pay enough attention to the clock."

Teegan inhaled. "Love that smell." She meant the scents wafting out of the boxes.

"It's Haiku. Avon cologne. My neighbor is a dealer. I really like this fragrance. It's not expensive."

"Nice."

"I have an extra bottle at home. I always order two when they're on sale. I'll bring you one tomorrow."

"Thanks, but you don't have to." Teegan keyed the deputy to pass on Candace's house; she had arrived safe.

238

Candace's royal blue pants had a crease pressed down the front and the cuffs grazed the top of her beige brogues. Her suit jacket matched the pants and set off the white ruffled blouse. She wore a long simple chain with an onyx fob; a wreath pin on her lapel had tiny blue stones set in it, maybe costume, maybe real aquamarines. The facets sparkled in the fluorescent light shining above the dispatcher desk.

"My husband's coming home for Christmas," Candace gushed. "He got leave. I heard yesterday. So I've been baking baking baking baking, setting cookies aside, trying new recipes. He loves cookies. I love baking them."

"A good arrangement," Teegan observed.

Candace let out a long breath and sucked in another, batted her overlong lashes. Teegan noticed she wore a pale, creamy gold eyeshadow. "I brought some of everything to share. Can't keep too many at home or I'll get fat."

Cookies! Teegan wanted cookies and wasn't afraid of the calories. "Been quiet tonight, Cand, except for a drunken brouhaha on Sycamore. Everyone's out on patrol for the firebug. Sheriff is on her way in. David Halm will likely call you wanting his hoodlum son checked on. He's got a nasty mouth, the kid. What kind of cookies did you make?" Teegan had missed out on the selection Candace brought in yesterday.

"Milk punch cornmeal, chocolate gingerbread, spiced ginger-bread, classic sugar, triple chocolate peppermint, and Tortellini Dolci al Forno—Italian fruit stuffed. I used strawberry preserves." Another big breath. "Tomorrow afternoon I'm making cranberry Moscow mule gingersnaps and brown butter-cardamom spitzbuben. I need to do some rum balls, too, but I have to buy rum."

Teegan wanted to taste at least one of everything. The extent of her baking was buying a roll of refrigerated chocolate chip cookie dough at the grocery, slicing, and throwing it all in the oven at 350, save for a glob of dough she'd eat raw.

"I'll set these on a break room table and hunker down at the desk here so you can go home. So very sorry I'm late. I'll make it up to you with Haiku."

Teegan had her coat on when Candace returned. She wanted to get home, make sure her fixer-upper was safe. "I'm gonna take a couple cookies on my way out, if you don't mind."

"Please do. Make sure you get one of the triple chocolate pepper-mint rounds. I think they're my favorite." Candace sat behind the desk and reached for the headphones.

"I should bring something in, you know. Maybe one of those almond kringles the bakery carries. Gotta go shopping tomorrow anyway so, yeah. Oh, and Cand, Sheriff wants everything on Roger Carlson. I think most of the stuff is in the system, but there're prob-ably a few folders in the file cabinet, things that haven't been entered yet. The case is on-going." Teegan grabbed a half-dozen cookies and left out the back humming "'Zat You, Santa Claus?"

C andace smoothed her blouse, arranged things on the desk the way she liked them, and clicked off Teegan's selection of Christmas music. Candace enjoyed Christmas; this year would be especially merry with her husband coming home on leave. But she was sick of Christmas music. Stations had started playing it since a week before Thanksgiving, and the stores had been piping it in well before that. In fact, she could pretty well do without any kind of music, it was all contemporary clamor. Her husband? He liked indie rock, Pixies and Arctic Monkeys. She had an industrial-grade pair of noise-cancelling ear plugs she employed when he was home.

Roger Carlson. She needed to pull up his records. Looked like Teegan had started on it, said there would be more in the file room. The phone was quiet, only a little radio chatter. She'd grab a cup of coffee, find the physical files, check the prisoners on the way, and start to work. A bathroom stop first. She had to pee badly, should have gone before she left the house, but she'd been in a hurry, already late.

. . .

C andace was washing her hands at the sink when she heard something like a shotgun blast, magnified by a thousand. It was followed by a sustained roar. She felt the building jerk, and the wave of noise grew into the screams of furious jet engines. It hammered her eardrums, becoming louder still, impossibly and painfully. The floor wobbled and she fell to her knees, her chin striking hard against the edge of the sink. Blood in her mouth, pieces of teeth. Chunks of the ceiling dropped on her and she fell back, something heavy pinning her legs. The walls shuddered and the sink broke free of the wall. Water sprayed from the severed pipe and rained from the sprinkler overhead.

The building's smoke detectors keened.

Gas, she could smell it. A gas line likely ruptured and caused an explosion; she'd read about such things happening, about the number of people who died in the blast ... and about the people they couldn't find afterward.

She tried to get up, had to get to the dispatch desk, call for help, call all the cars, the fire departments, Sheriff Blackwell. Call everyone. A gas-rupture explosion, the only explanation, and it was her job to dispatch the units. Only not dispatch them *from* the department this time. *To* the department. Candace struggled, freeing one leg, then the other, and crawling closer to a door that she realized would not open. No windows in here, it was the door or nothing. It pulled inward, and a section of ceiling and ductwork had collapsed, blocking half of it and trapping her. She'd need an axe to get out.

The image of her husband flickered. He'd come home to bury her, not to celebrate Christmas and New Year's. Stepped away from the desk to the bathroom and hell was unleashed and she couldn't do her job and dispatch help. If only she hadn't been late to work, had peed before she came in. She would have been at the switchboard, she could have summoned all of them.

She needed help.

Prisoners ... the two were farther back in the building. Were they all right? The awful sound had traveled from there, hadn't it? They needed help, too. Someone outside had to have heard the explosion. And would have called 9-1-1. She was certain were it not for the racket of jet engines and the building falling apart, she would have heard the phone ringing.

9-1-1. "What is the nature of your emergency?" a dispatcher would have asked.

"I'm trapped," Candace would have answered. "The building has collapsed. Help."

But she was 9-1-1. And there was no one to answer the phone.

The roar crescendoed, and then stopped.

Candace couldn't hear anything, like all the sound had been swallowed from the world, leaving behind a terrifying emptiness. Slapped a hand against the wall, couldn't hear it. Shouted, no noise. The floor vibrated, dust filtered down from what was left of the ceiling. The lights blinked, the water continued to spew soundlessly from the broken pipe, then the lights popped out altogether. She moved her right arm, twisted and brought it down to her side, fingers finding her soaking wet jacket pocket and reaching inside.

Feeling her cell phone.

She smelled smoke and burning things, acrid and pungent, dusty and damp, her mouth dry, her face wet. She was crying, sobbing, and she felt the tears. She gulped in the horrid air like she was starved for it.

The blackness around her quivered, full of frightening energy, threatening more of the building would come down. Her trembling fingers danced over the smooth surface of the phone, finding the back with the almost flush camera lens and the little indentation where her index fingertip went to wake it up. She did that, seeing a flicker of light, shook the phone so the flashlight kicked on and she could see the keypad. 9-1-1, she wanted to dial, an exercise in futility. She was 9-1-1 and she wasn't there to pick up the call.

Someone outside had to have heard.

She had numbers programmed in, and she managed to find the contact screen, press the number for Sheriff Blackwell. Candace couldn't hear it ringing, still couldn't hear anything, sound didn't exist. But she hoped Sheriff Blackwell had answered and could hear her.

Over and over, Candace said: "Help, an explosion at the Spencer County Sheriff's Department. Help, an explosion at the department. Gas rupture. Explosion. Help." She felt the words leave her mouth, worked up some saliva and kept up the mantra. "I'm trapped in the bathroom. Prisoners trapped. Help, an explosion at the department. Gas. Help, an explosion—"

The world wobbled as a chunk of something noiselessly dropped on her and she silently let out a cry of pain. Another chunk, the phone falling from her fingers and going dark, too.

Someone had to have heard.

Everything went black.

35

11:50 p.m.

Flames and a thick column of smoke spiraled from the crumbling Spencer County Sheriff's Department building.

Piper screeched to the side a few blocks north to leave room for fire trucks, threw open her door, and ran down the center of the street toward the chaos. Her chest felt impossibly tight. She forced her way through a wave of disbelief, breath trailing away in the cold.

This wasn't real.

Her department. Her responsibility.

Smoking and crumbling.

The ground shimmied, and somehow she kept her balance.

Piper drew in the ash-filled air and dodged a Rockport police cruiser arriving on the scene. Another followed it, and farther away she saw the taller shape of a department Explorer. Their sirens competed for prominence. The cacophony and lights bounced off buildings like the downtown was a big, horribly brilliant pinball game. Yet more sirens, distant, none of them sounding like a fire truck: she could tell the difference.

This couldn't be real.

A nightmare, and any second she'd wake up.

There'd been no warning. A sustained and massive boom of thunder to the south, though not a cloud in the sky, had heralded her arrival in Rockport heartbeats ago. A panicked Candace had reached out on her cell phone, crying, shouting about a gas leak and explosion and being trapped. Then Piper had heard a rumble and Candace cut out.

Piper had tried to call her back. Nothing. Had tried to radio her dispatcher, but instead reached the 9-1-1 operator for Warrick County to the west. Spencer's emergency dispatch rolled over to Warrick if the system failed. "Dispatch Rockport fire and police," she'd told the operator. "And ambulance. Send them all to the Spencer County Sheriff's Department."

She'd cranked the speed of her Explorer far faster than was safe as she'd searched her phone directory, calling her father at home. "Bring some units, and Santa Claus's fire trucks," she'd shouted. "Bring them to the sheriff's department now!" She'd disconnected before he could ask questions. No time to talk. Then she'd called the Rockport volunteer fire chiefs on their cells, confirming they were on their way, that Warrick dispatch contacted them, and wondering what she'd see when she arrived.

She saw hell.

She focused on the building, *her* building, what stood of it.

Two more police cars arrived, officers spilling out, someone shouting and waving.

A booming honk and still more sirens, a fire truck barreled down the crossing street and she jumped on the sidewalk to get out of the way. Rockport had two volunteer fire departments, one near the downtown, certainly responding first. Another fire truck was coming after it, the response blessedly faster than she expected. Maybe they'd been out on another call. She prayed other volunteer fire departments would join, that Warrick was radioing for more help.

No way was this real.

Piper slid to a stop on the corner across from her building, the front quarter of which still mostly stood, windows blown out by a concussive blast. The building reminded her of bombed out places she'd crawled through in the Middle East. Gas leak? More like a bomb. She paused by the bench that Lefty Jay liked to occupy only to suck in a deep breath of foulness and determine her path. Then she raced across the intersection toward the building, leaping over a fire hose that was being stretched. The phone in her pocket vibrated; she couldn't hear its ring with all the strident sirens and shouts. She pulled it out: her father. No time to answer.

She vaulted onto the opposite sidewalk, feeling the heat coming from the building, the air seeming solid and nasty and making her heave. A hand clamped around her arm and yanked her back. She fought to stay on her feet.

A fireman. He shook his head and gestured toward the trucks. He said something to her, but she couldn't hear him. Didn't need to, she knew he was ordering her away.

Defiant, she wrenched free of his grip, ran to the front door and threw it open, the metal handle not scalding, no fire directly behind it. Safe to enter. Safe? No, it wasn't that, but she had no choice.

The clamor of the rescue units grew louder, sirens multiplying. Another deep breath of the nasty air and she darted toward what had been the dispatcher station. All the smoke detectors were singing, but the smoke here seemed minimal, a wispy suggestion that hovered at the broken ceiling. No sign of Candace. Part of the ceiling had fallen on the desk, obscuring the headset and laptop, the desk lopsided because the impact had broken one of its legs. The power was out, but the wildly flashing police lights and the lit Christmas decorations on poles and buildings across the street provided a riot of color to see by. The sprinklers worked, they doused her, and the winter air seeped in through the broken windows. Her teeth chattered.

She'd been a damn fool to run into a burning, unstable building with no protective gear. But she couldn't lose valuable minutes trying to talk a fireman into loaning her the proper jacket and helmet and to risk them keeping her out. This was *her* department, *her* responsibility, *her* dispatcher who was trapped.

She pulled at the lower right-hand desk drawer. It resisted, but she yanked with everything and got it open. Fingers fumbled inside for the keys. The firemen wouldn't have known where to find the keys, and they were busy with the fire.

Piper had always run toward danger in the Army. On her first tour she and a medic dashed into a burning pottery shop, part of a block that had been bombed. They managed to save three people that night.

Tonight she wanted to save three more: Candace and the two prisoners in the jail.

Was anyone else inside? Had Teegan gone home? If her night shift deputies had not been on patrol looking for the arsonist, at least one of them would be here. She would have been here, too, obsessed with this case.

The sprinklers cut out.

She darted down the hall lined with historic photographs of city hall and past sheriffs and into murky shadows where the outside light barely reached. Jail keys in one hand, cell phone in the other, she ignored the call coming in and turned on the flashlight function. Past the break room where more chunks of ceiling had fallen and more windows had broken, past her office. A glance inside showed the wall behind where she always sat had collapsed and pieces of masonry covered her shattered desk and chair. The poinsettia was on its side on the floor, spilled from the pot. It had been the largest, prettiest one in the store.

Ahead was rubble, the air so thick with dust she could see it drifting in the beam of her flashlight. It hurt to breathe, but she pressed on, stepping over bricks and chunks of plaster, passing another office, Detective Meredith's, and coming to the women's restroom door. She tried to push it open, but something blocked it. Water spilled out from under the crack making the floor slick. Was Candace in there?

Piper pounded on the door. "Candace!" She pressed her ear to the wood, detecting the shushing spray of water. She shoved her shoulder against it harder, budging it an inch or two. "Candace?" Still nothing. She'd come back to it, grab a fire extinguisher and use it to batter the door open.

Other sounds intruded. Sirens, men shouting, an irregular thumping and thunking seemingly coming from outside. The whack of tools against brick?

She bent over gagging, the air palpable and cloying with awful burnt scents. Keep going. Piper picked her way over a section of buckled hallway, trying to keep her balance as she stepped on pieces of plaster and bricks, ducking under a hanging piece of ceiling tile. Electrical wires dangled, and she avoided them. The power seemed out, but she was cautious nonetheless. More thunking and thumping from outside, maybe firemen trying to get at the fire, which appeared centered at the back of the building where storage and the file room were. And just before them, the jail cells.

That's why Piper had rushed in here, for the keys to get the prisoners out of the cells. Maybe the firemen had something that could bust the bars; she didn't know, not acquainted with all of the volunteer departments' equipment. If she made it out of here, she'd familiarize herself. But this was her building, her responsibility to get the prisoners to safety. And Candace. The dispatcher was in here somewhere.

Her chest grew tighter, the air hotter. She saw light ahead and shook her cell phone to turn off the flashlight, shoved it in her pocket so she'd have a free hand.

The light was from something on fire. A few yards forward and to her right were the cells; whatever burned was beyond them, playing with the shadows and twisting them into malevolent shapes.

"Get me out of here, you bitch!" Jerome Halm was alive, his cell intact.

The cell past it, where Vincent Lasko was held, had not fared as well.

"You bitch!"

"Shut it, Jerome!" Piper hollered, in no mood to deal with him or his mouth. She stopped in front of his cell. He grabbed the bars and continued to curse at her as she fit the key in the lock and turned it. "Go out the front. Be careful," she cautioned. "Take it slow. And stay put. You're still under arrest."

He pushed past her, deliberately knocking her down, the back of her head hitting the wall across from the cell.

"I see the sheriff!" This came from where the fire burned. "Can't get to her. Too far."

Piper struggled to her feet, teetering on a chunk of fallen ceiling and stretching to the other cell.

"I'm all right!" she shouted, hoping the firemen could hear her. Doubtful. The crackling of flames and the whoosh of water from their hoses took over. The smoke detectors stopped wailing and she heard something sputter. Piper fitted the key in, turned it, and wrestled with the door to get it open despite the debris that had fallen in its path.

"Vincent! Vincent Lasko!" The shadows were thick in here, and once again she pulled out her cell phone, shaking it to get the flashlight and moving the beam until she found the man half-buried under bricks.

It was like the pottery building on her first tour. Dangerous. But she had someone with her then to share the risk. Not now. She muscled her way to him, dropped to her knees, setting the light on the floor, and tearing at the bricks. He moved.

"C'mon, Vincent, we have to get out of here." Piper worked faster, slicing her fingers and the palms of her hands, ignoring the pain, and pulling still more of the rotten air deep into her lungs. Finally clear, she tugged on him and he roused. "You have to help," she panted. "I can't carry you like this."

She'd done fireman carries before on tour, but she wasn't as battered and exhausted. "Vincent!"

He got to all fours and she levered him up, pulled his left arm over her shoulders and took his weight on her right side. Couldn't tell how badly injured he was, but he managed to shuffle beside her, didn't say a word, but moaned with every step. His head dropped down, chin against his chest. She guided him. Difficult over the rubble, and when they reached the women's restroom, she propped him against the wall, grabbed a nearby fire extinguisher, and rammed it against the door.

"Candace!"

She thought she heard something. A murmur, gasp. She hit the door again and again, cracking it, but not breaking it open.

"Candace!"

She'd get Lasko out; he looked terrible, then she would return for her dispatcher.

Water continued to pour onto the floor under the restroom door. The pool had spread past her office and reached inside the break room by the time she managed to get Lasko out the front door. She fell on the sidewalk, taking him down with her.

Hands pulled her up by her armpits, and then someone lifted her.

"Vincent," she said.

"We're getting him."

"Candace." She pushed a hand against the police officer who carried her. "My dispatcher is in the restroom, trapped. I have to get her out. Candace—"

"We'll get her!" Someone else called. "We got the sheriff!"

"Is anyone else inside?" This from another officer who rushed up.

"Candace." She nodded as she was carried away from the building. "Candace," she repeated. "In the bathroom. Maybe Teegan's somewhere. I don't think anyone else. But I'm not sure."

Piper saw the ambulance she was being carried to. "Put me down. Now." She intended to go back in.

"No," the cop returned. "I am not going to put you down. I don't work for you."

She briefly struggled, but gave up. So damn tired, so hard to breathe. Her head throbbed. Every inch of her hurt.

"Why the hell did you go in there? What were you thinking?" This came from James "Jimmy" Wollach, chief of the Santa Claus Volunteer Fire Department. He loomed over her. "What the hell were you thinking?"

"You didn't know where the keys were," she gasped, every cell in her body aching. "But I did. I had to get the keys to the jail."

36

1 a.m. Thursday, December 17ᵗʰ

P iper sat on the back bumper of an ambulance, refusing transport but accepting the care of a paramedic. She knew a trip to the ER would be a good idea; all the fumes and dust she'd inhaled had likely done something rotten to her lungs. Breathing still seemed onerous even though she'd sucked down a lot of oxygen through a mask. She didn't have time for a hospital. Not yet.

The cuts on her fingers and palms had been treated with ointment and wrapped with gauze. She had a gash on her forehead and a knob on the back of her head. Somehow she'd sliced through the sleeve of her heavy winter jacket and cut her arm; she hadn't felt that. They'd bandaged that wound, too, argued that she should have stitches, and wrapped her in a blanket. The sprinklers had thoroughly soaked her.

"You really should let us take you—"

"I'll go to urgent care," she rasped to the paramedic, "after this is over. Some things I have to do first." One of those was a quick call to Nang, begging him to stay home and that she'd talk to him again soon.

Dry clothes would help. She had a spare uniform in her locker. But it looked like that area of the building had been destroyed, and she wasn't about to lose time with a trip home to change. Piper let out a hollow laugh. A lot of things were gone. That beautiful poinsettia, the photo in the silvery frame of Nang and her from their wedding reception, pictures on the wall of past sheriffs, including her father. The fancy coffee maker gifted the department, along with some if not all of the records from the rubble that remained of the file room. Maybe evidence from the bodies found in the Laubenstein house was gone too. The drone. Candace's fancy cookies. The flash drives filled with video footage.

Before that, Millie had lost everything in the apartment fire. Oren had lost his house and all his treasures. Her father had lost his garage and the apartment above it.

A pumper tanker pulled close from around the back of the building, and Piper watched another hose unrolled and dragged toward the parking lot. The fire still burned.

A part of her wanted to deny the destruction. But the stink of burned and blasted things and the exhaust from the fire trucks and police cars hammered the rotten reality into her brain. Through the racket of firemen shouting and dousing the building, cops yelling orders to each other, and a paramedic hollering: "anyone else need help?" she picked up the buzzing chatter of disbelief.

"Was that the sheriff's department?" asked the ambulance driver. Piper guessed he was unfamiliar with Rockport. "Police department? One of those, right?"

"Looks like a missile hit it." This from a tall man on the corner, pajama bottoms visible beneath his long winter coat. "Ain't no fixing that. It's toast."

"If anybody was in there, bet they're dead," said a skinny woman next to the pajama man. "They're in pieces."

"You put out that cigarette, Henry," demanded a man Piper had often seen downtown. "Not right to smoke outside a fire. Salt in a wound. And it's bad for you."

Other comments swirled, coupled with all the sounds and sights making Piper dizzy and taking her back to her Army days. This piece of her little rural county looked much like the bombed-out wreckage she'd crawled through on her first tour more than sixty-five hundred miles from here. The Middle East. This shouldn't happen in Spencer County. Couldn't. She'd had trouble breathing back then, too, with all the dust and smoke from bombs.

The streets around her building's carcass remained bright with Christmas decorations and the flashing lights and headlights of the trucks and cruisers. Garish and ghastly. Brilliant and horrible. A mini war zone frosted with stubborn clumps of snow that clung to the edges of sidewalks and empty buildings.

A nightmare holiday tableau forever glued in her brain.

Her head pounded and her fingers ached. She turned down a painkiller, needed to stay sharp.

Vincent Lasko and Candace had been whisked to the hospital in Owensboro across the river, both with life-threatening injuries. Fire Chief Wollach said she'd saved the prisoners' lives, as shortly after she'd gotten them free, the part of the building with the jail collapsed. The firemen wouldn't have gotten to them in time.

Her father had taken Jerome Halm to a holding cell at the Santa Claus Police Department. Jerome would go to a regional jail after his arraignment tomorrow … she knew DA Scales would rail against any proposed bail amount. Jerome's father confirmed his son had been a detassler for Roger Carlson. Certainly where Jerome had gotten his marijuana, she thought, certainly why he was loyal to Carlson.

"I didn't believe him, but Sherlock was right," Tug said. He appeared around the corner of the ambulance, wearing the sheriff's department jacket she'd given him and a Chicago Bears knit cap. His sweatpants covered whatever shoes he had on and dragged on the pavement. "Sherlock was definitely right. This chunk of Indiana is not boring." He paused. "And not safe, apparently, if you have a badge."

Piper wondered how Tug had heard about the explosion. Ah, Teegan. She hung back behind him. Piper knew the dispatcher had a police radio in her house, and even though Spencer County's system had cut out, there had to have been a massive amount of chatter from Warrick and all the cruisers, and that had drawn her and others here.

"I called Sherlock, let him know about all this," Tug continued. "He wanted me to pick him up and bring him here, Esme wasn't about to drive him. I wasn't about to argue with Esme. I said I'd give him an update and meet him around seven for breakfast and a ride into work. Wherever it is you say we're gonna work from. A helluva thing, this." He gestured to the ruined building.

"The Rockport Police Department is giving us a couple of rooms to use until we get something figured out," she replied, her voice weak. "Yes, this is a helluva thing."

"Bomb?" Tug pressed. "Looks like a bomb. Doesn't look like a gas explosion. I've seen both."

"Bomb," Piper said. "Delivered by a big pickup, six wheels, tandem rear axle. Right up to the back of our building through the parking lot. Probably rammed into it, gas pedal stuck down, the driver jumping out. We'll look for surveillance footage of the area. Not much left of the truck, but it was definitely a special-ordered farm vehicle. Wollach thinks it was loaded with fertilizer and who knows what else."

"Oklahoma City."

"Something like that," Piper said.

"You know who could—"

"Could? I *know* who did. Roger Carlson. I'm waiting for Diego and Thresher to get here, and then we're going after him." Piper wanted to stay here, see the last bit of the fire put out, thank all the firemen and police. Watch them run the yellow tape around the perimeter to keep people out. She'd post a deputy to help with that.

A plethora of Rockport and Santa Claus police officers busied themselves helping the firemen and keeping back lookie-loos who had emerged from their homes in the neighboring blocks, all drawn by the lights and chaos. She needed to thank everyone. But she also needed to catch Carlson. And call Candace's husband, somewhere on his way back to the United States.

Time to delegate.

Millie was here, a dozen feet away talking to Edward Graham, one of the Rockport volunteer fire chiefs. Izzy and Rocco stood across the street, perched on a curb, Rocco filming with his phone. Tug and Teegan looked to be staying around, but she'd need them in the morning ... later this morning.

"Go home," she told Tug. "Get some sleep, and then pick up Basil. You've got something to do before you come in."

"National news, this is going to be," Tug mused. "A handful of years back George Floyd protestors burned a police department in Minneapolis. I think the only other time something like that happened was a hundred years before that, Milwaukee. National news will catch this, especially because it's a hate crime."

"A lot of hate." Except this wasn't hate based on race or religion. It was hate because the sheriff's department had put an end to Roger Carlson's pot industry and cost him everything. Everything except his hate.

"I don't want headlines," Piper admitted. "I just want to lock up that son of a bitch forever."

She took one more deep hit of the oxygen then pushed off the ambulance. "Get some sleep, Tug," she repeated. "I need you sharp tomorrow. Later this morning." She spotted Diego jogging down the sidewalk; he had Thresher in a bulletproof vest on a leash.

"Millie," Piper called, waving to get her attention. "A Hazmat cleaning service will have to deal with this. Don't know when we can get one here. But as soon as the fire departments give you the okay— ask Wollach and Graham, you, Izzy, and Rocco go in and grab as many files from the cabinets as are salvageable. If they're soaked, fine, we'll dry what we can. The rest is all for Hazmat. Just get the files."

Millie nodded and Piper headed toward Diego, holding up her bandaged hands. "I need you to drive."

She also needed to find an address for Roger Carlson and has family; his farm had been shuttered and he was living in a rental somewhere in the county. She'd wake up DA Scales and get that information, then contact Warrick dispatch to put out a BOLO on the Carlson clan, including all their vehicles in case they were trying to flee.

As Diego pulled away from the curb, Piper ignored her aches and watched the smoke continue to rise from what had been the Spencer County Sheriff's Department building. The radio chattered with news of the explosion in Rockport. Bile rose from her stomach as she fought against the burnt and smoky taste she couldn't get out of her mouth.

37

4 a.m.

S pencer County covered four hundred and ten square miles, a dozen of that water. 738 miles of county roads. 147 highway miles. Deputies were driving all of them, with an assist from Rockport and Santa Claus police. The state police were looking, too. BOLOS had been sent out to neighboring counties in Indiana and Kentucky with detailed descriptions of the Carlsons and their vehicles. Gas and hours were being spent, and Piper suspected a lot of coffee was being consumed in various efforts to stay alert.

They'd picked up Carlson's wife and son an hour ago at a rental house in Huff on the eastern edge of Spencer County. No sign of Roger or his black pickup and no leads to follow. But there were a few gas canisters at the back of a storage shed on the rental property, and a map tacked on the wall with several locations circled, all residences of sheriff's department employees. Deputies and police were regularly patrolling past those areas.

Piper's gut told her Roger Carlson hadn't left Spencer County, that maybe he intended to burn more houses before he left this world, but she covered the bases by checking with Evansville, Owensboro, and other nearby cities.

Milton Strong, a Santa Claus officer, reported seeing Carlson's pickup leaving Grandview, then lost track of it. A Rockport cop spotted it in Rock Hill and chased him into Enterprise in the south before losing him on a side street. It looked like Carlson was sticking with rural roads.

Another sighting came in Buffaloville, not far from Rockport. Piper heard sirens through the radio.

"That's close," she said. "We're going there."

Diego hit the lights and siren and pushed the Explorer past the speed limit. Piper hated being the passenger, wanting to drive and be in control. Smarter, letting her deputy do this, her hands bandaged and her breath raggedy. Thresher, the department's sleek Belgian Malinois, was in the back, alert, muzzle twitching with the anticipation of action. She hoped they wouldn't need the dog, but she was glad to have him along.

"Got him." This from Strong. "Got the truck south of Lincoln City, turning on 162 north of Lincoln State Park. Closing on him. He's really cruising."

Diego pushed faster. They'd seen no cars this early in the morning, the streets deserted, the county roads empty. Too late for celebrants, too early for first-shift workers. They sped past Gentryville and up to 162, slipped east and opened it up even more, farm fields screaming past Piper's window, the sirens and chatter dancing over the radio. The few farm houses they passed were dark.

"I want him," Diego said, his voice hard. Diego's place had been circled on the map. He'd also been on the scene when Carlson's marijuana facility was discovered.

Piper didn't reply, just stared out the front window and willed the Explorer to catch up with Strong and Roger Carlson. She wanted him too.

"Pulling him over," Strong reported over the radio. "No, wait. He's back on the road."

Radio chatter indicated deputies and police were joining them on 162, a convention of flashing lights and sirens.

Short minutes passed and Piper held her breath.

"There!" Diego leaned forward.

Ahead were the blue strobes of Strong's Santa Claus police cruiser.

"Get ahead of him," Piper urged.

"You got it." Diego swerved left, the Explorer protesting, and laid the gas pedal flat. The car juddered and Piper gritted her teeth. Thresher whined.

They passed the Santa Claus cruiser and caught sight of the back of Carlson's pickup. The plates had been muddied, only half the numbers visible, but they knew it was the right vehicle. Who else would be fleeing from police at this hour, and with gas canisters in the bed of a truck with a gray mesh tailgate? Perched higher in the Explorer, Piper could see the tops of the canisters—four of them.

They were gaining on him when flashing lights came from the other direction. Piper rolled down her window and leaned out, the cold wind whipping her hair and stinging her eyes. She managed to grab the mic, flipped a switch, and shouted into it. The Explorer had an external speaker.

"Roger Carlson, pull over. Pull over now!" She repeated it, not knowing if he could hear her, his windows rolled up, sirens piercing the air. He was heading toward Santa Claus, and she wanted him stopped before he could get there. A car chase in town would be too dangerous. They wouldn't pursue at high speed, and could lose him.

Piper was about to give Diego instructions, but stopped herself. Diego knew what he was doing. He inched even with Carlson, the lights in the opposing lane closing. Jinking the steering wheel to the right, the Explorer's front fender brushed the back of the pickup, pushing it off the lane and onto the shoulder. Carlson forced the truck back on the pavement, but that didn't last. Diego pressed forward and again shoved the pickup, this time with more force, a textbook maneuver.

Piper heard the scrape of metal on metal and felt the jolt of the collision. The truck went off the shoulder and down a low embankment, and the Explorer half spun before Diego righted it and slammed to a stop on the side, gravel flying and sounding like bullets ricocheting in the wheel wells. Piper was out of the seatbelt and out of the car before Diego had turned it off.

She turned on her body cam, heard him start to radio a report, the words lost to the chorus of sirens that seemed to come from all directions. She barely registered the cold as she scrambled down the embankment, losing her balance and picking herself up in time to see Roger extricate himself from his pickup that had gone nose down over the side.

"Stop!" she hollered with as much power as she could muster. Piper's voice lacked authority, her lungs compromised, breathing still an effort. She should be in urgent care, not trying to run through waist-high dead weeds in a farm field after a maniac. "Stop!" The scents of rotting vegetation and wet ground burrowed into her senses.

Carlson kept going, but he wasn't fast. The ground sodden and uneven, the weeds tangling, he struggled to gain distance.

"*Nimm ihn runter!*" Diego shouted from behind her.

It was German for "pull him down." Thresher had been trained in that language.

The brown and black dog shot past Piper, cutting through the weeds like they weren't there. Then he leapt, flying, seventy pounds of dog slamming into Carlson's back and dropping him. Piper hurried, holding her side and gasping for air. Diego charged after her, passed her, and skidded to a stop next to Thresher, drawing his gun.

"Stay down!" Diego shouted. To Thresher: "*Freigeben.*"

The dog released Carlson and Diego holstered the gun, grabbed Carlson's right arm and then the left, wrenched them behind his back and clicked the cuffs.

"Your collar," Piper panted when she caught up. "You read him."

She was proud of her deputy, of the Malinois, of her whole department, thankful to be a part of it. She had good, competent people, and despite everything, the fires and the bomb, they'd won this day.

The sirens had stopped but lights kept flashing from a half-dozen cars, blue and red strobing crazily across the slush-dotted field and disappearing against a black sky that was graying at the edges. Sunrise was an hour or two away.

Diego pulled Carlson to his feet.

Carlson glared at Diego, and then turned his icy stare to Piper. "You ruined me," he grated "Ruined my life. My family, farm. Ruined everything!"

"We didn't ruin you, Mr. Carlson." Piper worked to keep her voice flat, almost businesslike. "We just arrested you, shut down your operation. You ruined everything all on your own."

38

---

8 a.m. Friday, December 18ᵗʰ

T he blueberry pancakes were damn tasty, Sherlock. Esme and the kids went all-out for us. Eggs, orange juice, not enough coffee to stop me from yawning. Good coffee, though. But all you drank was that herbal shit." Tug yawned and slapped the steering wheel as he pulled out of Basil's driveway. "I stayed on the scene too late last night. Ha! Too late this morning. It was something. I told the sheriff you're right. This county is not boring. We get done with this shift, I'm going to bed. My sister's here. She can handle stuff at the bar, look after Angel for me while I catch all the Zs I need."

Tug continued to chatter and Basil growled. He had wanted to be at the department when all hell was breaking loose. No one agreed to drive him. He almost attempted to drive himself, but his boot-contraption would have made that impossible, not able to tell how much pressure he was putting on the gas or the brake; an accident waiting to happen. A taxi was out of the question since the county didn't have any. He would have had to call one in Dubois County to the north, or Owensboro, KY, to the south, either costing more than was practical. There was Uber, but they turned him down because of the early hour.

Tug drove to the small brick guard post and nodded to the sentry, Kenny Caine. Caine raised the bar and waved them to pass through. But Tug stopped even with the post and turned off the engine, set the flashers.

"This might be fun," Tug said.

Basil opened the passenger door, and with some amount of effort got out, grabbed his crutches and hobbled over to the narrow door, rapped on it. Tug followed.

Caine hesitated before opening it. "What? Something wrong?"

"You know about equal liability, right?" Basil looked over his shoulder, asking Tug.

"Yeah. A deputy is the alter ego of the sheriff. If we do a thing, it's as if she did a thing. So we gonna do this thing?" Tug grinned. Softer: "Want me to play good cop?"

Caine looked puzzled. "Something wrong?" he asked again. "You know you just can't park there. You're blocking the exit gate."

A pine scent and Christmas music spilled out, Kasey Musgraves' "Christmas Makes Me Cry." On the floor behind Caine, the grizzle-faced chocolate Labrador curled in a bed. He raised his head with vague interest and regarded Basil. Kenny pointed to Tug's car. "Bill Shaw's coming up the street. You better move so he can get to work."

"Mr. Shaw is going to have to wait." Basil gestured and Caine stepped farther inside. Basil had to go in sideways and was immediately appreciative of the heat. It was in the mid-thirties outside, at least thirty degrees higher inside. Tug squeezed in after him and shut the door. There was barely enough room for the three men, dog, desk, and mini-fridge.

"We need to know the names of the two people who died in the Laubenstein house fire." Basil fixed Caine with a stare. His foot throbbed and he felt unsteady, regretted not taking a pain pill.

"What? Why would I know that?" Kenny's lip quivered ever-so-slightly. A tell.

"You let them into Christmas Lake Village," Basil said. "This month. This past summer. Other times. You know them. Give us their names."

Caine sputtered.

"Sure, we'll get their names eventually," Tug put in. "DNA, dental records. But that's taking time, must be some sort of backlog, and we want this wrapped up with a bow before Santa slides down the chimney. It'd be in the holiday spirit to help us. And I can tell by the music you play and all the little decorations that you're in the holiday spirit."

Basil watched the old Labrador rest his head back down and snort. The dog kept his eyes open, tracking Caine.

Kenny reached behind him and turned off the music, looked out the window at a beige Chevy Tahoe, no doubt Mr. Shaw behind the wheel. The car horn sounded.

"I need to let him through." he pointed to the Tahoe. "Mr. Shaw's running late. Don't need to make him—"

"About the two people who died in the Laubenstein house," Basil interrupted.

"Listen, I don't know anything about those people. What makes you think I—"

"They didn't need a card to get through the gate. You let them into the Village without one, and you cut the sections of video that showed their car driving around," Basil said. He wasn't one hundred percent on that, but he was sure enough to press. "Because if you'd passed the video to us unaltered, we would have seen the Rabbit come and go through your gate, drive around the neighborhoods, and that would have incriminated—"

The Tahoe honked again, and then the driver backed it up to go out one of the other access points.

"They didn't hurt anybody," Caine said. He fidgeted with his pen and clipboard, and stuck his chin out in a vague show of bravado. "They just needed a place to stay for a few weeks. Didn't hurt anybody. Didn't hurt the Laubenstein's house. Didn't hurt any house. And they didn't set the fire. I guarantee they didn't do that."

"So give us their names." This from Tug, who'd bent over to scratch the old dog's ears. His tail thumped appreciatively.

"We'd like their names so we can notify any relatives. Wrap it up in a bow before Christmas, just like my partner said." Basil's voice was low, even, and carried a threat. "You don't want your friends to stay in a drawer in the morgue do you? Lonely. Unclaimed. Don't your friends deserve better than that?"

"I wouldn't call them friends, exactly," Kenny cut back. His fingers fidgeted faster and he rocked from one foot to the other. Basil caught a sheen of sweat on the young man's forehead, and he dropped his chin down as if admitting defeat. "Just people I got to know. My roommate, Mason, he introduced them to me. They were friends of his, all of them from someplace in Arizona."

Basil recalled from Piper's notes that Mason Knowles had the three-to-eleven shift after Caine, four days a week.

"Phroggers," Tug put in, as he stood shoulder to shoulder with Basil. The little post seemed to shrink.

"That's not a nice term, Phroggers," Caine said. "Renters is better."

"But they don't pay rent," Tug said.

"Well, no. They just stay in houses while people are on vacation. They even vacuum and stuff, feed the fish in aquariums. Keep everything tidy. Leave it all just like they found it. Maybe better than they found it. She was always a clean freak."

"You have the right to remain silent," Tug started. While he rattled off all of the Miranda, Basil watched Kenny, figured he was close to soiling himself.

"So see, you don't have to talk to us, Mr. Caine. You have that right to be silent. We can all go down to the station and you can get an attorney," Tug explained. "And if you can't afford one, there'll be one assigned to you. And then you eventually have to talk to us. Or you can give us an early Christmas present and talk now. Up to you."

"A present like the names, Mr. Caine." Basil was uncomfortable, the welcome heat becoming too warm, and with no easy way to get out of his jacket. His armpits ached from the damn crutches. "My patience is pretty skinny right now. It's gonna be skeletal in a—"

"Craig and Libby. Libby, Olivia Moore. I don't remember Craig's last name, but Mason knows it. He was friends with them, I told you, from Arizona. He used to phrog with them. It's how I met Mason. I didn't go to Arizona. Mason just popped up here one day."

"So you let Mason and his two friends come in to the Village," Basil prompted.

Caine shrugged. "Well, just Mason at first. That was, oh, two or so years back. The Simpsons on Jingle Bell were on a Mediterranean cruise, gone a month, and Mason stayed there. Mason liked Santa Claus and decided to settle here, said he liked our little bit of snow. I needed a roommate, and there was an opening for a gate guard. Then he invited Craig and Libby to come to the Village. It worked out for everyone."

"Not for Libby and Craig," Tug observed. "It didn't work out at all for them."

Kenny dropped his head even lower. "Yeah, I feel bad for them. And Mason, he's real broke up about it. Couldn't stop crying when he let the network know. Craig and Libby had recently gotten engaged."

"Network?" Basil didn't like the sound of that.

"The network, a bunch of people who phrog—rent space—across the country. They post reviews of places, tell other phroggers spots to avoid. I only ever phrogged once, but the network was helpful."

Basil shook his head and mouthed "Wow."

Tug said, "A phrogging network. Sadly dope."

"Mason knows Craig's last name." Basil didn't pose it as a question.

"Yeah. He told me before, but I'm not terrific with last names. Have a hard enough time remembering the last names of people in the Village. I just remember Libby's. She was pretty. Real pretty. Real shame, that fire. Wished we would have picked out a different place for them to rent, but the Laubensteins were going to be gone the longest. We thought we'd all spend Christmas together. Already have a huge turkey bought. It's taking up the entire freezer."

Basil repeated the Miranda warning.

"Yeah, yeah, I heard you the first time," Caine said. "But I helped you, right? Gave you their names. And when Mason comes in to relieve me this afternoon I'll ask for Craig's last name and let you know."

Tug took out his handcuffs.

"Hey! Hey!" Caine tried to back up, but he was already against his desk, nowhere for him to go. Rocket whimpered. "I helped you. I gave you their names."

"And admitted that you picked out the places for them stay," Basil said.

"They never hurt anybody."

"They stole from people."

Kenny made a face. "The people in here, they got money, not going to miss underwear drawer dollars or a few pieces of jewelry and such. No real harm done."

"And I suppose you got some sort of a take," Tug said. "A little share for finding them the digs? Right?"

Caine didn't reply. The quivering lip was the tell.

"Put your coat on," Basil said.

Caine stared slack-jawed.

"Put it on now, and then put your hands behind your back." Tug shook the handcuffs.

Kenny cried, his shoulders shook. Rocket whimpered again. "You can't arrest me. I didn't do anything wrong. Not *much* wrong. I don't want to go to jail. Bette. My girlfriend would kill me. We're going to move to Portugal. I didn't hurt anybody."

"Accessory to burglary, several counts. Accessory to trespass," Tug said.

Basil caught his friend's eyes glimmering; Tug enjoyed this.

"We'll probably come up with some more charges to tack on." Tug clicked the cuffs on him.

"My dog. Rocket. If you take me to jail, what'll happen to him? He can't go to the shelter. He's old. He'll get the needle. You can't—"

"We won't take Rocket to a shelter." Basil's tone softened. Millie was picking up the cats today. He'd been thinking about getting the kids a puppy. This could be a starter-dog. "Maybe I'll watch him for you." And if that didn't work, he figured he could talk Sheriff Blackwell into adding to her animal collection.

"He likes that bed. He has toys at the apartment. He—"

"We'll get that stuff from your apartment when we go to arrest Mason," Tug said.

"Arrest Mason, too?"

"Maybe with a good attorney you'll get out of prison while Rocket is still alive and you can take him back," Basil said. "Let's go." He gestured with his head toward the door.

Tug leaned over and clipped a leash to Rocket's collar.

"Dog better not pee in the car," Tug said. "If he does, I ain't cleaning it."

39

1 p.m. Tuesday, December 22nd

"G ornisht helfn," Oren grumbled.

Oren didn't look any better to Piper's eyes than when she'd visited him ten days ago. But Dr. Mattingly said there was considerable improvement.

She sat next to his bed, wearing a gown and gloves instead of the PPE outfit she'd had to don before. Nang waited outside because visitors were still limited.

The antiseptic scents didn't seem harsh today. Or perhaps her sense of smell was still dampened from her foray into the collapsing, burning building.

"I need you to promise me," she said. Piper wanted to set her hand on his arm, a physical connection, but had been told to keep a distance of a few feet. She'd also wanted to bring flowers, but they weren't allowed yet, so she settled on a bouquet of helium-filled balloons. His room had a plethora of them, most wishing him well. The trio of purple bats was likely from Teegan.

"I don't know," he said, voice still raspy. "*Gornisht helfn*. I just don't know."

"Well, *I* know," she insisted. "I know that you have to come back to the department. You have to promise me that."

"Sixty-six," he said.

"Twenty-four," she replied, well aware that she was forty-two years younger than the chief deputy.

Oren made a puttering sound. She watched the lines on his monitor jump slightly.

Millie had been up over the weekend, and had told him about the bomb and subsequent apprehension of Roger Carlson and his wife and son. She didn't have to go over that news. But she'd talk about the motive.

"Roger Carlson said he went after you first, revenge because you'd showed up at his property and found his marijuana. Said you tossed his friendship away when you arrested him. Basil was targeted because he was with you. Millie was at his barn, so she made the list. Apparently I had too many security cameras to warrant an attempt to burn my house."

"And the department?"

"He went after the building, all of us, because we'd arrested Jerome Halm."

"My neighbor's asshole kid."

"He hoped to kill Jerome. The kid knew Roger was behind the arsons. And Roger thought ...no, *knew* ... Jerome would testify against him. Wanted to punish him for that."

"Carlson was a good man once. Or I thought he was."

"He'd been running his pot industry a lot of years, using corn detasslers to help him," Piper said. "Undetected for way the hell too long."

"Indiana has the death penalty," Oren returned. "Looking at life for the trafficking. Looking at death for burning buildings and killing people."

Piper held the arms of the chair. "Said it didn't matter that we caught him for the fires. That he'd rather die than spend the rest of his life in prison. An unbalanced, angry man. His wife was involved with the arsons, too, she bought all the canisters and filled them with gas."

"Never was a good man, then. Fooled me for a long time." He let out a hoarse breath. "The bomb was fertilizer, right? A farmer, he'd have enough, or know where to get more. Millie said she figured it was fertilizer."

Piper nodded.

A nurse came in, looked at his monitors, drew a vial of blood, all of it saying only, "Good afternoon Mr. Rosenberg."

Piper waited until the nurse left.

"I signed mutual assistance contracts yesterday. With Warrick for dispatch and Rockport police. Teegan and Zeke are taking some shifts in Warrick as part of the agreement. The rest of the time they, and everybody else, are working on our restart."

A huffing noise this time.

"In two weeks we're moving into the old furniture store downtown, going to work out of it until our new building is finished."

"And when will that be?" Oren sat up a little, and brightened.

"Insurance is still shaking out, and the budget is being worked up. We've just started going over design options with the county board, looking at architects. I'd like to bring some schematics up in a few weeks, get your input. I want a shower and a room with a couple of cots in case people work late, double shifts, need to stay around. There are other things on my wish list."

"Same lot?"

"After everything is bulldozed. Yeah, same corner."

"What about Candace?"

"She's being released from the hospital Thursday. Her husband got here yesterday on leave. I met him when I stopped in to see her. Nice guy." Piper frowned. "Candace gave me her notice, said she's going to open a bakery downtown. Said baking is safer work."

Neither said anything for a while, the beeps and hisses of the monitors playing between them, the clatter of a cart being pushed down the hall outside. She saw Nang look through the window and smile.

"It's going to take too long," she said. "It'll be two or three months before the board signs off on any floorplans. Then bids will go out and construction can start, and that'll probably take another ten months, maybe a year before it's all done. Hazmat was busy with our old place over the weekend, yesterday. They moved what was left of our furniture, file cabinets, equipment out to the parking lot. Good thing it didn't snow, but it's in the forecast. Everything's been covered with heavy plastic. Some of it will be cleaned and can be reused. But they warned it might cost more to clean it rather than replace it. We'll see. Weapons, some of the uniforms, they can be cleaned."

"I don't know," he repeated with a huff. "Sixty-six."

"Twenty-four. I need your experience," she countered. Piper thought she was doing this for him, not her. The department could move along fine without Oren Rosenberg. She could hire another deputy and promote someone from in-house to chief. But he needed a purpose, something to help counter his deep loss. And … admittedly he was a good chief deputy. Maybe she was also doing this for herself.

"I need your experience, especially with rebuilding everything, ordering new equipment. I need your advice. And when you get back, I need you in charge so Nang and I can finally go on a honeymoon." They'd discussed the honeymoon possibilities last night, thinking of combining the trip with a cooking contest Nang could enter … New York, Los Angeles, Vegas, London, Sydney … the big cities that hosted the shows. Depended which one accepted his application video.

"I don't—" Oren's voice trailed off and he turned his head, glanced away and saw Nang looking through the window. He sighed. "I guess I'll need something to do. I guess the cats and I are going to stay with Millie in your husband's trailer until I have a new place built in the Village. Different neighborhood though, still near one of the lakes because of my boat. I can't live across from David Halm any longer."

Piper wouldn't want to live across from David Halm either, too many memories of his son involved with the Carlsons and the arsons.

"Doesn't need to be quite as big," Oren went on. "For just me and the cats. Don't need a third bedroom. And I want a walk-in shower and a study."

Piper listened to him talk for a while. His voice was much stronger than when she'd visited shortly after his fire. There weren't as many bandages. Still, she knew it would be a couple of months before he came back to Spencer County. She anticipated that.

"Figure I'll be back about the time construction starts," he said. "I suppose I could look at your building plans, give my two cents."

"I'd appreciate that," Piper said. She stood and placed a book on his tray table: *A View From A Broad* by Bette Midler. She'd found a signed copy for a reasonable price on eBay. "I really am going to need your help."

"I doubt that," he said. "I double-doubt that. But thanks for saying it."

She walked to the door.

"Merry Christmas to you and Nang," he said.

"*Chag sameach*," she replied.

She and Nang stopped at the Lego store before leaving Indianapolis, picking up the building block sets Basil had intended to buy for his kids before the golf course incident. Then they found a baby shop and bought a blanket and some onesies for Tug's grandson born two nights past.

They didn't get home until after dark, the stores crowded, the traffic difficult, all the lighted homes beautiful to see along the way.

They settled on the floor in front of their tree, Camaro stretched out on the red skirt. Tater took up the couch. Marmalade preened on an oversized cushion. Tim Janis's instrumental Christmas music played softly.

"Supposed to snow tomorrow," Piper said.

"Hope so."

"I didn't think you liked snow."

Nang cocked his head. "I sell lots of shovels and scrapers at the Quick Mart when it snows. I met you when it snowed."

She nestled against him. "Just a little snow," she said. "Enough to cover up all the burned things. Make those places smell better."

He kissed her forehead. "I think we'll need to get a couple of feet for that."

She smiled sadly, happy to have his warmth, his strength, his optimism.

"You still shine," he said.

ACKNOWLEDGMENTS

Piper Blackwell is a good sheriff because of: Robert Scales, who provides expert advice on all of her legal issues; Mike Black, a fine writer and former police officer, who knows all the ins and outs of law enforcement; and Bill Gilsdorf, who helped shape her from the beginning and taught her how to properly wear a badge.

Much appreciation to Carol Clarkson and Juliana Wence, nurses supreme, who expertly treated Oren Rosenberg in the burn unit.

A nod to Lance Larkin who came up with the name for the restaurant: Nang's Uptown Wok.

Thanks also to:

Mindy Clodfelder for her expertise on golf courses and golf carts.

Daniel Kramarsky, for an assist with Millie's Indianapolis visit.

Jessica Zindar, for helping to injure Basil Meredith.

Julie Benningfield for sharing her insights on Santa Claus and Christmas Lake Village.

Vicki Steger, the best beta-reader ever.

Paula Cristina Simões for pieces of Portugal.

The Kenosha Writers' Group for being an awesome sounding board—Steve Sullivan, Steve Rouse, Warren Langlois, and Christine Verstraete.

Echo Shea and Mindy Mymudes for their incredible promotions, encouragement, friendship, and blueberry preserves.

SPENCER COUNTY, INDIANA

It's a real place, about as far south in Indiana as you can go. The towns, roads, and some of the businesses I reference in this novel exist. There really is a Santa Claus—it's nestled between the Ohio River and Interstate 64. On my visit to the Christmas store there I picked up some walnut fudge, a quirky Green Bay Packers ornament, and a Boston terrier ornament that I had personalized with Missy's name. Rockport is about twenty miles from Santa Claus, and is where the real Sheriff's Department sits. I've fictionalized the county, taking considerable liberties, including with Christmas Lake Village and the adjacent golf course. I used to live in Indiana—Evansville, during my newspaper reporter days. Spencer County isn't far from there. The place is a good home for Piper Blackwell and company.

ABOUT THE AUTHOR

I write…a lot.

I write with dogs wrapped around my feet. I get to wear sandals or bedroom slippers to work, and old, comfortable clothes. When the weather is fine, I get to write on my back porch. I love summer. I started getting published when I was twelve, studied journalism at Northern Illinois University, and then went to work as a news reporter…eventually for Scripps Howard, where I managed their Western Kentucky bureau. Getting itchy feet, I moved to Wisconsin and went to work for TSR, Inc., the then-producers of the Dungeons

& Dragons game. I wrote Dragonlance novels and reached the *USA Today's* Bestseller list several times.

I've written fifty or so novels (including a couple of ghosted projects … shhh!), more than a hundred short stories, and I've edited more magazines and anthologies than I care to count. Right now, it's all about mysteries…thrillers, suspense, and uncozy-cozies.

I am a recipient of the Faust, the Grand Master Award from the International Association of Media Tie-In Writers. My novel, *The Bone Shroud*, won the 2019 Illinois Author Project competition. And *The Love-Haight Case Files*, written with Donald J. Bingle, hit #1 on Amazon and won three Silver Falchion awards. That is more than enough to Snoopy dance about.

I am a geek about boardgames and rpgs, I visit interesting and odd museums when I get the chance, and at every reasonably good opportunity I toss tennis balls for my cadre of dogs. I'm pretty damn good at tossing tennis balls.

Writers and dogs go great together. Mine get me away from the keyboard and show me how very important it is to chase butterflies, roll in patches of dandelions, and bark at passing trains. Piper Blackwell has dogs. I'm thinking Basil Meredith needs to get one. Maybe that's for another book … or maybe this one.

Visit me at jeanrabe.com
Facebook.com/jean.rabe.1
https://twitter.com/jeanerabe
https://www.amazon.com/stores/author/B01LZ9IP5A

BOONE STREET PRESS NOVELS BY JEAN RABE

The Dead of Winter

The Dead of Night

The Dead of Summer

The Dead of Jerusalem Ridge

The Dead of Autumn

The Dead of Sled Run

The Bone Shroud

Pockets of Darkness

The Cauldron

Fenzig's Fortune

The Finest Creation

The Finest Choice

The Finest Challenge